THE
SEVEN KINGDOMS

THE
SEVEN KINGDOMS

THE DARKENING LANDS

HARRY G. SHERWIN

authorHOUSE®

AuthorHouse™ UK Ltd.
1663 Liberty Drive
Bloomington, IN 47403 USA
www.authorhouse.co.uk
Phone: 0800.197.4150

Published by AuthorHouse   05/15/2013

ISBN: 978-1-4817-9213-4 (sc)
ISBN: 978-1-4817-9212-7 (hc)
ISBN: 978-1-4817-9214-1 (e)

Library of Congress Control Number: 2013907230

About the Book

For the first time in over a thousand years the Seven Kingdoms of Justava are at peace with each other. As age old tensions melt away, the people are able to rest easily in their homes, safe in the knowledge that war will trouble them no longer. But a new power is growing in the heart of Justava, an unseen malice that threatens to destroy the fragile peace and throw Justava back into chaos and war.

With the evil Necromancer Empire spreading to every corner of the Seven Kingdoms, it falls upon two young elves who lost everything to this new evil to make a stand. Together, Brenik and Nalia must overcome age old prejudices and travel deep into the wilds of Justava in order to raise their banner and ignite the fires of rebellion.

For Niamh, who has never stopped believing.

And with thanks to Sarah Hanson, Peter Rolls and of course, Mum and Dad.

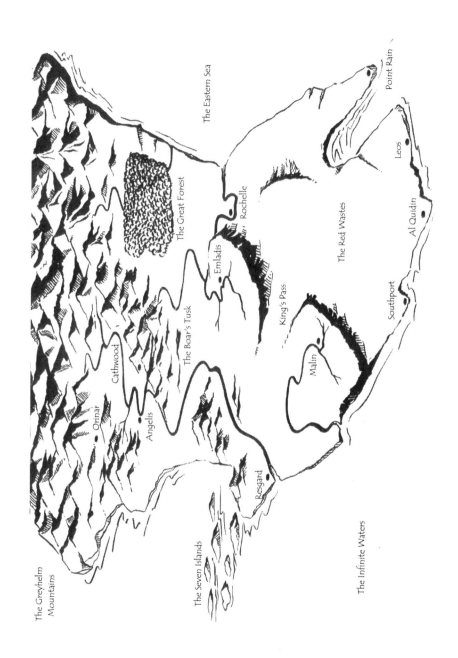

Prologue

A gentle summer breeze drifted lazily between the tall, grassy shoots of the vast, moonlit meadow. Other than the soft rustling of the long stems the meadow was quiet, the tranquil scene spreading out to the tall mountains that lay watchfully in the distance.

A small mouse suddenly sprang from between the grass and scurried excitedly through the grasslands on its way home. There was something about the way the mouse kept glancing back over its shoulder though, the way that his eyes were sat so wide in his tiny head and how his ears were pressed against his body. The mouse was afraid.

The mouse's tiny legs pounded against his sides as he raced through the meadow, dodging and weaving his way around sticks the size of fallen trees and stones the size of boulders. His tiny heart raced in his chest as his pursuer hissed violently from behind him.

A hawk cried out as it circled watchfully overhead. The mouse glanced up, wishing that it was only the hawk that was chasing him instead of these things, these monsters.

A thin ray of light suddenly penetrated the thick grass and the mouse squeaked in triumph as he leapt from the tall shoots into the small, earthy clearing where his burrow was dug. With one final, desperate push he jumped forward and dove into the safety of his hole.

From outside there came a sharp hiss of disdain and what little moonlight that entered the hole was suddenly blocked as a long, skeletal hand reached into the burrow after the mouse. The mouse pressed himself against the back of the wall, his eyes wide in terror as the pale hand probed the depths of his home, getting closer and closer. A series of loud shouts suddenly filled the air and with an angry hiss the ragged hand slowly withdrew back into the outside world.

The mouse breathed heavily, sucking in great lungfuls of air as the adrenaline that had filled his body during the pursuit began to seep away. He could relax; the chase was over; he was alive. But deep down in his tiny chest, the mouse knew that that was not the case. For nestled away at the back of his small brain he knew what he had escaped.

The darkness was coming.

Chapter 1

In the centre of a small, square courtyard, surrounded by beautifully carved arches of white stone, sat a small fountain. Cool, clear water trickled gently from a stone urn held in the arms of a delicately crafted woman and splashed soothingly down into the pool of water that surrounded her bare feet. Despite being made of stone, the woman appeared radiant, her skin soft and shining as the water below reflected the warm light of the night's stars up into her round, unblemished face.

The sharp 'click' of boots on stone suddenly disturbed the peaceful scene and the woman's face became hidden as a dark shadow fell over her stone body. The lone figure that appeared in the courtyard was wrapped in a cloak of shimmering, violet silk which clung tightly to the angular lines of his sharp armour. He paused beside the fountain, glancing suspiciously around at the various entrances to the small courtyard before passing quickly through one of the stone arches that led out onto a balcony that overlooked the elven capital city of Cathwood, his strong leather boots still clicking sharply against the uneven stone floor.

Satisfied that he was alone, the figure reached up and threw back the hood that veiled his face. The combined light from the twinkling stars and the two torches attached to the wall behind him revealed the man's long face with his pale skin and large, hooked nose. His green eyes flared in the flickering flames of the torches and his pointed ears twitched slightly from underneath his long, straight, black hair.

Like all elves, the man was blessed with keen vision and his sharp eyes quickly scanned the streets below him before settling on a lone, shadowy figure silhouetted against the entrance to a dark alleyway. The elf turned to his left and pulled the nearest torch from its bracket on the wall before waving it from left to right three times. He watched the black figure below and a sly grin pulled at his thin lips as a small flame appeared within the folds of the figure's black cloak.

"Guillard?" someone called suddenly.

Guillard Terune jumped at the mention of his name and spun around abruptly, the torch slipping from his hand to fall the distance to the cobbled street below. Three figures were making their way across the courtyard towards him. The first was Brenik Lithuik, Guillard's closest friend. A tall elf with neatly trimmed brown hair and a handsome face, Brenik carried himself with a quiet confidence and an undeniable charm that made him a natural leader and a trusted friend. On Brenik's left drifted Nalia Sommer. Clad in a white dress that left her arms and shoulders bare, she appeared more beautiful than Guillard had ever seen her look before. She smiled softly at Guillard and her ice blue eyes twinkled as they reflected the pale light of the evening stars. Finally, on Brenik's other side, walked Jaythun Iradu. Unlike his companions, Jaythun looked scruffy and out of place alongside the regal pair. His long brown hair was wild and untamed and his light green tunic bore a stain from whatever meal he had last eaten. He grinned broadly at Guillard who wouldn't have been overly surprised to learn that his friend had had a little too much to drink with his evening meal.

Brenik frowned as his friend stared open-mouthed at the small group. "Is everything all right, Guillard?" he asked.

Guillard glanced nervously back over the balcony, relieved to see that his shadowy ally had disappeared into the maze of streets that ran through Cathwood City. He turned quickly back to his friends and moved towards where they stood in the courtyard. Smiling, he cleared his throat by way of composing himself. "My friends!" he said in his usual, casual manner. "What are you doing out at this hour?"

"We could ask you the same thing," Nalia purred with a playful smile.

Guillard could not help but smile at Nalia's alluring voice. Ever since Guillard had first met her, he had been in love with Nalia. Time and time again he had tried to charm her but Nalia had always turned him down as gently as she could. She had other interests Guillard thought as he glanced at Brenik.

"We just thought that as the summer months are coming to a close we would enjoy a walk in this lovely evening," Nalia continued.

"That is true! It is a fine evening." Guillard took a deep breath of warm, summer air and smiled broadly. "Alas! I would join you but I have work that I must attend to. Why not continue your walk and we can talk more in the morning? I am sure that the weather will hold."

Brenik raised a thin eyebrow, his dark, midnight-blue eyes boring inquisitively into Guillard's own pale green eyes. "Work? What business is urgent enough to keep the Captain of the Guard out this late at night I wonder?" he asked.

Guillard ran a nervous hand through his dark hair. "One of our caravans was attacked by a tribe of raiders," he lied.

"Really?" Brenik said thoughtfully. "I was not aware we were moving any supplies at this time." Brenik glanced thoughtfully across at Nalia. "And it cannot be Nalia's parents returning as they are not due back from the country for several days."

Guillard cursed himself silently. Although Brenik was not officially a part of the elven military, his primary job being a physician, he was the son of a Lord and one of the most skilled warriors in the Kingdom. Brenik's skills were a result of his father, Rothule Lithuik, who was one of the most influential Lords in the Kingdom of Cathwood and was grooming Brenik to eventually take his place. It was because of this that Brenik had been given the best training in riding, combat and diplomacy and why he also had access to all the military movements and records of the elves of Cathwood City, which he kept a close eye upon at the insistence of his father.

"No, you wouldn't have known about it," Guillard blurted out. His voice came quickly and he forced himself to slow down. He had never been a good liar. "It was organised as an afterthought, shortly after the dossier on our week's activities was released. The King decided to deliver the supplies to the outpost earlier this year, whilst the weather remains favourable. I assume that there will be a full report released with next week's list."

After a brief pause Brenik nodded, apparently satisfied with Guillard's explanation. Whether his friend actually cared about it or not, Guillard could not say.

"So I assume you are rounding up a battalion to investigate?" Brenik asked steadily.

"Well I'm in!" Jaythun chuckled, raising his right fist in a mock salute. "I could . . ." But Jaythun was suddenly cut off by the sound of a scream followed by a loud explosion.

"What was that?" Nalia frowned.

Brenik pushed urgently past Guillard and rushed out onto the balcony, his friends only a few paces behind him. As the four of them looked out over the city walls they saw thousands of tiny lights flickering to life across the meadows that lay before the city's mighty gates. They watched in horror as huge chunks of stone, some coated in oil and burning brightly, flew effortlessly over the walls and crashed into the streets below, blowing holes in walls and crashing through buildings.

Screams of terror rose up from the streets of Cathwood City and in the distance the ominous war drums of the enemy began to beat to the steady pace of the invaders' advance.

Chapter 2

Brenik burst into the armoury of his family's estate and quickly began to gather up his equipment from the varied racks of weapons and armour that had been passed down through the Lithuik family over their many generations. First he strapped a plain pair of tanned leather vambraces to his wrists followed by a pair of matching shin and shoulder guards. Next he slipped a padded, leather jerkin over his loose, white shirt before fastening a dark blue cape around his neck with a pin bearing his family crest, an open circle of golden rope surrounding the bough of a reflin tree, a type of oak tree unique to Justava. The golden branch stretched across the circle and the spindly tips of its smaller branches touched the edge of the rope in seven separate places.

As Brenik slung his bow and quiver full of white feathered arrows over his back he noticed Guillard standing nervously in the entranceway to the armoury. Unlike his friends, Guillard was the son of a simple tailor and not of noble blood. Guillard had always felt out of place amongst the members of Cathwood's nobility and the way he was rocking on his heels and casting his eyes down towards the floor showed how, even now, Guillard was still uncomfortable amongst the grand buildings of the elven lords.

"This city is well protected Guillard," Brenik said by way of distracting his friend. He picked his elegant sword from its polished wall rack and drove it defiantly into the sheath hanging from his belt. "Whatever we face, we will stand against it together."

Guillard looked at Brenik, his unfocused eyes staring into the distance, and nodded curtly. "What of your parents?" he said, suddenly coming back to the present world.

Brenik frowned slightly, noticing that Guillard's hand was resting uneasily on the hilt of his curved scimitar. Both of Brenik's parents had been blessed with the power of magic. Brenik's father in particular was an extremely powerful wizard and his magic had contributed to many victories in the years that he had led Cathwood's military. They provided inspiration that only the King of Cathwood could match and often their mere presence on the battlefield was all that was needed to provide their soldiers with the courage to defeat their enemies.

"They will be with the soldiers at the main gate," Brenik said reassuringly. He stepped forward and placed a firm hand on Guillard's shoulder. "Do not worry, my friend. My parents will stand and defend the city by our side, no matter the cost."

Guillard's face set in grim determination. "Then we must hurry to them. They will need our help."

Brenik nodded and the two elves hurried out into the empty street to find Nalia and Jaythun waiting for them. Nalia had removed her dress in favour of a white blouse, black trousers and sturdy, dark grey boots. Around her stomach she wore a black, leather corset and upon her wrists were a pair of dark, leather vambraces, of which the left was slightly longer than the right. She held a longbow in her hand and a black quiver full of white and yellow feathered arrows was strapped across her back. Jaythun stood eagerly beside her, shuffling his feet excitedly. He wore gleaming silver armour made of overlapping layers and etched with the symbol of an eagle's talon. He also wore a long, orange cape that flowed down from the shoulder plates that it was fastened to.

The two nodded at the approaching pair and together they turned to face the growing sounds of battle. A heavy silence fell over the group as they made their way quickly down the cobbled streets of the city towards the main gate, all of them focusing on the battle ahead.

As they pushed down the sloping street, dodging the falling rubble from buildings as they were hammered by the enemy's artillery, they came across streams of frightened civilians retreating to the safety of Cathwood City's deep caverns. Men, women and children pushed past the four of them as if they weren't even there. Some limped along with lost expressions on their faces whilst others desperately dragged their wounded friends behind them, doing what they could to stem the tide of the streams of hot blood that poured from the fresh wounds. They all looked terrified.

A woman suddenly lunged at Brenik, knocking him sideways. "Please! You have to help me!" she wailed frantically.

Brenik gently pushed the woman away. "We are trying, Miss," he said calmly. "Please, continue to the upper level. You will be safe in the caverns."

The woman ignored Brenik's words and continued to claw at his arm. "They bit me!" she sobbed. "They bit me!" She thrust her bloodied arm under Brenik's nose and the elf grimaced as he saw the ripped flesh and the stained white of her bone beneath.

Brenik looked back up at the woman, noticing how pale her skin was from the loss of so much blood. "Who did this to you?" he asked swiftly.

"Demons! Demons in the market!" The hysteric woman suddenly began to sway on her feet. "Please, help," she whispered before her legs gave way and she collapsed.

Brenik grabbed the woman in his arms as she fell forwards. "Miss? Miss?" he called urgently. Gingerly he reached up and pressed his fingers against her neck in search of a pulse. After a short while his eyes slid sadly shut.

"What do you think she meant by demons?" Jaythun asked in a low voice as Brenik lay the dead woman gently on the cobbled street.

Brenik brushed the woman's hair from her face and stared determinedly down the dark street before them. "There's only one way to find out," he muttered as he got to his feet.

The four of them began to run again, racing down the streets towards the market squares in the lower level of the city. As they ran, none of them bothered to look back. Had they done so, they would have seen the dead woman raise herself stiffly to her feet and her dead eyes slowly slide open once again.

* * *

"Look!" Nalia yelled over the roar of the enemy catapults as they reached the lower levels.

They had found their way into one of the city's many market squares, a place that was normally bustling with strange merchants from far-off cities selling delicate trinkets or farmers from the outlying villages laden with their freshly grown produce. Today, however, the long, open ground was strewn with the bodies of dead elves. Huge chunks of rubble littered the green strips of grass that were used to divide the market square into sectors and flames tore through the charred shells of the wooden stalls. In the centre of the chaos stood a large group of idle figures.

The four warriors slowed to a stop, ducking down out of sight behind a chunk of rubble in order to observe the figures from a safe distance.

"Who are they?" Jaythun whispered curiously as he peaked over the rubble that they hid behind. Since the Treaty of Emladis, one hundred years ago, there had not been a full scale war in Justava. Although there had been minor disputes, the different races had at long last begun to live in harmony and strive towards the creation of a united country. Jaythun was eager to discover which race had had the audacity to break the agreement and attack his people.

Brenik shook his head slowly. "It can't be," he whispered to himself in disbelief.

The figures stood dotted randomly about the square, some lumbering slowly forward whilst others stood still, swaying unsteadily on the spot. There was nothing uniform about the group of invaders; some held axes whilst others had bent swords or twisted clubs. Some wore tattered shirts or rusted armour whilst others stood bare chested. The only similar thing about the group was their stance. None of the figures stood upright; some were hunched over whilst others leant back so far it was as though their spines had been ripped from their backs. Furthermore, none of the invaders seemed to have control over his or her head and as Brenik looked around he saw the skulls of the figures lolling randomly from side to side on top of their useless necks as they trudged along.

The four elves crept over to another piece of rubble and as they did so a low, ghostly moan rolled across the courtyard to fill their pointed ears.

"Brenik?" Jaythun said, his usual, cheerful manner all but vanished.

Brenik scowled as he surveyed the enemy. "They are the Kerberyn," he whispered in grim explanation.

"The what?" Jaythun hissed back. The young elf could see by their faces that his other two friends knew what Brenik meant. Jaythun on the other hand, was not as learned as his friends, preferring to focus his skills on what he considered to be the more important aspects of life, such as fighting and drinking.

"In the common tongue it means demon of the earth. You will know them as the undead. Zombies." Brenik shrugged indifferently. "Call them what you will, they are all the same essentially."

Jaythun snorted loudly at Brenik's response and immediately regretted doing so. Even as he attempted to cover his outburst one of the creatures turned suddenly to face them, it's yellow, unblinking eyes fixing upon the four figures crouched behind the broken rock. A thick string of saliva fell from its drooping jaw before the creature lunged forwards and let out a screaming howl of rage.

Brenik leapt to his feet and plucked an arrow from his back as the rest of the creatures responded to the howl and charged towards them.

"Defend yourselves!" He cried as he drew back the arrow and let it fly from his bowstring, watching as it sped through the air before embedding itself in the lead creature's heart. If the arrow had any effect on the creature it gave no sign and Brenik watched in shock as the Kerberyn continued to charge wildly towards them.

"Aim for their heads!" Nalia called from beside Brenik as one of the Kerberyn crumpled to the floor when one of her arrows pierced the spot between its glowing eyes.

Brenik drew back a second arrow and let it race from his bow to strike a Kerberyn in the beast's forehead. His third arrow lodged itself in the open mouth of a roaring Kerberyn, dropping the third creature with a garbled scream. With the other beasts drawing closer, Brenik drew his sword and nodded to Nalia as she fell back up the sloping street in order to continue her barrage of arrows. He then gritted his teeth and spun his curved sword in his hand as he returned to face the charging horde.

Guillard looked uncertainly at the crazed beasts. "Do we have a plan?" he asked in a level voice.

"Nothing different to usual," Brenik said with a slight grin as the three men readied their blades against the approaching tide of undead warriors. "Just don't let them bite you," he added quickly.

The swarm of howling monsters lunged towards the three warriors in a frenzied mass of teeth and rotting flesh. Jaythun had never faced an enemy anything like the hoard of undead Kerberyn which he now battled; he was used to his enemies falling when he drove his sword through their hearts or cut a deep gash across their chests. This was not the case with the Kerberyn. When cut they bled black blood but they did not fall. Blow after blow rained down upon the beasts but still they kept coming and slowly the sheer number of undead creatures began to force the three warriors into a fighting retreat that took them back up the winding hill.

Jaythun grunted with exertion as he lunged forwards, driving his weapon through the nearest Kerberyn's heart. The creature hissed as the elf held the sword in its body but it did not fall. Instead, with its left hand the creature attempted to claw at Jaythun's face whilst it swung its club wildly in its right hand, all the while driving itself farther along the sword.

Jaythun grimaced as the beast came face to face with him. Up close the Kerberyn were a terrifying sight to behold. Their skin was a foul, pale grey-green colour and in many places was covered in black scabs or peeling away to reveal the battered, yellow bones below. Their features were drawn and skeletal, with hollow cheeks and eye sockets that held bright yellow eyes with no visible pupils. All over the zombies' rotting bodies were collections of pus filled boils and when the creatures opened their mouths to roar, small flecks of brown pus and saliva would fly out from behind their mismatched rows of blackened teeth.

To call them zombies was technically incorrect. Zombies could not be controlled nor could they think for themselves, their only ruler being their ever-empty stomachs. The Kerberyn, however, were much more deadly. Unlike zombies their brains remained partially intact, allowing them to be given orders which they carried out with unquestioning loyalty. They were still mindless beasts of course, but a beast with half a brain is far worse than one with no brain at all.

Jaythun gagged as he leant away from the disgusting creature and the smell of excrement that wafted from its stained clothes. The Kerberyn wore the tattered remains of a blue-grey dress and the wisps of blonde hair suggested that the beast had once been a woman, had maybe even been quite pretty once. These thoughts were driven quickly from Jaythun's mind as the creature continued to slide down his sword and he saw a small group of maggots crawling from the Kerberyn's left nostril up into a hole in the top of its skull.

"They're disgusting!" he cried before sliding his sword from the Kerberyn's gut and slicing it in two at the waist.

Beside him, Brenik neatly decapitated the creature he was attacking, sending the head bouncing to the floor where its boils burst in a shower of sticky pus.

"Just be thankful they aren't good fighters," he muttered back, looking down in disgust to see that a large amount of pus had splattered onto his left boot.

Guillard said nothing as he swung his scimitar back and forth, chopping limb after brittle limb from his enemies' rotting bodies. He knew that the creatures did not rely upon their weapons to attack but instead used their teeth as their primary weapon. The undead, be they zombies or the demonic Kerberyn, had only one purpose in life: to feed on the flesh of the living. A bite from the creatures could lead to infection from a range of deadly diseases or worse yet, the victim becoming that which had bitten them. Guillard had no intention of suffering either fate and as he fought he made certain to keep as little of his skin exposed as possible.

Suddenly two Kerberyn leapt at Guillard. With a flick of his wrist he smashed the first beast's skull with the hilt of his sword but the second was now clinging manically to his sword arm. The Kerberyn howled as it bit down on the leather braces that were wound around Guillard's wrists. Blood poured from the creature's vice-like mouth onto Guillard's arm as the resistant leather held firm against the beast's teeth.

"Get away!" Guillard yelled in disgust, very aware that he was in danger of becoming swamped by the other advancing Kerberyn.

An arrow suddenly flew past the elf's ear and embedded itself in the Kerberyn's left eye socket, dropping the beast immediately and freeing Guillard's arm. He glanced over his shoulder at Nalia and nodded his thanks, catching her grin and returning it with one of his own rare smiles.

"Are you paying any attention to this fight?" Brenik said cooly in Guillard's ear.

Guillard turned around and jumped in surprise when he found himself face to face with a Kerberyn, teeth bared and ready to sink into his exposed flesh. But the beast was dead and as it toppled forwards Guillard saw Brenik standing behind it, examining his bloodied sword.

"How many is that that you owe me now?" Brenik asked casually, referring to the number of times that he and Guillard had saved each other's lives.

"No more than I owe you," Guillard replied flatly as he dove back into the fight.

The battle was fierce and bloody. Although the Kerberyn could not match any of the four elves for skill, their numbers had forced the warriors to retreat halfway back up the long hill. However, the encounter had shown the elves what they were up against and once they had learnt how to kill the Kerberyn, their greater skill had eventually overcome their enemies' and they had claimed their victory.

The elves walked slowly back down to the market square and looked around at the carnage they had wrought. A sudden howl drew their attention and they turned to see a lone, female Kerberyn advancing from behind them.

"Looks like you missed one," Jaythun said jokingly to Brenik.

Brenik tutted. "How careless of me," he said.

The elf spun his sword and stepped forward, swinging his blade in one fluid motion that dropped the creature to the floor.

"Happy now?" Brenik asked sarcastically.

But when Brenik looked down, he felt a sinking feeling in the pit of his stomach as he saw the creature's face. This Kerberyn was not like the others. Its skin was pinker and there were no boils or scabs to speak of. As Brenik looked at the former woman's arm he sighed sadly as his eyes settled on the torn flesh from where the woman had been bitten.

"The woman from the street," Nalia said sadly. She looked slowly about the square before toeing a ragged head that sat by her feet. "How is this possible?" she whispered.

Brenik turned away from the dead woman and wiped his sword clean on a tuft of grass before sliding the blade into its sheath. "It is old magic," he said, voicing his theory. "When my father was younger he stumbled across a shrine hidden within the lower regions of the Greyhelm Mountains. The shrine was dedicated to a forbidden order of witches and wizards who had discovered a way of using their powers to commune with and summon the spirits of the dead."

"Necromancy?" Nalia breathed in obvious horror. "I thought that was just a myth though?"

Jaythun snorted as he kicked a rotting, armless hand across the square. "Yeah, and I thought zombies were a myth! Looks like we're all learning something new today."

"The entire episode was kept very secret. To be honest, I don't think my father should have told me about it." Brenik shrugged before continuing. "At the time, most people thought as you do, including my father. When they realised that the magic the books contained was in fact possible they were locked away, hidden from the world so that their horrors could never be unleashed." Brenik glanced back down at what remained of the woman at his feet. "It would appear that someone has managed to uncover them, however."

Guillard glanced impatiently around and cleared his throat. "We waste time speculating. We must get to the main gate."

The others looked at their friend and nodded. Sheathing their weapons, they stepped over the corpses of the Kerberyn and ran in the direction of the main gate and the sounds of battle.

Chapter 3

Like all elven cities, Cathwood was renowned for its stunning architecture, wide, colourful parks and its proud history. The capital of the first Elven Kingdom, the city sat at the western feet of the Boar's Tusk, a short stretch of small mountains that jutted out from the main range of the Greyhelm Mountains that ran across the entirety of Justava's northern boarder. The mountains were named after the legendary orc warrior, Greyhelm the Boar, who had united the orcs and goblins under one common banner, bringing an end to hundreds of years of pointless war that had plagued the mountain creatures.

Nestled at the south of the Tusk, Cathwood's tall, white walls formed a two tiered semi-circle with the rocky mountains at the rear. Streets set at a constant, sloping angle rose from the main courtyard at the gate up to the lone Council Tower at the city's highest point and the Royal Palace and estates that flanked it on either side.

Due to its importance, the city was obviously well defended. Large towers with red roofs speared the sky at regular intervals around the two walls, each one capable of housing a score of archers and artillery during the rare times of war. The main gate was made of reflin, an evolved form of oak tree that grew only in Justava, particularly in the Great Forest that lay to the east of the Tusk. Reinforced with strong iron bands and heavy locks, the gate had never been breached by an attacking army.

Until now.

When Brenik and his companions had pushed their way through the ranks of defenders into the centre of the circular courtyard they found the wooden gate lying splintered before them. The right half of the gate had been completely destroyed whilst a huge chunk had been blown from the left, leaving the splintered shards to dangle precariously on the few surviving hinges. The remains of the gate lay scattered about the entrance to the courtyard, mixed in with the shards of rubble that had fallen from the besieged walls and the lifeless bodies of the defenders of Cathwood.

Nalia nudged her friend. "Bren! Your father!"

Brenik looked over to where Nalia was pointing to see his father stood upon the statue in the centre of the courtyard. The statue was of Orlin Ferus, the founder of the Kingdom of Cathwood and its capital city. The stone elf stood roughly four metres high, leaning on his iconic magical staff as his wise face looked on approvingly at the entrance to the city. Standing on the plinth at the feet of the statue was Rothule Lithuik, Brenik's father. He stood with his legs slightly apart and his arms stretched out before him as he launched a series of searing hot fireballs from the tip of his crooked staff. In the heat of battle, Rothule was an impressive sight to behold. His olive skin shone with perspiration and his long, silver-grey hair flowed wildly behind him whilst his bright red robes billowed about his thin body, disturbed by the arcane powers that flowed through the air surrounding the wizard. But the thing that stood out most of all were Rothule's eyes, pools of deep, shining blue that were almost identical to Brenik's. They glowed brightly against his dark, sweat soaked skin, flickering in the fires that burst forth from the wizard's staff.

"Come on!" Brenik called eagerly as he hurried across the bloodstained cobbles.

The four of them shouldered their way through the courtyard, passing by wounded soldiers limping to safety and ducking under attacks from the lumbering Kerberyn. When they reached Brenik's father, Nalia, Jaythun and Guillard formed a defensive semi-circle around the statue's plinth to allow Brenik time to talk with the wizard.

"Brenik!" Rothule called out in his ever calm voice as he glanced down at his approaching son.

"Father!" Brenik replied. He glanced around nervously. "Where is mother?"

Rothule nodded to an open shop behind him where Brenik could just make out his mother stood within a group of soldiers. Whilst Rothule's power was primarily in the offensive arcane forms of magic, Brenik's mother's power was focused on the art of healing. As he watched, he saw her bend over a wounded elf and hold her hands out over a gushing wound on the elf's leg, stemming the red tide with a soothing, white light.

"We are vastly outnumbered, son," Rothule said quietly, bringing Brenik's focus back to the battle.

"We've been through worse," Brenik said, trying to sound confident. "Remember when we got stuck on the Seven Islands?"

"I was younger then," Rothule said with a tired smile. "And the people we were facing actually died when you killed them!"

"I suppose that did help," Brenik muttered. "Well, we haven't given up yet," he said defiantly. "Where is the King?"

Before Rothule could answer a loud blast of a horn sounded across the courtyard and several men sitting atop great stallions rode into the courtyard.

Brenik and Rothule bowed low as the horsemen approached them. "Sire," they said in unison.

King Lanir X smiled at the two men as he looked down from his horse. Lanir was ten years older than Brenik and had a wild personality. He was a small but muscular man with sharp, handsome features and long, blonde hair. In one hand he gripped his golden helmet whilst he rested the other on the hilt of his sword.

"Rise, my friends," the King said kindly. "We don't have time to be polite!"

Rothule nodded as he stood up straight. "Yes, Sire. The enemy has taken up positions along our walls but so far we have able to funnel them to this spot. Their catapults continue to bombard us but our walls are too thick for their shots to penetrate."

"Excellent!" Lanir exclaimed as he pulled his helmet over his head. "We shall hold them here and use our superior skill to push them back."

Rothule watched nervously as the King rode off with his Royal Guards, the royal horn echoing in their wake. Lanir was a good

King, but had never been challenged by war. Rothule feared that complacency and legends had caused the boy to become arrogant.

"Father," Brenik said slowly. "What would you have us do?"

Rothule's expression hardened as he watched the King and his Royal Guards crash into the enemy lines. "Fight, son! Don't let these demons claim our home!"

Brenik nodded and tightened his grip on his sword. He stepped forwards to stand beside his friends, glancing at Nalia as he did. "Stay together," he cautioned his friends. "And kill as many of them as you can!"

Jaythun grinned broadly. "Now that's my kind of plan!" he called as the Kerberyn charged towards them.

*　　*　　*

For over an hour the battle for the main courtyard raged back and forth, with one side appearing on the verge of forcing the other back when the tide would suddenly turn against them. There would be moments when the elves felt as though they could hold out no longer until a sudden burst of courage would give them the strength to drive their enemies back to the gate, forcing the enemy to retreat and giving the elves a precious few minutes to regroup, gather their strength and remove their dead before the next assault began, driving the elves back until the Kerberyn were exhausted once more.

Throughout the entirety of the battle, Brenik and the others remained fixed at the base of the statue of Orlin Ferus, protecting their great city's founder from the wrath of the dead whilst Rothule summoned every power in his arsenal to force back the attackers. In the meantime the King rode proudly through the ranks of his soldiers, his inspirational banner flying high above them all and his horn blasting out into the night. The sight of the Lords of Cathwood was enough to rally the other elves around them, and despite the overwhelming odds, not a single elf turned in terror. If the enemy wanted Cathwood, they would have to kill every last one of her defenders.

A particularly long pause gave the warriors time for a much needed rest. The elves were sat at the base of the statue, addressing the few cuts and bruises that they had received, when Brenik's mother floated gracefully over. Dressed in a gown of the dark blue livery of the Lithuik household, she radiated a calm and graceful beauty. Her black hair was pulled back into a long ponytail and the elegant streaks of silver that betrayed her age glowed brightly in the flames of battle. She looked over the tired elves with soft, green eyes and smiled up at her husband.

"Maleena," Rothule said happily, stepping down from the plinth as his wife approached. The two embraced each other for a time, holding each other close before Maleena turned to greet her son and his companions.

"I have done all I can for the wounded, Rothule," Maleena said sadly as she adjusted the Lithuik pin on her husband's robes. "I have never seen wounds so severe though. I do not know how much longer they can last."

"Where are the other Lords?" Rothule asked, knowing the answer already.

Maleena looked down sadly. "Lords Temal and Saska were in the observatory when the attack began. It was one of the first buildings hit. Apparently there were no survivors."

"And Lord Iradu?" Rothule asked hopefully, referring to Jaythun's father, the only remaining Lord other than the Lithuiks and Nalia's parents.

Maleena shook her head. "He was defending the gates before you got here. The Kerberyn were too many for him though. They carried him off into the night, there was nothing that we could do." She turned sadly to Jaythun. "I am sorry, Jaythun," she whispered.

Jaythun nodded mutely. He and his father had never been very close. Jaythun's mother had died giving birth to him and Jaythun knew that his father blamed him for her death. There was no love lost between the two of them but, nevertheless, Jaythun could not help but feel a pang of regret at the loss of the only real family he had ever had.

"They seem to have no end to their forces," Nalia murmured in defeat.

"Have faith, young Nalia," Maleena said kindly, cupping the young girl's chin in her hand. There was a brief flash of white light and a small cut that ran along Nalia's left cheek suddenly sealed shut.

"The night is almost over and whilst we still hold true to each other, no storm can touch us."

Nalia ran a hand over the invisible scar and smiled at Maleena, feeling her hope return at the woman's kind words.

"Why do they wait so long?" Guillard muttered impatiently.

"Perhaps they're out of dead people?" Jaythun joked without smiling.

Brenik took a long sip of water and watched the King ride slowly through his soldiers, shaking hands and offering words of encouragement. Despite his arrogance, Lanir X had always known how to treat his men and even Brenik could not deny the heightened sense of courage that he felt from watching his Lord mingling with the common soldiers.

Someone let out a cry of alarm and all eyes turned skywards as a single, bright green light shot up into the air from outside the gates. They watched in awe as the light rose higher and higher into the night sky before it exploded into a shower of green sparks.

"Ready your weapons," Rothule called grimly as he climbed back up onto the plinth. "We face a new enemy."

The elves stood slowly and drew their weapons, spinning swords in their hands and stroking the fletching of their arrows uneasily. Nervous eyes turned to stare into the green mist that lay beyond the gateway and ears twitched as they searched for any sound of the enemy. For a long while there was no sign of movement and the only sound came from the occasional shuffle of the elves as they waited tensely for the enemy to come.

Jaythun turned to the elves around him. They stood proudly in light, golden armour and white clothing, gripping curved spears, swords and bows firmly in their hands. Jaythun was a captain in the army, on his way to becoming a general, and he knew his words would carry some weight amongst the soldiers around him.

He smiled reassuringly at the men under his command. "Stand fast, friends!" he called. "We got through the last wave and we'll get through this one!" His voice took on a strong tone of authority that he lacked when speaking to his friends and he saw the elves straighten as he spoke.

From outside the gate, something heavy hit the floor. The loud *'thump!'* echoed loudly through the gateway, stirring the dust that hung in the still air. There was brief pause before a trio of armoured giants suddenly came thundering through the entrance. Each one stood at least fifteen feet tall, their fat, pinkish skin adorned with tattoos and wicked battle scars. They wore bits and pieces of crudely fashioned armour over equally crude clothing. Two carried massive clubs made of bone with bits of jagged metal driven into them for added damage. The third one, the one heading towards Jaythun, carried a long scythe which was also fashioned from bone.

"Spread out!" Jaythun yelled to the group of elves beside him. "Keep moving! We can confuse him!"

Jaythun set his jaw as the elves carried out his orders, breaking ranks and scurrying either side of the lumbering giant. The giant roared in confusion as the elves dodged and dived about him, his slow mind struggling to keep up with the agile figures.

The beast roared angrily as its eyes fell on Jaythun and he lunged forward in an attempt to crush the elf underfoot. But the young elf was too quick for the dim witted beast and he dove forwards, rolling out from behind the giant's leg and narrowly avoiding being squashed by the beast's hairy foot. As Jaythun stood he swung his sword out behind him, feeling the blade slow as it cut a deep gash in the beast's leg. The giant roared and spun around, swinging his scythe at Jaythun as it did so. Jaythun dropped awkwardly to his knees, feeling the rusted blade pass closely over his head. Several elves were not so quick and let out garbled screams as the massive blade bisected them across their waists. The giant stamped his feet in approval and let out a deep, booming laugh.

Snarling with determination, Jaythun jumped back onto his feet and charged between the giant's legs, swinging at the backs of its knees once more. The giant howled in pain as Jaythun's sword sliced through the tendons in its legs, causing the beast to tumble unceremoniously to the floor.

"Got you!" Jaythun grinned in triumph.

The elf scrambled onto the beast's stomach by using its arm as a step and hurried towards its head. However, the giant suddenly reached up with one massive hand and plucked Jaythun from his chest. Despite its pain the giant managed another deep chuckle as he held the helpless warrior in his iron grip. But just as the giant was about to squeeze the life from Jaythun, it let out a gasp of surprise.

Jaythun opened his eyes as the giant's grip relaxed and he tumbled onto the beast's soft, pink stomach. Looking up he saw Brenik, sword in hand, standing on the giant's head, a river of blood streaming down from the wound in the beast's bald skull.

"What are you doing here?" Jaythun asked accusingly.

"Saving you!" Brenik cried defensively as he hopped down onto the giant's stomach.

"Hey! I had the situation under control," said Jaythun as his friend pulled him to his feet.

"Oh, of course," Brenik said in mock seriousness. "But I saw the opportunity and thought I might save you the trouble." The elf chuckled as his friend thanked him. "Come on. This battle isn't over yet."

Chapter 4

The elves stood silently in bloodied courtyard, bathed in an increasingly pale light as one by one the torches that surrounded them burned through the last of their fuel. The courtyard floor was littered with the rotting corpses of the Kerberyn and the massive forms of the three dead giants that lay sprawled amongst the carnage that they had created.

Brenik sighed as he gently slid the eyes of a fallen elf closed and moved the body to the side of the battlefield. He was about to move another when the sharp sounds of horses' hooves filled the quiet night.

The elves hurried to their positions and watched as a group of four horsemen rode through the broken gates. Two of the four were humans, both cloaked in black with ornate gold and silver trinkets decorating their dark robes. The third rider was of the orc race. He wore a sleeveless, black leather vest with a long, black, fur cloak draped over his broad shoulders and his red hair was pulled tightly back into a long ponytail.

The final rider was the leader as far as Brenik could tell. The man, for Brenik was sure that that was what he was, was draped like the others in black robes. However, his robes somehow seemed darker and grander, making him by far the most imposing of the riders. The sharp points of the man's spiked armour protruded out from amongst the folds of his dark robes and atop his head, under the shadows of his hood, he wore a silver mask. The mask imitated a face, with hollow, black eye sockets and a small rectangular gap between the thin, metal lips. Two bands of short but sharp spikes wound their way around the mask's forehead and the chin itself ended with two long, vicious spikes that curved down and in on each other. At his waist hung a wicked longsword and in his right hand he gripped a black, metal staff tipped with a deep purple amethyst.

"So," King Lanir X said across the stillness of the courtyard, "the cowards finally stand before us."

The masked figure laughed, his deep chuckles echoing in the confines of his metal mask. "King Lanir. It is a pleasure to finally meet you."

Brenik felt a chill run down his spine as the man's icy voice filled his ears.

"Who are you?" Lanir demanded.

"A mere messenger of the Emperor," the man said dismissively. "There are those who call me the Emperor's Fist. I prefer to be known simply as the Masked Man."

"Why are you here?"

The Masked Man spread his arms wide. "We come before you today with the promise of order and power."

"Yet all we see here is chaos and cowardice!" Maleena countered dryly. "Who is your Emperor? What does he want with us?"

"The Master is the Emperor," the Masked Man said cryptically. "He can offer you power, strength and dominance over Justava and the weaklings who inhabit her."

Maleena raised a silver-black eyebrow. "You come here offering us power? You burn our city and you send waves of your undead soldiers to fight us, yet here we still stand. I think that we have shown our own power to be superior to whatever you have to offer."

"You have indeed fought bravely today, old woman," the Masked Man snapped in his deep voice. "But you are tired. Your city is in ruins and your army is near destruction. You cannot possibly hope to survive the night."

Brenik stepped forwards to stand proudly beside his parents. "Everything you have thrown at us, your walking dead soldiers, your great giants. Everything. We have fought and defeated it all." Brenik fixed the Masked Man with a cold stare. "We are but a small force. Once word reaches the other elven cities of what you have done here, then you will find that there will be no escape for you. The elves will stand united against you and your Emperor! We will not be destroyed by some upstart claiming a title that he has no right to hold!"

The Masked Man chuckled and turned to the King. "Are you really so weak that you let a child and an old woman speak in your place?"

"They are Lithuiks!" Lanir countered. "They have my respect and are free to speak with me!"

The Masked Man looked curiously at the Lithuik family. "It is good to have allies whom you can trust," he said thoughtfully.

"Why are you here?" Lanir demanded again. "Have you come to destroy the elves?"

The Masked Man tilted his head as he looked at the King. "You poor, naive little boy," he said in amusement. "You think this is about the annihilation of your species?" He chuckled and shook his head slowly. "No, this is something much bigger than you could ever hope to understand. A new order is rising. You will welcome it, or it will destroy you."

"Your plan, whatever it might be, has failed today. Your armies are weak, this city will not fall!" Rothule's commanding voice rang out across the courtyard and the remaining elves straightened at his resolve.

"You are wrong," the Masked Man hissed. "It is your men who are weak, your King who will fall!"

Lanir urged his horse forward. "You fight us with the broken souls of dead men and mindless beasts who do not know their left from their right! Our army is vastly superior to yours!"

The Masked Man laughed and urged his horse forward so that he drew level with Lanir. "We understand the capabilities of our army, King Lanir. That is why we have a plan." The Masked Man stopped and turned to regard Guillard. "General, it is time," he said softly.

There was a brief ring of steel followed by the sudden sound of metal scraping against metal. A gasp of surprise rang out across the courtyard and Brenik turned quickly around to see Jaythun standing behind him, the bloodied tip of a scimitar protruding from his chest. Nalia gasped in horror as their friend raised his hand towards them and tried to speak but instead only a small trickle of blood passed from behind his lips. The scimitar slowly retreated from Jaythun's lifeless body, allowing the young elf to drop limply into Nalia's arms.

Behind him, gripping his bloodied blade in his hand, stood Guillard Terune.

"Guillard!" Nalia breathed as she cradled Jaythun's lifeless body. "What have you done?"

Guillard looked down at Jaythun's cold body, refusing to meet Nalia's eyes and trying to ignore the horror in her voice. "I am doing what is best for our people." His voice was a whisper but as he raised his eyes and fixed Brenik with a hopeful stare it grew in volume. "You must see, Brenik! The world is weak! All the Kingdoms of Justava are ruled by weak, undeserving Lords! If things continue the way they are now then we will lose everything! I cannot let that happen!"

"And so you would betray your friends; you would betray your people and side with these . . . These demons?" Brenik spat in disgust.

"They are not demons!" Guillard protested. "They see life for what it truly is! We are shackled by the chains of society! The strong are held back in order to support the weak! Those who have the power are not able to use it because they are forced to bow down to the weak; to help those who do not help themselves!"

"That is their duty, Guillard!" Brenik shouted. "The strong must protect the weak!"

"No!" Guillard said firmly. "The weak must become strong or perish in their attempts! That or they must serve the strong. When my parents died I had nothing! My father was a tailor, I did not have the luxury of a title! But I worked my way up through our society. I worked and I trained and I earned my place amongst our people! I did not sit back thinking it was the duty of others to look after me! These people," Guillard said, moving in front of the horsemen, "they can change the world! Make it a place where those who work for power are rightfully rewarded! You must join with us Brenik! We will forge a new age of peace and prosperity together, as brothers!"

Brenik shook his head. "Your words are not your own Guillard," he said quietly. "You think that siding with a group of people who talk you into murdering your friend, betraying your soldiers and who raise the dead without a second thought will bring about peace? Guillard, you are wrong. And we will never join you."

"If you do not surrender," the Masked Man growled threateningly, "you will die."

Lanir turned back to the Masked Man, anger flooding his face as he reached for his sword. "No, you will die!" he roared.

Lanir's sword slashed through the air but just as it was about to strike the Masked Man's head from his body there was a flash of green light and the King of Cathwood was thrown from his horse. Cries of pain rose up from the gathered elves as their King's broken body hit the floor and he lay still.

The Masked Man lowed his staff, the amethyst still smoking gently. "I gave you the chance to join us," he whispered. "You still shall, but first there will be pain."

The horsemen raised their staffs and beams of energy filled the air as they launched their spells into the lines of nervous soldiers. The elves screamed in terror as green fires burst from the ground and strange, ghostly mists began clawing at their skin.

"Retreat!" Rothule roared from the plinth. "Get to the catacombs!"

Brenik ran toward the soldiers, shouting for them to fall back up the streets. As he turned his eyes widened as the orc fired a ball of green fire in his direction. Brenik dove aside, tackling Nalia to the floor moments before the spell raced over their heads to crash against the wall behind them.

Brenik grabbed Nalia's arm and they edged their way over to the porch of a ruined shop. "Stay down!" he yelled in Nalia's ear as more fireballs and bolts of blue and green lightning flew over their heads. "There is nothing we can do here."

They watched as the two elven magi fought side by side against the collected group of riders. The few elves that had remained, the majority of which were the Royal Guard, charged uncertainly towards the horsemen but were either shouted away by the Lithuiks or incinerated by the spells of the enemy.

Nalia and Brenik remained fixed in their alcove, watching the epic battle that was unfolding before them. Maleena fired off bolts of pure energy towards the riders and summoned barriers to protect her and her husband when the riders retaliated. In the meantime, Rothule summoned the power of fire and lightning, engulfing their enemies in blinding tornadoes of arcane magic. The riders fought back with green fire and lightning and bolts of crackling energy that drained the heat from the air in front of Brenik and Nalia as they zipped past them.

The Masked Man hurled a giant green fireball towards Rothule but the elven wizard quickly threw up a protective barrier, redirecting the fireball so that it raced back towards the riders and engulfed one of the surprised humans, leaving nothing but a small pile of ash behind.

The orc rider snorted and rode forward, waving his gnarled staff horizontally before his twisted face. Brenik saw the air before the orc begin to shimmer and watched as the attacks of his parents slammed into the invisible barrier without effect, some rebounding towards them. A lump of rock bounced onto the floor before Brenik and he looked up to see the shattered remains of Orlin Ferus' nose, blown from the statue by a bolt of lightning that had rebounded from the orc's shield. Behind the orc, the Masked Man raised his staff into the air and began chanting in an language that Brenik could not understand but recognised as the tongue of the Necromancers.

"What's happening?" Nalia yelled in Brenik's ear.

Before Brenik could reply, a streak of pure, dark purple energy shot forth from the black staff, passing unhindered through the orc's energy barrier and slamming into a surprised Rothule's chest. Brenik turned around in horror and watched his father disappear in a flash of purple light, leaving only the small pin of the Lithuik house and the shattered remains of his crooked staff behind.

"No!" Brenik cried as he scrambled to his feet and raced towards the statue. He dropped to his knees in front of the plinth, staring through his tears at the place where his father had last stood. He felt anger rising in his chest at his helplessness, a feeling he had only felt once before, and he clutched madly at his father's pin.

"Brenik!" The sound of his mother's voice snapped him from his trance and he turned around to see her still defiantly battling the horsemen. "Brenik you have to leave!" she said calmly.

"Mother, no!" Brenik said, reaching for his sword.

"Yes, my son, you must! I will not stand here and watch you die pointlessly. The world will need you my son. You and Nalia! I can buy you both enough time to get out but you must run and not look back!"

"I won't leave you to them!" Brenik protested.

Maleena smiled. "Curse your bravery my dear son. Think about it, Brenik. You have so much to live for! You can stop this, save Justava! But you must leave now!"

"But . . ."

"Brenik." Nalia's soft voice filled his ears and he felt her squeeze his hand reassuringly. "She is right."

Brenik turned to his mother, fighting once more against the tears that stung his eyes. "I will stop them," he promised bravely. "I love you."

"And I love you, my son," Maleena said gently.

A bolt of lightning struck the statue behind them again, sending a shower of small rocks clattering down about them.

"Go now!" Maleena yelled. As the two young elves made a break for one of the alleyways Maleena smiled to herself. "Be safe, young ones."

"You think you have saved them?" the remaining human sneered loudly. "Against the coming darkness, there is no safety!"

"Perhaps not," Maleena admitted.

A frown crossed the human's face as Maleena suddenly became cloaked in a blinding, white light. Drawing in her power, the elf suddenly unleashed it in a massive wave of energy. The human was thrown from his horse, slamming into the city wall with enough force to break his neck and end his life. The other horsemen and Guillard were thrown painfully to the floor, bruised but not seriously injured.

As Maleena Lithuik lay on her back, her energy and power completely drained, she looked up into the clouded night sky and smiled as the light from a lone, distant star shone through a break in the grey clouds.

"But there is always hope," she whispered as her eyes slid shut for the final time.

* * *

Guillard stepped over Maleena Lithuik's body without giving the old woman who had treated him like a son a second glance. "We should go after them," he demanded, staring down the alleyway which Brenik and Nalia had disappeared into.

The Masked Man rode up beside him. "Normally, yes. But might I remind you of the Master's very specific schedule, General Guillard?"

Guillard Terune, General of the army of the rising Necromancer Empire, looked down at Maleena Lithuik's family pin and placed the heel of his boot on the shining symbol.

"Yes. There will be another time," he whispered as he drove the pin into the courtyard's floor.

Chapter 5

Brenik and Nalia ran as fast as they could along the cobbled streets of Cathwood City. The city itself lay in ruins. All around them they could see buildings that had stood for hundreds of years now with huge chunks blown away by the enemy's catapults. A large fire was burning out of control in the northern side of the city and with the flames that were blazing all around them, Brenik was sure that the southern side would soon be engulfed in a similar inferno.

They ducked down a side alley and sprinted onwards until Brenik's sharp ears suddenly picked up a new sound. He turned and shoved Nalia backwards as a flaming chunk of rubble slammed into the building above them, showering the street with pieces of rubble and razor sharp shards of glass.

Nalia scrambled to her feet, coughing in response to the dust that had been thrown into the air. "Brenik?" she called, unable to keep the panic from her voice.

"I'm fine!" Brenik yelled from the other side of the flaming wreckage. "Go up three streets, we can meet up there!"

"Alright!" she called in relief. "Just be careful!" Nalia turned on her heels and hurried back down the deserted street that they had just climbed, passing the first two side alleys which led to dead ends before turning into the third street.

She froze in her tracks as her eyes met those of the lead Kerberyn of a group of about twenty creatures. Without thinking, she retreated back down the street and dove through the splintered door of a damaged house. She pressed herself up against the front wall, holding her breath as the pack of Kerberyn stumbled past the window, moaning in confusion.

After several long minutes, the group seemed to have passed when suddenly one of the undead beasts threw itself against the window. Nalia clamped her hands over her mouth as the drooling monster peered into the gloom of the deserted house. For what seemed like an eternity the creature remained staring dumbly through the window, long strings of yellow saliva inching their way down the dusty window-frames as the Kerberyn pressed its face against the glass until it eventually gave up its search and limped quietly off in pursuit of the rest of its pack.

Nalia lowered her hands and let out a long sigh of relief.

"Nalia!"

Brenik clamped his hand over his friend's mouth as she shrieked in surprise. She turned on him, fixing him with angry eyes as he pressed a finger to his lips and led her quietly through the back door.

"Sorry," Brenik said apologetically when they stepped into the adjacent street.

"Sorry?" she hissed. "You scared the life out of me!"

Brenik shrugged half-heartedly, not meeting her eyes. Either he was trying not to laugh or he was too distracted to notice his friend's distress.

"Sorry," he said again. "Come on, it's not far now." Slipping his hand into hers, Brenik led Nalia back into the maze of destroyed streets.

As they ran they stumbled past more hordes of Kerberyn, some standing motionless whilst others chewed at the corpses of their fellow zombies or of the elves they had killed. In both cases the two elves did not stop to fight. The Kerberyn were too distracted by the fresh corpses at their feet to worry about chasing two elves into the night so Brenik and Nalia were able to slip past them easily.

As they turned down a narrow street, Nalia frowned. "This is a dead end!" she called out as Brenik ran ahead.

"No, it's not." The young elf slowed to a stop as he reached the smooth rock surface of the mountain that the elven capital city was built against. Brenik ran his hands steadily over the stone wall before leaning his weight against the rock, resulting in a loud grating sound as a section of the stone wall gave way and swung inwards.

"You just have to know where to look," he said as he took a torch from the wall beyond the doorway.

Nalia followed Brenik into the dark tunnel, waiting as he closed the entrance behind them, trapping them in the long tunnel with nothing but the deep, orange light of the torch for guidance. Nalia was much shorter than Brenik and whilst her friend was forced to stoop over against the low roof of the tunnel, Nalia was able to stand fully upright. Even so, the cramped conditions and lack of light made her feel very claustrophobic.

"This tunnel was decommissioned many years ago," Brenik explained as he lit a second torch and handed it to Nalia. "There were concerns about the area to which it led. Whatever is there though, it can't be worse than what we faced back there."

"How do you know about it?" Nalia asked nervously as she took the torch.

"I came across it in one of my father's old record books. I've been meaning to explore it for years but never got round to it."

Nalia stopped short. "So you have no idea where it goes to?"

Brenik shrugged. "No, not really. But I'd rather face whatever's at the end than the hoards back there," he said, jabbing a thumb back towards the city.

Nalia chewed her lip uncertainly. "Fine. Lead the way," she said reluctantly before falling into step behind Brenik as he led them into the gloom.

*   *   *

For several hours the two elves trudged endlessly and silently through the cold tunnel. Occasionally Nalia would attempt to start a conversation, desperate to get her friend to talk of his parents or of Guillard's betrayal. However, Brenik's answers were short and unrevealing and the conversation would die down as quickly as it had begun. Normally, the two elves could spend an entire day just sat in each others' company, discussing the world and everyone and everything in it. The two of them had always been there for each other and even in Brenik's darkest hour he had not refused her help as he was doing now.

Nalia was just about to attempt another stab at a conversation when a thin shaft of white moonlight appeared ahead of them.

"Finally," Brenik muttered and with renewed energy the two elves quickly covered the short distance to the tunnel's exit.

Blinking as they stepped out into the bright light of the moon, they looked around and surveyed the area. The tunnel came out upon the top of a group of hills that rested against the tall mountains. From their position, Brenik guessed that they had walked straight through the thick stretch of the Boar's Tusk. The exit to the tunnel had been dug into a small recess in the mountains and the high, jagged walls that curved out on both sides of the hill where the elves stood provided them with shelter from unfriendly eyes. The top of the hill was dotted with two pairs of young reflin trees and a handful of dry gorse bushes. Down below, stretching out before them like a great pool of shadows, they could see the western boarder of the Great Forest.

"We should get away from the tunnel." Nalia's voice was low and had taken on a sudden edge. "And from that," she whispered as she nodded towards the forest.

"No," Brenik said, shaking his head. "They won't follow us, I am sure of that. We aren't important enough. Besides, we are sheltered from the wind here and we have a good view of our surroundings."

"What about water?" Nalia protested, desperate to get away from the threatening expanse of woodland.

Brenik pulled a small flask from his belt and tossed it towards her. "Don't drink too much," he cautioned. "We might have to make it last for a long time."

Nalia watched as Brenik turned his back on her and wandered back towards the tunnel, away from the crest of the hill. Slipping the flask onto her belt, she turned on her heels and followed him.

"Hey," she said softly, placing her hand on Brenik's arm when she caught up to him. "Talk to me, please."

Brenik sighed but did not turn around. His parents' deaths had struck him far harder than he had ever thought they would, leaving him with an overwhelming desire to avenge them and make their final stands worth the price that they had paid. But it had left him with something else as well; the realisation that those whom you love can be taken away with a mere click of the fingers. He looked back at Nalia and opened his mouth to speak. No words came out, however, she was just his friend, nothing more. Telling her how he felt about her would only make things more difficult for the both of them.

So instead, when Brenik turned around he simply forced a smile and said: "I'm fine. I'm just trying to process everything that has happened today."

Nalia looked up into her friend's deep blue eyes and without thinking, placed a hand on his warm cheek. She smiled at him and for a brief moment considered telling him how much she truly loved him. But she stopped herself, thinking that it would only bring more troubles to Brenik's already troubled mind. "Well, whatever you need, I am right here for you," she said instead.

Brenik smiled and touched her hand with his. "I know you are," he said, a small smile touching his lips.

Chapter 6

Brenik awoke suddenly, the sharp snap of a twig easily rousing him from his light sleep. He lay perfectly still, keeping his eyes half closed as he scanned the area around him. Nalia was asleep on his left side, in front of him lay a collection of the gorse bushes scattered around two of the juvenile reflin trees.

A shadow glided past in Brenik's peripheral vision and his eyes darted nervously in its direction. He was sleeping with the hilt of his sword a few centimetres from his face and he slowly moved his left hand onto the cool, leather grip.

"I wouldn't do that if I were you."

Brenik jumped at the sudden voice, scrambling to his feet and drawing his sword from its leather sheath. "Who's there?" he demanded, searching his surroundings for the owner of the voice.

"My dear boy, try to relax. I am up here."

Brenik glanced up into the intertwining branches of the nearest tree. A man was crouched on one of the largest branches, examining the two elves with great interest. He had short, black hair that was slicked neatly back over his head and his skin was as white as the snow that peaked the distant mountains of the far-off main range. He wore dark grey trousers with thin pinstripes running down the legs and an ornate silver breastplate underneath a long, black overcoat which was trimmed with fine silver buttons and lined with rich velvet and deep pockets. The man tilted his head curiously before dropping agilely from the branch to the ground. There was something unnatural about the movement, however, it was too fast, too smooth to be human.

"Forgive my intrusion on your rest," the man said as he stood slowly and extended a long-fingered hand towards Brenik. "I was merely curious as to who might be travelling in these forgotten lands." He had a thick accent which made his w's come out as v's.

Brenik kept his blade pointed at the man's white neck, ignoring the hand that remained extended in his direction. "We are not here by choice," the elf said coldly, very much aware of the dark forest spanning across the land behind the man. "Who are you?"

The man bowed deeply, pulling one side of his overcoat across his body as he did so. "My name is Yukov," he said politely. "Please, you have no need for your weapon."

Brenik lowered the blade to his hip but made no attempt to sheath the sword. "And what exactly are you doing here, Yukov?" he asked suspiciously.

"Well, this is my home!" Yukov exclaimed as he spread his arms out to indicate the vast expanse of the Great Forest that lay before them. "But forgive me! I am forgetting my manners. I have not asked your names! Or why two elves are so very far from their homes?"

"We have no home anymore," Brenik mumbled, unable to keep the sadness from entering his voice. "A group of magi practiced in the arts of Necromancy destroyed it."

Brenik's words were like a chain reaction in the man that stood before him. As soon as they left his mouth, Yukov's face contorted with anger. He hissed violently and drew back several steps and as he did so, Brenik noticed the two elongated fangs that were hidden behind the man's thin, purple lips. The elf immediately stepped back, tripping over Nalia's prone body as he rushed to regain his grip on his sword.

"Brenik?" Nalia said groggily as she sat up. Her eyes fell on Yukov. "Who are you?" she asked in confusion.

"Nalia, stay back!" Brenik called urgently as he stepped defensively in front of his friend and levelled his sword at Yukov's throat. "He's a vampire!"

Yukov the vampire ran a shaky hand over his slicked back hair as he quickly composed himself. "My apologies," he said slowly. "But I am familiar with who and what you speak of. These Necromancers, I know what they are like."

"Of course you do!" Brenik spat. "Vampires practically use Necromancy themselves!"

Yukov hissed violently again, causing both elves to jump in fright as his dark eyes burned a blazing orange and his fangs reappeared. "No!" he yelled, fighting to compose himself once more. "I understand that you do not trust me, but do not insult me in this way!"

"But you are of the undead. Your kind revolve around the powers of Necromancy!" Nalia exclaimed.

Yukov shook his head angrily at Nalia. "You know little of my kind. We, like many of the beings who roam the depths of the Great Forest, are descendant from the elder races. It was the old magic that gave us our strength and our power. Not this wild pathetic power that now plagues the world!"

Nalia looked down at her feet. "I'm sorry," she said. "I did not realise."

Yukov sighed and shook his head. "It is not your fault. The world has grown weak, the old magic forgotten. When I was a boy, this Necromancy would never have been tolerated. Ah, the power that the witches and wizards had in those days! The power that we vampires had as well!" He sighed again and looked at the floor. "Alas, like all of the elder races, our power has faded. And like so many others we must bow to lesser beings. I am truly sorry about your home, I know what it is like to lose everything that you love."

"Do you?" Brenik yelled, finally giving way to his grief. "Do you know what it's like to see your friends die? To have your parents killed without being able to do anything to help? You are a monster! You could never understand what we are going through!"

Yukov waited patiently for Brenik to finish before fixing the elf with a disarming stare. "Can't I?" he whispered. "Two hundred years ago, when I was only young, the three Kingdoms of Men began to hunt my kind. They claimed that we were an abomination against their Gods, a manifestation of their Devils. We were rounded up, placed into camps and executed." Yukov turned sadly away and looked down on the forest. "I was in my home, hidden at the western feet of the mountains, when the men attacked our village. I watched my parents and everyone I loved fall to the blades of their so called paladins, their holy warriors. There was nothing I could do to stop the attacks. Two days after I escaped my village, your people called for the attacks to stop. What was left of my kind were driven deep into the Great Forest, where we have remained until this day." Yukov fixed Brenik with a level stare. "I may seem like a monster, master elf. But I am still capable of all the same feelings as you are."

Brenik felt suddenly ashamed at his earlier outburst. Yukov had made no attempt to attack either of them, if that had been his plan he could have easily killed them both in their sleep.

Brenik lowered his sword and bowed his head slowly. "Forgive me, I have dishonoured you," he said softly, looking down at the ground before him. "I am Brenik Lithuik, and this is Nalia Sommer. We are elves from the City of Cathwood."

Yukov smiled as he shook both of the elves' hands in turn, the sadness that had touched his face earlier now vanishing. "Ah so this is where this tunnel goes to. I have always been curious to know." He smiled warmly at Nalia who could not help but smile back.

"We truly are sorry," Nalia began.

"Nonsense!" Yukov cried. "I am aware of the reputation of my kind, and you two look like you have faced a very challenging night. Your reaction was more than understandable."

"The Necromancers have completely destroyed our city," Brenik explained. "I fear they plan to do the same to not only the elven cities but to the entirety of the Seven Kingdoms as well."

Yukov nodded solemnly. "Yes. They have come to the forest many times with the promise of power. They recruited many creatures, vampires, werewolves, banshees and many others. If we refused they tried to kill us." Yukov chuckled and licked his lips. "That did not go so well for them."

"So there are some of you left?" Brenik said eagerly. "People who are willing to stand against their armies?"

Yukov chuckled and held up his hands. "Steady, Brenik. Standing up to an army and refusing to be recruited to one are very different things, my friend." The vampire shook his head before smiling again. "But we are getting ahead of ourselves and the grumbling of your stomachs is telling me there are more important matters to tend to."

Brenik and Nalia looked at each other, both suddenly realising how hungry they were.

Yukov glanced quickly up at the distant, pale orange sky; the sun was beginning to rise. "Come with me," he said quickly, a slight edge creeping into his voice, "I can take you back to my home where I have food and shelter. And I promise, I will not eat you," the vampire added, grinning at the two elves.

Brenik licked his lips nervously and looked at Nalia. She looked back expectantly, waiting for him to make the decision.

"Well," Brenik said slowly. "I suppose it's better than sleeping out here where anything could attack us. The next vampire might not be so accommodating."

Nalia grinned at her friend. "And he did promise not to eat us," she reasoned cheerfully.

Brenik turned to the vampire. "Lead the way, Yukov," he said, scarcely believing his own words.

Chapter 7

General Guillard Terune stood on the wide balcony of the tall Council Tower that overlooked Cathwood City, feeling very out of place. To his left stood the grand Royal Palace, still shining proudly in the morning sun despite the scorch marks that now stained its white walls. On Guillard's right were the Lords' estates, their high walls reduced to rubble as looters scoured their hallways. Then there was the tower that Guillard stood in. the tower was where the city's nobility had once come to discuss political issues such as new tax legislations or military movements. Guillard was surrounded by the nobility and he did not like it.

Trying to divert his attention, he looked out at the city. He sighed as he looked at the charred remains of buildings and areas that had been completely flattened by the Empire's catapults. He had known that the invasion would not leave the city undamaged, however, he had not realised just how brutal the damage would be.

Guillard shifted his feet uncomfortably and glanced down into the tower's wide courtyard which was packed with the citizens and warriors who had survived the battle that had raged through their city. They were huddled closely together, families holding each other protectively as the feral Kerberyn roamed slowly around the terrified elves, licking their cracked lips longingly.

"Strange isn't it? That even the greatest of civilisations can be reduced to nothing in the blink of an eye."

Guillard jumped at the deep, ragged sound of the Masked Man's voice. He was standing just behind Guillard, his hands clasped behind his back as he surveyed the circle of elves and the broken remnants of the city behind them. Like almost all who knew of him, Guillard had no idea as to the Masked Man's appearance, let alone his race or name. For all Guillard knew, the Masked Man could have even been the Masked Woman, although he seriously doubted that.

Realising that the Necromancer was waiting for an answer, Guillard quickly nodded at the black figure. "Yes," he whispered.

"You did well today, Guillard," the Masked Man said, placing an armoured hand on the elf's shoulder. "It would seem that I was right to select you for this task. You have more than earned the position of General, my friend."

Guillard smiled and bowed his head graciously. "Thank you, My Lord." He glanced at the captives in the courtyard below. "What will happen now?"

The Masked Man stepped to one side, clearing the space before the doors to the inside of the tower. "Watch, and you will see."

The small group that stood on the balcony, all of whom were witches or wizards with the exception of Guillard, suddenly fell silent and stepped back, forming a walkway that led from the tower doors to the front of the wide balcony.

Slowly, one of the tall, brown doors creaked open to reveal a slight figure clad in a heavy, black cloak and hood. The cloak fell tightly around his thin frame and the tips of the drooping sleeves brushed gently over the smooth, stone floor as the figure glided forward. When the cloak parted, Guillard could see the blood red lining on the inside of the black folds. A silver clasp depicting a hand gripping the top of a cracked skull fastened the cloak around the figure's neck and in his left hand he gripped a black staff tipped with a blood-red ruby clasped by three claw-like spikes. The figure walked slowly and leant heavily on his staff, but even so, he exuded an air of complete dominance over all the other beings gathered on the balcony.

The Masked Man stepped in front of the figure and bowed deeply. "Master," he said softly, his voice filled with respect for the shadowy figure.

Guillard straightened at the cloaked man's title. The Master was the leader of the Necromancers, the self-proclaimed Emperor of the

Necromancer Empire and the orchestrator of the plot to overthrow Justava's many rulers. He was a man who few had seen and even less had spoken to.

"You have done well, my friend," the Master said in a frail voice, placing a withered hand on the cheek of his dark lieutenant's mask. Under his hood he turned his head to face Guillard. "As have you, my new General."

Guillard quickly dropped to one knee. "Thank you, Master," he stammered quickly.

The Master chuckled softly to himself and continued along the line of Necromancers, greeting some fondly and offering congratulations to others. When he came to the edge of the balcony he stood silently for a while, examining the scene below him. Then he spoke in a deep, booming voice that sounded far from the initial frail voice that had first congratulated Guillard.

"Citizens of Cathwood!" the Master began, commanding an immediate silence from the captives below. "Today you have been given a great honour! You are the first of many who will join my Empire! The Necromancer Empire! Your time has come, at last you will serve true power and you will be rightfully rewarded!" The Master laughed harshly. "Oh but I know, you are elves, proud people! I know you will resist."

Guillard watched the crowd shuffle uncomfortably below. Some were glaring up at the Master with bold defiance and hatred etched upon the faces, bristling to reclaim their homes. Others looked down fearfully, the threat of the strange powers that they had witnessed sapping their spirits.

"But you would be foolish to do so," the Master continued. "You are perhaps the greatest civilisation to have graced our fair Justava. That is why you will be the first race to join me. You will become my scholars and my elite warriors! My enforcers, my iron fist against the tyranny of man and dwarfs alike! You have only but to bow to me and I will restore the power that was once yours!" The shadowed half of his face showed the Master's cruel smile as he finished his speech and spread his arms invitingly out before him.

"Murderer! Why would we bow to scum like you?"

The outburst was so immediate, so defiant, that it took a moment to register amongst the Necromancers who quickly began whispering urgently and craning their necks to get a look at the bold offender.

The Master scowled from under his hood but waited patiently as the crowd parted to reveal a lone male elf staring defiantly up at him.

"You have spirit," the Master said dryly, cocking his head so that the light fell on his smooth chin. "Tell me, what is it that you do?"

"I am a defender of Cathwood! A member of the Guard!" the young elf yelled proudly. "I watched your creatures butcher my family and burn my home! I ask you, why should I bow to you? Why would I ever want to serve you?"

The Master turned slightly to glance back down his line of lieutenants. "General, come up here," he instructed.

Guillard blinked in surprise, momentarily forgetting his new title. A gentle shove from the Masked Man, however, brought him back to his senses and he hurried up to stand beside the Master.

The Master placed a surprisingly firm hand on Guillard's shoulder as he turned back to face the former guard. "Do not bow because I am asking you to. Bow because he is asking you!"

A collective gasp rose up from the people of Cathwood as one by one they began to recognise their own Captain of the Guard.

The elf guard took a step back in surprise, his brow furrowing in confusion. "Captain?" he said slowly. "What are you doing? What's going on?"

"What is right, Ethnar," Guillard replied cooly, recognising the man as one of the men who had been posted in his personal unit of guardsmen. "These people can offer us a chance to grow strong once more! We all know our history. Long ago it was the elves who ruled Justava! But then that power was passed on to lesser beings. The Necromancers can give us a chance to take back what is rightfully ours! We can rule the lands as we did so many years ago! We will have our rightful place restored to us! You must bow to him, Ethnar!"

The Master smiled coldly as an urgent whisper rose up amongst the prisoners as they saw their captain standing so confidently beside the invaders. Guillard's belief in the Empire would serve the Master well in his conquest of the rest of the elven Kingdoms.

Ethnar looked hopelessly down at the ground as the men and women around him began to question their standing. However, as one woman began to bow his face suddenly hardened and he turned his cold eyes upon his former captain. "You have betrayed your oath, Captain!" he shouted back at Guillard. "You have surrendered your honour and I for one will not serve under a betrayer!"

"If you will not serve, you will die!" the Master said harshly, growing tired of the elf's performance.

Ethnar dropped to his knees and spread his arms wide. "Then let me die!" he yelled defiantly.

The Master tightened his grip on his staff and slowly raised his free hand. "So be it," he whispered.

A flare of green energy burst forth from the Emperor's fingertips and snaked down to strike Ethnar in the chest, lifting him up into the air. The young elf screamed as he became engulfed by the green light. His blonde hair began to turn a dull grey and shrink back into his skull. His smooth skin began to crease and wrinkle and his eyes became clouded. Within seconds the bright, young elf was stripped of his life. The Master took in a deep breath as he absorbed the energy that he had drained from Ethnar. There was a final flash of light and Ethnar's dusty bones clattered onto the cobbles of the courtyard. The Master exhaled slowly and closed his eyes in satisfaction as he lowered his blackened, smoking hand.

The demonstration had had its desired effect. Slowly, one by one, the other elves began to drop submissively to their knees.

A cruel smile spread across the Master's unshadowed mouth as he claimed his victory. "Welcome to the Empire!" he roared in triumph. He then turned to the Masked Man who had approached them without Guillard's notice.

"The first city has fallen, My Lord," the Masked Man said quietly as the three men began to walk slowly back towards the tower doors.

"Yes," the Master sniffed as he stepped into the room behind the doors. The office had once belonged to Rothule Lithuik and was decorated with plush red furniture and beautiful works of art. The Master walked over to Rothule's massive desk and settled himself into the golden chair behind it, resting his staff against the back of the chair and his arms on the cushioned armrests.

The Masked Man stood opposite the Master, leaning on his staff. "And with Cathwood under our control, the Kingdom of Rochelle will fall quickly."

"Do not get carried away, my friend," the Master cautioned. "Remember, we must ensure dominance over this Kingdom first. The other Necromancers have their orders, as do you."

"What are my orders, My Lord?" Guillard asked carefully.

The Master ignored the elf. "Whilst you see to the second stage of our plan, they will secure the rest of the Kingdom," he continued to say.

The Masked Man glanced back out of the doors to where the captives were held. "Are we ready to begin the second stage?" he asked uncertainly.

The Master nodded curtly. "Yes. Better we test it on a few before we find that what we are attempting is not possible." He glanced thoughtfully down at the symbol of the Lithuik household etched into the beautiful desk. "Take the prisoners to the dungeons and begin the conversion process." The Master paused thoughtfully. "Test it on the children before you do the soldiers," he added.

"What of my suggestion? Am I to proceed as we discussed?" The Masked Man asked slowly.

The Master glanced at Guillard and nodded. "Yes, I think the General has shown sufficient loyalty. You may proceed with your experiment."

Before Guillard could ask what was happening he felt a strange sensation pass over him. His eyes felt heavy and he was suddenly aware that he was falling. By the time Guillard hit the floor he was already unconscious.

Chapter 8

The banshee screamed a horrible, high pitched note that caused Nalia's ears to ring and her blood to freeze in terror. The creature stood about two metres tall with flaming red hair that fell down around her cracked, pink-grey skin. When she screamed, her mouth stretched unnaturally wide and her eyes burned with orange fury.

"Get back!" Yukov yelled as he dropped low and charged towards the creature.

The banshee screamed again, clutching her contorted head before ducking down and charging the vampire in return. The two met in a fury of teeth and claws, lashing out at each other with wicked nails and hungry mouths.

Brenik dove to one side as the fighters flailed towards him, passing him by and crashing into a tree where they hacked and slashed their way through the vines that threatened to entangle them. Suddenly Yukov had the banshee pinned against the trunk of the tree, holding her tightly by her thin neck as she thrashed uselessly against his iron grip. A strange look came over the vampire's face; his pale eyes blackened and his sharp fangs slipped out from behind his lips as his jaw opened wide and he began to feed.

Brenik held a defensive arm out before Nalia as the vampire crouched over the banshee's now lifeless body, doing his best to ignore the slurping sounds that rose up from their guide as he drained the twisted woman of her blood.

"Yukov?" Brenik said cautiously, his right hand dropping to the sword at his hip, his body tensed and ready to fight.

Yukov stood slowly and turned. His pale mouth was stained red with blood and his eyes were as black as night. He took a threatening step towards the elves before snapping his coat up to cover his face.

"Get ready to run," Brenik whispered urgently.

Yukov's coat dropped away and he was stood as he was before, bright eyed and clean faced. "I am sorry you had to see that," he said with regret. "I can't imagine it helped to improve your image of me."

Nalia relaxed slightly as Brenik lowered his arm uncertainly. She glanced behind the vampire, looking nervously at the body of the banshee. "What is it?" she asked.

"A banshee," Yukov replied. "They are cursed men and women and the only people in the forest who will not see reason." Yukov glanced at the creature's blood drained body. "If I had not killed her, she would never have stopped hunting us."

"What would she have done to us?" Nalia whispered.

"She would have killed you, Nalia," Yukov said bluntly. "Banshee's have no interest in members of the same gender."

"And us?" Brenik asked.

A dark shadow crossed Yukov's face. "We would have been her prize. Never to leave her domain until we died or became mad ourselves."

Both Yukov and Brenik shuddered at the thought of becoming a slave to the maddened woman.

"Come," Yukov said as he stepped back onto the twisting path that ran through the forest, "we are not far from my house. We will be safe there."

*   *   *

Nalia let out a sigh of relief as Yukov's small hut came into view. For hour after hour the three companions had marched uneasily through the knotted trees of the Great Forest, constantly alert to any signs of attack from another banshee. Throughout the entire march none of them had said more than a few words; Brenik's hand had never left the hilt of his sword and Nalia had kept a tight hold on her longbow. Even Yukov's cheerful disposition had dulled, replaced instead by a grim determination born from years of living within the confines of the deadly forest.

"You can relax now," Yukov said as they stepped into the small clearing. "This area is safe from intruders."

The two elves nodded quickly but kept their weapons close until they slipped past the stone wall that surrounded Yukov's home. Against the bleak darkness of the forest, the small house looked warm and inviting. The single storey building stood on a slightly raised platform and a small veranda sat outside of the front wall, bearing a single cushioned rocking chair and some well tended plants. The wooden walls of the house had been roughly painted in white and a grey, stone chimney sat against the wall on the far side. The small garden area surrounding the hut was covered in neatly trimmed grass and a stack of firewood leant up against the far wall. Despite being in a clearing, only patches of sunlight were able to reach the house due to the broad covering of the tall reflin trees that bent over and intertwined with each other, blocking out the light from high above the building. Despite the lack of sunlight, however, the house still looked cheerful and Nalia could not help but laugh softly at the thought of the monster who they'd just seen suck the blood from the banshee living in the quaint little home.

Inside, the house appeared even more comfortable than it had on the outside. A stone fireplace sat against the far wall of the main room and plush, red and purple cushions and rugs had been placed neatly around the stone hearth. Tapestries depicting strange symbols and carefully woven figures hung from the smooth wooden walls and thick, dark curtains draped down either side of the arched windows. A small door off to one side led into what Nalia assumed was Yukov's chambers; the door was shut and a large imposing lock prevented any unwanted visitors from entering the room.

"Come in!" Yukov said cheerfully. "Welcome to my home!"

"It's wonderful, Yukov!" Nalia exclaimed as she stamped the mud off of her boots before stepping over the threshold.

Brenik looked suspiciously around as he stepped through the doorway. "You are well stocked for someone who lives in a forest," he commented sourly as he noticed the dining area and the pair of expensive, silver candles that sat on the large, round table.

Nalia chewed her lip awkwardly. She could see that Brenik still had very little trust for their new companion and she could hardly blame her friend. The episode with the banshee had reminded her just how potentially dangerous their new ally could be. However, Yukov was proving every story that she had ever heard about the vampires to be wrong, meaning that either the scholars were wrong or that Yukov was not what he seemed.

"If you are implying that I stole these items," the vampire said, a wry smile crossing his pale face, "then you would be correct. What you see are items that I recovered from the villages of my people. We, the other vampires and myself that is, were able to briefly return home after being driven away. We all took as much as we could and returned everything to its rightful owners." Yukov looked at the candles sadly. "Of course, not everything had an owner to return to."

"Do vampires not live together anymore?" Nalia asked. She knew from the legends that vampires tended to live in small groups, with one vampire claiming dominance over the rest through regular demonstrations of strength and agility.

Yukov shook his head. "It is too dangerous for us now. Besides," he added sadly, "many of us prefer to live alone now, where we can be at peace with our grief."

Nalia nodded slowly. If Yukov had taught her one thing about his deadly race, it was that the bond that ran between a pack of vampires was one of the strongest that she had ever encountered. She could sense that behind his surprisingly friendly personality, Yukov was hiding a man stricken with the two hundred year old grief of the loss of both his pack and family.

Brenik shifted his feet, eager to discuss the possibility of gaining support from the other residents of the forest. "Before, you mentioned other vampires. Do they share your views on Necromancy?"

Yukov laughed softly. "Brenik, my friend. You think that you can raise an army over night even though you are close to exhaustion!"

Brenik shrugged, refusing to acknowledge his heavy eyelids and empty stomach.

Yukov smiled and placed a kind hand on Brenik's shoulder. "The time for fighting will come soon enough. But now you must eat and you must rest. Now sit!"

Yukov gently pushed Brenik onto one of the cushions beside the fireplace and disappeared off into a small door that Nalia had not noticed at first. "Tend the fire if you want something to do!" the vampire called over his shoulder.

Brenik sighed in defeat as he picked up the poker and began prodding half-heartedly at the few remaining embers in the fireplace. For a moment Nalia watched him try fruitlessly to restart the fire, then she knelt down beside him and placed a hand on his broad shoulder.

"Hey," she said softly into his ear. "We are going to be fine. You know that don't you?"

Brenik snorted and threw the poker down into the grate, tired of trying to ignite the fading embers. "Oh sure!" he spat with anger that seemed to surprise even himself. "We've lost our homes and our friends and we're currently lodging with a man who could potentially start drinking our blood whilst we sleep! Sounds just fine to me!"

Nalia shifted so that she could look into Brenik's deep blue eyes. She knew that his sarcasm was not meant to hurt her. Her friend was angry, not at her, not at the men who had destroyed his home, but at himself. Guilt had a terrible effect on her friend and it was a burden which, unfortunately, he readily accepted.

"Bren, you did everything you could," she said, her voice soft and calming.

"How can you be this calm?" Brenik asked in exasperation. "Your parents are supposed to be leaving your estate to return to Cathwood City tomorrow! Are you not afraid for them?"

Nalia looked up at Brenik, tears stinging the corners of her eyes. "Terrified," she admitted.

Brenik watched as she sighed and took hold of the poker, gently prodding the embers together around some unburnt kindling.

"But I know that if we survived the attack, if we escaped capture and that if we encountered someone who we thought to be a murderer but then in fact turned out to be a man simply offering us food and shelter." She paused and looked deeply into her friend's eyes as the fire flickered to life. "Well if that is the case then I know that there is hope for their survival as well as ours."

Brenik smiled at the fire and looked up at his friend, realising how much his words had unintentionally stung her. He leaned forward and pulled her close to him, and for a long moment, the two friends simply held each other in their arms.

From the door to his pantry, Yukov smiled at the sight of the two young elves embracing each other. They had been through so much he thought. The support that they could provide each other would be invaluable over the long days that were to come. Yukov liked them both. Brenik was understandably suspicious of the vampire, but Yukov felt confident that, given time, he could make the elf see that his intentions were pure and that he truly did want to help.

Yukov suddenly found himself thinking of his own family, and he felt the familiar twinge of guilt run through his body at their memory and of his final hours with them. However, looking out upon the two young elves, he could not help but notice that the guilt that he felt was far less severe than usual. Perhaps, way out on the boarders of the Great Forest, Yukov had finally found something that could make him happy once more.

Chapter 9

Guillard awoke with a start, his breath catching in his throat and causing him to cough violently. He was lying on a smooth, wooden board, looking up at the ceiling. His wrists and ankles were shackled to the wood with thick, iron bands. He strained to lift his heavy head and look around.

He could tell that he was in the dungeons under Cathwood's Council Tower, where all prisoners were kept in varying degrees of captivity. The room that he was in was square and built from slabs of roughly cut, dull, grey rocks. Opposite him, a thick wooden door with heavy, iron bolts denied him any chance of escape. Two small torches flickered either side of the doorway and from the small, barred window built into the door he could hear the sound of people screaming.

"Good morning, General," said a familiar voice.

Guillard twisted in his shackles but was unable to face the voice that came from behind him. "Where am I?" he spluttered.

"The dungeons, my friend." The Masked Man's armoured boots clicked against the flagstone as he moved slowly to stand beside Guillard. "It is only a temporary position, do not worry."

"What is happening? Why am I here?" demanded the General.

The Masked Man leant slightly on his tall, black staff, the jagged lump of amethyst that tipped the black rod shining brightly in the torchlight. "When we say that the elves are the most advanced civilisation in Justava, we do not lie. But even so, there is room for improvement."

The Masked Man gently touched a spot on Guillard's arm. The elf glanced down and frowned. His skin was pale, very pale, and was tinted a faint, grey-white colour. He could clearly see his veins, each one a line of purple streaking across his white skin, all converging on this one spot that the Necromancer was touching.

"Does it hurt?" the Masked Man asked curiously as he indicated the small scar on Guillard's arm.

Guillard shook his head. "What have you done to me?"

"The reason the elves were attacked first was because you posed the greatest threat to our plans," the Masked Man said, ignoring Guillard's question. "But as you know, the Master never intended to destroy your people. We knew that you had the potential to become our greatest allies, if you could be turned."

Guillard frowned. "But they did turn! You saw them bow to you outside! You only need to show them fear and they will be yours!"

The Masked Man snorted. "You know that fear does not make for a stable relationship, General. No, you elves are a stubborn people and the Master knew that you would not turn willingly."

"So you are going to chain us up in here and brainwash us? I was loyal to you already!"

"In a way General, you are not far wrong," the Masked Man said slowly. "Within the scrolls that teach the power of Necromancy we found the power to alter the physical state of both the body and mind. Due to my advanced ability in the magic of illusion, particularly teleportation, I was able to help the Master recreate the ritual, allowing us to turn your elves into the ultimate fighting force. They will be physically strong and completely obedient to whatever orders we give to them. They have become the perfect soldiers."

With a wave of the Necromancer's hand the shackles holding Guillard to the table clicked open and the Masked Man helped the elf to sit up.

"I feel strange," Guillard mumbled, rubbing his wrists and blinking as the blood rushed to his head.

"The effects of the magic," the Masked Man said dismissively as he helped Guillard off of the wooden table. "We altered your body but left your mind untouched. I felt your loyalty was already assured."

Guillard allowed himself to be guided to the rear of the room where the Necromancer placed him before a covered mirror. He swayed unsteadily on his feet, his bleary eyes coming in and out of focus as his brain tried to make sense of everything.

The Masked Man watched the General carefully as he moved slowly behind the mirror and took hold of the sheet. "Now look, and see yourself reborn!" he declared grandly as he threw back the sheet.

Guillard gasped as the white sheet fell away from the mirror, revealing his reflection. Guillard's body had changed. He was taller and broader than before, the muscles of both his arms and legs thicker and clearly defined so that his skin rippled with strong contours and well defined features.

Guillard grunted as he flexed his fingers. "I feel broken," he whispered as his fingers clicked in protest to the movements.

"A natural reaction," whispered the Masked Man. "You will regain control over your limbs soon. With time you will become used to the changes. You will be faster and stronger. You will also find your eyes are sharper and your hearing even greater than before."

Guillard looked at himself in the mirror. Although he was more muscular his face appeared more drawn than ever, seeming almost skeletal. His lips were thin and stained purple and his hair had become thick and greasy. His eyes were also different, having lost their former colour, his irises were now completely black with only small flecks of green remaining, making it almost impossible to tell where the pupils began.

The Masked Man saw him examining his face. "Channelling so much power into a single being rarely leaves the person unscathed. Like the hand that withers from the spell, your appearance contorted as your body grew."

Guillard looked at his deformed face, raising a hand and running it over his hollow cheeks and high forehead. Then he looked down at his body, his muscles bulging with strength that he had never before known. He nodded slowly. The improvement was worth the cost.

The Masked Man watched Guillard silently before placing a gloved hand on the elf's shoulder. "Come, I have a gift to give you. Something fitting for the General of the Necromancer Empire."

Guillard followed the Masked Man obediently out of his cell and into the corridor outside. His legs felt shaky as he walked and on more than one occasion he lost his footing and stumbled forwards to the dusty floor below. But gradually he began to feel more normal and his sense of balance slowly returned to his altered body. The Masked Man was right. He did feel stronger.

As they walked down the long, empty corridor, Guillard realised that he had been held in one of the solitary cells, reserved for political prisoners or the more deadly criminals of society. As they made their way into the main complex they passed the general prison cells which housed the imprisoned citizens of Cathwood. Upon the sight of their former captain several of the elves recoiled in fear at his strange, new appearance whilst others threw him disgusted glares. In both cases Guillard ignored the prisoners, their angry cries falling on deaf ears.

Leaving the general cells behind them, they continued on and passed a corridor that led down to the interrogation rooms. It was here that the screams were coming from.

"To alter the mind, it can be a painful process," the Masked Man said in response to Guillard's questioning look.

Guillard nodded and followed the other man into a small corridor, trying to recall the process of his change. "I remember no pain," he said eventually.

"That is because we did not alter your mind. As I said before, I was confident in your loyalty."

"How does one alter the mind and body?" the General inquired.

The Masked Man looked briefly at Guillard before answering. "It is a long process. First one must consume the essence of another who has the desired traits. Then that essence must be transferred to another and manipulated in such a way that it becomes dominant over the host's original traits. In some ways it is not dissimilar to teleportation, only in this case, one leaves the body behind and transfers only the soul."

Guillard frowned thoughtfully. "Where did you find the desired traits?"

The Masked Man shrugged. "The Kerberyn. Their blind obedience and general hatred of everything that doesn't bring them food made them a perfect choice for the mind transfer."

"But the Kerberyn lack intelligence," Guillard protested.

"That is why we only take the desired traits," the Masked Man said slowly as if he were talking to a child.

"What of the body transfer?" Guillard asked after a short pause.

"The giants. Their essence is great enough that it can be divided between several bodies and still produce the desired results."

Guillard nodded slowly as his mind began to process the information. He almost walked straight into the Masked Man before he realised that they had come to a halt. They had stopped in the middle of a long corridor which eventually led to a large cavern that was used as both a place of storage and a place of safety during war. It was here that the women and children had fled to during the invasion. They were stood beside a small wooden door, standing a few metres from the exit to the cavern.

"Your gift. A General deserves equipment befitting his position," the Masked Man said slyly before pushing the door open.

The room beyond the door was small and square, made of the same dark stone as the rest of the prison cells. A table and chair sat in one corner with a set of simple black clothes folded on the table's surface. What caught Guillard's eye, however, was the straw mannequin that stood against the opposite wall.

The mannequin was draped in a beautiful set of armour. A shining breastplate of silver sat loosely on the chest, bearing an image of a hand resting atop a large, cracked skull etched upon the otherwise smooth surface. Matching vambraces and shin guards were strapped to the mannequin's wrists and shins and on top of its head stood a tall conical helmet that left the mouth and eyes free whilst providing protection to the cheeks and nose. On top of the helmet was a dark purple plume that flowed down to the bottom of the mannequin's back. All of the armour pieces glinted in the light of the torches that lit the room and Guillard noticed that each piece was adorned with ornate golden filigree. Accompanying the armour was a purple skirt that fell down from underneath the breastplate to end just above the knees and a long, purple cape that was attached to the shoulders of the breastplate by golden clasps in the shape of skulls.

Guillard stepped forwards and ran his hand over the breastplate. "It's beautiful," he whispered, staring with the same wonder that a child might possess when in a toy store.

"And armour of such a standard should be accompanied by a weapon to match it," the Necromancer whispered from the doorway.

From under the folds of his cloak, the Masked Man produced a long scimitar which he held with the hilt pointing towards Guillard. The elf stepped gingerly forward and took hold of the weapon. It was perfectly balanced; the blade glinted in the torchlight as he turned it in his broad hands, aching to be used. The hilt itself shone with the same gold that decorated his armour and the moulded leather grip felt comfortable in his strong fingers.

The Masked Man handed Guillard a belt with a loop in to sheath his new weapon. "Arm yourself, General. You go to address your men shortly," he said proudly.

Guillard nodded, taking the belt as the Masked Man disappeared outside. He eagerly removed his ragged clothing and donned the black trousers, shirt and boots that waited on the table. Taking care not to smudge the gleaming silver, he slipped the breastplate and skirt over his head before fastening the straps at either side. He then pulled the vambraces and shin guards tightly around his limbs and secured the purple cloak to his shoulders. Finally he buckled his belt about his waist and sheathed his scimitar. Due to the weapon's curve the scimitar had no full sheath so the blade was left to hang openly at the General's side, a constant threat to any who might oppose him. As Guillard left the room he took the helmet and tucked it under his left arm before running a hand through his long hair. He looked in the mirror and smiled, for the first time since his betrayal, Guillard's doubts over his actions had vanished completely.

"How do you feel?" the Masked Man asked knowingly when Guillard re-entered the corridor.

Guillard smiled dryly. "Much better."

"Good. Then I think you are ready to meet the men that you will command."

They walked silently down the remainder of the corridor, the ringing of their armour the only sound in the long hall, before stepping out into the huge vaunted cavern.

Stalagmites and stalactites littered the floor and ceiling of the cave, casting strange shadows in the light of the many torches that lit the rocky walls. Guillard and the Masked Man came to stand on a large balcony with stairs leading down to the main level at either end. Below them was the wide open floor of the cavern. Today it was filled with hundreds of soldiers.

The soldiers stood in units of twelve, four men wide and three men deep. In the elven society women were allowed to join the military, but Guillard could see very few women in the male dominated ranks that stood before them. The soldiers wore similar armour to Guillard's, although theirs was far less ornate. The breastplates were smooth and undecorated and did not shine in the same way that Guillard's did. Each one wore vambraces and shin guards, but whilst Guillard wore clothing underneath his armour, the elves' skin was bear, the only clothing that they wore being the purple skirts and cloaks similar to Guillard's and a padded vest under their breastplates. The material of the soldiers' clothes was thinner than Guillard's, however, making the colour appear less rich but proud nonetheless. The cloaks were also much shorter that the General's, ending at ankle height rather than dragging behind the wearer as Guillard's did. Each soldier stood holding a vicious looking halberd in their right hand whilst their left hand rested on the hilt of the short sword hanging from their belts. As Guillard and the Masked Man came to a stop the assembled soldiers straightened and saluted with their left hands, placing a closed fist over their twisted hearts.

"They are almost ready," the Masked Man explained. "We took from the prisoners those most suited to become soldiers and initiated the changes. We estimate we will achieve at least twenty more units from the prisoners. The rest will be put to use elsewhere."

"We would have had more had you not killed so many in the invasion," Guillard said bitterly.

The Masked Man conceded the point before resting his hand on Guillard's shoulder. "This is but one of the great elven cities, General. When we go to the next cities, when they see their brethren standing amongst our ranks, then more will join us."

Guillard nodded slowly as he looked at the elves with their drawn, pale faces and black eyes. They were far removed from their original appearances. "What do we call them?" he asked.

"They will be known simply as the dark elves. The elite warriors of the Empire! And they, General Terune, are yours to command."

Guillard Terune looked down upon his warriors and rested his free hand on the balcony. "Soldiers!" he bellowed in a commanding voice. "Whom do you serve?"

"The Empire!" the dark elves chanted in unison, raising their halberds in salute of the newly formed Empire.

A thin smile touched General Guillard's lips. "Yes," he said softly to the Masked Man. "I think they will do nicely."

Chapter 10

"Let's take a look at things shall we?"

Nalia quickly pulled the wooden bowl that she had been eating from out of the way as Yukov unfolded a large map between her and Brenik.

"Now, we are here," Yukov said, absently poking the map.

Nalia looked curiously at the small drawing of the Great Forest which sat in the northeast corner of the map. To the north ran the Greyhelm Mountains and the long Boar's Tusk speared downwards to the west of the forest. East of the forest lay the vast expanse of the Eastern Sea and southwards lay the boarders of the two Elven Kingdoms, Cathwood and Rochelle.

Yukov plotted the elves' journey from Cathwood to the forest and tapped the map thoughtfully. "We may be able to find help within this forest, but by no means will it be enough. We must look to recruit people from other regions," he reasoned as his eyes scanned the map thoughtfully. "Now, we could look to go south to the Neutral States but that means cutting through one of the Elven Kingdoms, and I assume that they will be crawling with the Necromancer armies. Therefore, I think we should head north . . ."

Brenik slammed his bowl down onto the map, cutting the vampire off and making both him and Nalia jump in sudden surprise. "We don't have time to recruit people!" the elf yelled in frustration. "Every hour we waste sitting around more people are being killed by the Necromancers! We have to act now!"

Yukov looked calmly at Brenik. "What do you plan to do Brenik? Do you think that the three of us might stumble up to the gates of the Necromancer stronghold and end this by our own powers?"

Brenik glared at Yukov, the vampire's tone only serving to further his frustration. "Once people see us fighting they will rise up and join us!"

"Oh yes, because three people throwing their lives away is clearly going to inspire the rebellion you are looking for!" Yukov's voice was now laced with an edge of sarcasm.

"How would you know? We have to try! We can't just sit here and eat and drink as though we have all the time in the world!"

"What would you have us do Brenik? Throw our lives away like martyrs in the hope that someone might do the same?"

"We aren't throwing our lives away!" Brenik protested. "We're making a stand, showing the people that they do not have to become slaves! Nalia agrees with me, don't you?"

Nalia looked suddenly up at the two men who were staring expectantly at her, waiting for her verdict. She swallowed and looked sadly at her fellow elf. "No Brenik, I don't," she said gently. "I am sorry but Yukov is right, Bren. We saw what the Necromancers are capable of. Cathwood was one of our best defended cities yet they still defeated us! We may have courage, but they have magic. Magic that we cannot fight on our own. If we attempt a last stand then we will be so utterly crushed that it will do the exact opposite of what you are hoping to achieve."

Yukov turned to Brenik in satisfaction, noticing the mingled surprise and anger in the elf's face. The vampire sighed and spoke slowly, his temper easing. He knew Brenik wanted to help, but he also knew that the elf was being driven by his anger, and that was often a fatal emotion to act upon.

"The Necromancers intend to rule their lands by fear, Brenik," Yukov said. "Their power, the creatures at their disposal, all of these things are meant to strike fear into the hearts of even the bravest warriors. Until you can meet them with your own army at your back, you will not be able to stop them."

"So we just let innocent people die?" Brenik said quietly. His voice had lost its volume and his anger was all but spent. He now seemed tired and defeated.

"Yes, unfortunately some will die," Yukov admitted sadly. "But the Necromancers are not looking to lay waste to the Seven Kingdoms. They crave power, that is what this is about! And what is power to tyrants if there is no one for them to suppress?"

Brenik ran a hand through his short hair and nodded. "You are right," he said at last, his voice sounding stronger. "But where do we begin?"

Yukov smiled and leant back over the map. He indicated the central lands, wide plains, fruitful forests, shimmering lakes and bountiful mines. These areas were controlled by the elves, the men and the dwarfs, divided into the Seven Kingdoms. Three Kingdoms belonging to men, two to the elves, one to the dwarfs and one shared realm in the centre of the country that was devoted to the Order of Magi.

"These areas will be almost useless to us," Yukov said dismissively. "It is here that the Necromancers will first attack. Assuming the Order of Magi has already fallen, they will undoubtedly attempt to destroy the elves first as you pose the greatest threat to their power. Given the attack on Cathwood I think it safe to assume that this is the case. Once the elves are subdued they will move on to attack the dwarfs and men."

"What about the orcs and goblins?" Nalia asked, pointing to the Greyhelm mountains where the fourth largest race in Justava lived. The orcs and goblins lived alongside their pets: trolls, giants and wolves, in large tribes that spanned the centre of the great mountain range that ran across Justava's northern boarder.

Yukov shook his head. "During the few recruitment sessions that I attended in the forest I heard some of their leaders talking. Many of the orc and goblin chieftains have joined the Necromancer Empire without question. Those who have not have vowed to remain neutral during their conquest. You will find no help from them."

"So we will find no help in the North?" Nalia said glumly.

"Don't be so sure," Yukov said, indicating the eastern side of the mountains. "Whilst the orcs and goblins control the centre of the mountains there are other tribal settlements on the eastern side."

"The Northern Clans?" Brenik scoffed. "They would not help us, even if we could get past the orcs to talk to them!"

Many years ago, the Northern Clans had once been part of the Kingdom of Resgard, the largest of the three Kingdoms of Men, until the then King had introduced a new Act which restricted public farming in order to benefit the Kingdom's nobility by increasing the amount of land which they owned and allowing them to invest in their personal farms, cutting jobs and restricting supplies. Many of the common people were against the Act as it came when Resgard was suffering economically, having just pulled out of a costly war against the dwarfs which had gained them nothing. The peasants eventually formed into a respectable force and marched through the Kingdom in protest, gathering supporters from the many villages scattered throughout Resgard. However, the march allowed the King time to marshal his forces and when the peasants returned to the capital they were confronted by the might of Resgard's royal army.

For several weeks the two forces engaged in bloody clashes that saw hundreds of rebels butchered. The King was ruthless in his attacks, all prisoners were executed, including the women and children who served in the rebellion.

By continuing his policy of brute force and by making several changes to the treasury the King was able to restore stability to Resgard. The rebel leaders were publicly executed whilst the remainder of the force was condemned and banished from the Kingdom. They attempted to join the other Kingdoms of Men but neither was willing to accept rebels. Without a home to go to, the survivors had climbed up and eventually settled in the Greyhelm Mountains where they went on to live a life of solitude, having next to no contact with the rest of Justava.

"What makes you so certain they won't help?" Yukov smiled slyly. "The northerners may have a troubled history with the rest of Justava, but their new Chieftain is young and has a good heart. I do not think that the Clans are ready to let their country fall so easily."

"But it's getting to them," Nalia said uncertainly.

Yukov shrugged. "Despite what I said about the orcs and goblins there are some even amongst their kind who do not wish to see the Necromancers rule. However, to be safe you will have to take the longer roads to get past their lands, that way if you do run into any of them they will most likely only be scouts. But who knows? You might even find some sympathetic ears."

"It will not be an easy trek," Brenik reasoned.

"No," Yukov agreed. "But amongst the foul beings of the Greyhelm Mountains you will find the core of your army. And who knows, you might even find something more powerful." He tapped the map before grinning. "Dragons!"

Nalia could not help but burst into a snort of laughter. "Dragons have been extinct for five hundred years!" she chuckled.

Five hundred years ago, the dwarfs had begun to offer great sums of money to anyone who killed a dragon after the great beasts began interfering with their mining processes. The giant beasts had been living comfortably around the western half of the Greyhelm Mountains until the dwarfs had begun to develop their mining operations, disturbing the dragons and resulting in them attacking the mines and their workers. The Great Hunt had gone on for a lengthy time, seeing many dragons slain until an unlikely alliance between elves and orcs had brought a stop to the attacks. Unfortunately, the end had come too late and within a few years the mighty beasts had at last faded from existence.

Yukov smiled at Nalia. "The thing about dragons, Nalia," he said, touching his nose and winking, "is that they are a very hardy species. You'd be surprised at what you might find, my friends."

"And just how do you suppose we'd even talk to one?" Brenik said, still unconvinced.

"Dragons and vampires are very similar in one respect, Brenik," Yukov said as he ran his fingers over the two fangs protruding from his lips and smiled. "People assume we are monsters and are therefore planning the best way to eat them from the moment we see them. I would suggest that you take your time and trust whatever it is that you might stumble across."

Nalia tilted her head to one side. "You talk as if you aren't coming with us."

The vampire shook his head. "No. I will stay here in the forest and spread the word of what you are doing. The people of the forest do not trust strangers, but they might be willing to listen to me. Now come, I have a gift for you. But first lets work out how you're going to get out of this forest."

Chapter 11

Nalia gripped Brenik's waist tightly as he guided the massive black stallion that Yukov had given them through the thick trees of the Great Forest. A pure-bred from the Neutral State of Al Quidin, Yukov had acquired the massive stallion from a Necromancer who had attempted to turn his black magic on the proud vampire.

Al Quidin was a small region in the neutral south of Justava, controlled by humans. Originally, Al Quidin had been part of the Kingdom of Malin, the third Kingdom of Men. Al Quidin was a barren land; hard soil and jagged fields of boulders made it unsuitable for farming and the high winds and storms that plagued the coastline made fishing all but impossible. What Al Quidin did have, however, was wide, open plains and a rare type of berry which grew specifically to the region.

In its solid form, the persharaa berry was incredibly toxic and for many years the inhabitants of Al Quidin had steered clear of the wild fruit. However, it was later discovered that when the berry was pulped into a paste and mixed with some of the local herbs, a nutritious meal was produced that was not only non-toxic, but also promoted growth, a trait that became particularly prevalent in horses. With the help of the berries the people of Al Quidin were able to breed some of the fastest, strongest and most beautiful horses in Justava. People from all races and walks of life came to Al Quidin in search of the animals and the inhabitants began trading with the Lords and Ladies that came to them, amassing a huge amount of wealth in exchange for their fine stallions.

Feeling betrayed by his people, the King of Malin attempted to seize control over the production and trading of the 'superior horses'. However, he found that the people of Al Quidin, supported by the other Kingdoms and races, resisted his order and forced his armies into an embarrassing retreat that turned them out of the region. Al Quidin quickly broke away from Malin and joined the other three Neutral States of the South, declaring its independence. Free from the heavy taxes of their disgruntled King, Al Quidin became one of the richest regions in all of Justava, known for its beautiful halls, expert riders and exceptional horses.

With her glossy black flanks, her wild mane, huge brown eyes and powerful legs, Ishalla was certainly no exception to the legendary reputation.

"How much farther?" Brenik called over his shoulder.

Nalia, who had been attempting to keep track of how far they had come through the forest, leaned in closer to Brenik. "We're about half way!" she called back.

The night before they had sat down to map out their route with Yukov and had quickly agreed that getting out of the forest was the most important thing to do first. The fastest way out was to go west, the way from which they had entered with Yukov, which would only take them half day at most. However, the vampire had pointed out that this was the most dangerous route and had urged them to head south, adding almost another three days onto their journey. It was at that point that Yukov had then gifted them with Ishalla, allowing the pair to take a third, slightly quicker route that would only add an extra day to their journey.

The final plan had the elves leaving the forest that day and putting some distance between it and themselves before setting up camp. The next day they would travel to the Cathwood Road, the road that joined Cathwood City with the elven country estates and finally the elven outpost at the feet of the Greyhelm Mountains, and camp somewhere out of sight before making a break along the road to the outpost on the following day. From there they would then have to sneak up the mountains through the many orc tribes before beginning their search for the Northern Clans. The route was long and filled with danger, but at least both of the elves knew that they would feel much better once they left the dark confines of the forest behind them.

*   *   *

Night fell on the fourth day of the journey. Ishalla's hoofs fell rhythmically on the stone floor and the two elves slumped tiredly in the saddle.

Brenik blinked and looked around, a smile of relief suddenly touching his weary face. "Nalia," he said softly as he nudged her with his elbow. "We're clear."

Nalia glanced up and smiled with her friend. They had been riding for several hours the previous day when they had discovered the flaw in their plan. The route which they had selected would take them around the tip of the Boar's Tusk and up past Cathwood City itself. Realising that they would never make it past the now Necromancer controlled city, they had turned Ishalla and ridden northwards, parallel to the Boar's Tusk, where they had begun to search the Tusk for a pathway that would take them out onto the road north of the city.

They had found a small track late in the afternoon of the second day and had ridden hard and fast over the rough terrain and craggy mountains that the track wound its way around. It had been a long, hard ride. In the lower regions, the mountains were filled with a thick dust that had coated their already ruined clothing and stuck in their dry throats whilst thin ledges and rocky ground forced Ishalla to walk through the higher regions. The torture did not end at night either, for when the skies went dark the howling of wolves and roars of mountain bears had made stopping to sleep a short-lived luxury.

Brenik eased Ishalla away from the brown rocks of the lower mountains and crossed over the wide, sand track of the Cathwood road to the opposite side where he continued the horse on to rest behind the cover of a clump of thick trees and bushes, ensuring that they were well out of sight of any travellers that might come by.

They quickly set about their duties, eager to eat something warm and then fall into whatever sleep that they might gain from the chilly night. Brenik set about attempting to put up the small tent that Yukov had given them whilst Nalia began attending to Ishalla.

"That tent really isn't worth it," Brenik muttered as he came over to stand by his friend.

Nalia smiled as she scratched Ishalla's nose and looked at the flimsy sheet of canvass. The tent was barely big enough to house the two elves and it was surprisingly difficult to put up.

"At least it will keep us dry," she reasoned.

Brenik nodded as he placed a hand on Ishalla's broad neck and handed Nalia an apple. He couldn't help but frown as his friend took it with only a quiet offering of thanks. She had been quiet all day and Brenik was growing increasingly concerned for her.

"Is everything all right?" he asked softly.

"I . . ." she trailed off and Brenik thought he could see tears forming in the corners of her eyes.

"Hey," he said, wiping a tear away as it rolled slowly down her cheek. "What's wrong?"

"We're setting out on an impossible task Bren!" she cried suddenly. "It was all well and good talking about it in Yukov's hut, but . . . I'm scared Bren! I'm worried about my parents! And worst of all I stink!" She smiled weakly as she attempted to make a joke about the state of their clothes. Although they had washed at Yukov's hut, he had had no spare clothes to fit the elves and they both still wore their torn, blood and mud stained clothes from the night of the invasion.

Brenik stepped forward and put his arms around her. He suddenly realised that he had been so wrapped up in losing his own parents and coming to terms with the task before them that he had been neglecting Nalia's own feelings. He pulled her in close, ashamed by his ignorance.

"We are going to be fine," he said strongly, gently rocking Nalia in his arms. "The world isn't going to let these demons walk in and just take over like this. People will join us and we will make things the way they used to be again. And as for your parents, I have no doubt that they are sat at your estate sipping wine whilst remaining blissfully unaware of what has been going on."

Nalia laughed at the thought of her parents drinking whilst she had been fighting for her life. "You think so?" she said softly, looking up at Brenik through her tears.

Brenik squeezed her tightly. "I'm certain," he said. "Now come on, let's get some sleep."

*　　*　　*

Brenik held Nalia tightly as she sobbed into his ragged white shirt. He could feel her tears soaking through the thin linen but he did not care. He slowly rocked his friend back and forth and stroked her soft hair whilst making gentle, soothing sounds.

Lying before them was an elven carriage. It had been tipped onto its side and stripped of its supplies and horses. Several bodies scattered the road around the carriage, elves bearing the white crest of the Sommer household. Amongst the guards was a man and a woman. The woman was no taller than Nalia, she had long blonde hair that was starting to turn a silver-grey and a soft face similar to her daughter's. Nalia's father lay beside her. He was a tall, slim man with shoulder length grey hair and well defined features. In his right hand he still clutched the hilt of his elegant sword whilst his left hand was reaching out to his wife who lay beside him.

Brenik had been very fond of Nalia's parents and seeing them lying side by side, their bodies scarred and broken, brought up painful memories of his own parents and once more he felt an overwhelming desire to avenge their deaths.

"I'm so sorry, Nalia," Brenik whispered, small tears rolling down his own face as he fought to keep his voice level.

Nalia gave no response, instead burying herself deeper into Brenik's chest. He continued to hold her until she had no more tears to cry.

"Come on," he said as he took her hands in his. "Let's give them a proper goodbye."

Nalia nodded through her tears and they began to break up the carriage, forming two funeral pyres with the beaten wood. Then they stripped the guards of their armour and piled them carefully onto the larger pyre before setting it alight.

Brenik watched the flames consume the bodies and began to speak a common prayer. "May the flames forever guard you against the darkness. May they light your way so that you may join the fires

69

of your ancestors. By the grace of Altria, creator of Justava, may you find peace and warmth everlasting. Amen."

Brenik lifted the torn banner and thrust it into the ground before stepping back from the pyre. He had never been particularly religious, but given the circumstances he was more than willing to put his doubts aside and pay his respects to the fallen warriors.

When the last guard disappeared into the flames, they turned to the smaller pyre that held Nalia's parents.

"Do you want to do it?" Brenik asked gently, holding his small tinderbox out to his friend.

Nalia nodded tentatively and took the box. She walked over to the pyre and looked at her parents. Tears came to her eyes as she said her final goodbye but it was not until the flames were burning strongly and she was back in Brenik's arms that she allowed them to roll freely down her cheeks.

"They were strong in life, Nalia," Brenik whispered. "They will find honour in the halls of your ancestors."

Nalia nodded softly and smiled as she reached down to touch the leather grip of her father's short sword. "They fought to the end, I'm sure of it."

Brenik squeezed her tightly. "Then let us honour their last stand and bring an end to this Empire!"

The two elves gathered up their equipment and climbed back onto Ishalla, Brenik spurring the great horse into a gallop to make up the time they had lost. Stopping to burn the bodies of Nalia parents and their guards had taken several hours and by the time night fell they had not yet reached the outpost.

They had ridden along the Cathwood Road for most of the day, passing through the rich countryside where the elven Lords and Ladies had built their beautiful country estates. Along the way they had passed by many of these great estates including their own. All of them had been ransacked; the only remains that were left standing were the blackened timbers and cracked foundations. Anything that was left of the two elves' former lives was now hidden in the ashes that blew across the meadows.

As they rode on both elves had fallen silent for the remainder of the day, Brenik giving Nalia a chance to collect her thoughts and come to terms with her loss, something that she had gladly done.

After a while Brenik slowed Ishalla to walking pace and looked at Nalia over his shoulder. "There are some caves over there, we can camp there for the night if you like?"

At Nalia's nod Brenik pulled on the reins and directed Ishalla towards the caves he had seen. They were getting closer to the outpost and the terrain had slowly become less green and more grey. The large trees that they had used for cover during the nights had been replaced by boulders the size of small buildings and the temperature had been dropping steadily throughout the day. The animals too had grown thin. The cheerful songs of brightly coloured birds falling silent to be replaced by the harsh squawking of rooks and crows.

The small rock face that Brenik had seen was dotted with a series of caves, ranging from huge, gaping holes to thin cracks embedded in the walls. They slipped into one of the smaller caves and found a relatively smooth patch of rock to sleep on. The dark confines of the cave made Ishalla nervous, however, so Brenik was forced to lead her back outside and secure her amongst a cluttering of boulders. He brought her an apple along with her food and draped her thick blanket over her body, ensuring that she was well fed and would be warm enough in the night.

"Don't you run off now," Brenik said as he left the horse for the night. Ishalla snorted dismissively and turned to the food that Brenik had left for her.

When Brenik slipped back into the cave he found Nalia waiting with their small rations of food. "What do we have?" he asked casually.

"Rice," she said.

Brenik turned the stodgy white rice with his spoon and grimaced as he forced it down. "No matter how hungry I am, this stuff will never taste good," he muttered.

Nalia smiled as she put her bowl to one side and lay back on the floor. "You never were fond of camping."

Brenik picked an uncooked grain out of his teeth and shook his head. "Oh no, this is great fun," he joked.

Nalia laughed as she pulled her blanket up around her. "It's so cold," she said.

Brenik stood and stepped over to the heavily laden saddle where he unrolled the thick green canvass of their small tent.

71

"Here, this should help," he said when he came back.

Nalia smiled as he lay down beside her, covering himself with his own blanket before pulling the canvass over the two of them. She pressed herself against Brenik's body, glad for the extra warmth he provided.

"Night," Nalia whispered.

Without thinking, Brenik leant down and placed a kiss on her cheek. "Night," he managed to reply before he felt Nalia turn and press her warm lips against his and wrap her arms around his body.

Chapter 12

The next morning the two elves awoke to the sound of rain hammering against the rock outside of the cave. The wind whistled loudly as it surged through the cave entrance, bringing a bitter cold that chilled the elves to their bones.

"It'll be freezing outside," Nalia grumbled as she threw Brenik a nervous glance.

"At least the rain will wash away our tracks," Brenik reasoned as he folded the canvass away. He felt awful. The night before was pressing on his mind but it was the last thing he wanted to speak about. Had they been wrong to go so far? Had he just been taking advantage of Nalia in what could have been a brief moment of weakness on her part?

Nalia fastened her bag to Ishalla's saddle and looked at Brenik. "Do you think we'll find anything at the outpost?" She wanted the to keep the conversation going, hoping to find a way to discuss the events of the previous night. But Brenik's silence was telling her a lot already.

Brenik helped Nalia up on to the saddle before unfastening his own cloak. "I doubt it," he said distantly. "But maybe we'll find some better clothes at least."

Nalia shivered against the cold and nodded. "I suppose that would be better than nothing." She watched sadly as her friend went about securing the remains of their gear, certain that the previous night had ruined the friendship that she held so dear.

Unable to do anything about the weather, Brenik rolled the tent and their sleeping mats up in his cloak as best he could before climbing into the saddle and setting off into the rain. He felt Nalia's hands on his waist and he recoiled involuntarily from her touch. With a pang of regret he felt her withdraw her hands and grip tightly to the sides of the saddle instead.

As they climbed higher up the mountain the temperatures continued to drop until the rain turned slowly into hail which pelted and stung their exposed skin. It was worse for Brenik who had given up his cloak to keep their sleeping equipment dry and although Nalia did her best to share her cloak between them both she could not stop her friend from getting slowly soaked through to his skin.

By the time they reached the outpost the weather had changed once again and a light shower of white snow fell about them. Brenik shivered as he jumped down from Ishalla's saddle, his boots sinking up to the ankle in the dusting of snow that covered the rocky ground. His face fell as he looked upon the outpost.

The elven outpost consisted of four tall watchtowers joined together by a wooden wall that stood about eight feet high. Behind the walls were four buildings: a barracks, a blacksmith, a hall used for dining and meetings and a stables. For hundreds of years the outpost had stood as the Cathwood elves' first line of defence against raiding parties from the orc tribes and they had always managed to repel any invaders that came their way.

However, as Brenik and Nalia walked towards the outpost, they could see that the fortress had not been able to withstand the Necromancers' brutal onslaught. One of the four towers had collapsed, falling into the hall and virtually cutting the building in two. The small gate in the centre of the south wall had been completely smashed open and a few feet down from the splintered remains they could see that another hole had been smashed through the wooden palisade.

As they moved inside their faces became grim as they saw the bodies of elves lying on the bloodstained snow, their lips and skin tinted blue from the cold. The stable was empty and the wooden doors clattered ominously in the breeze that kept alive the still burning embers that were the remains of the fire that had destroyed the blacksmith. The only building that remained largely undamaged was the barracks which sat in deathly silence amongst the ruins of the outpost.

Slowly the two elves walked into the barracks, their weapons held at the ready. However, like the rest of the outpost the building was empty and the elves were allowed to search it in peace.

When they emerged they had both donned new clothes. Brenik wore his light, leather jerkin over a dark, padded shirt and a warm vest and had his vambraces pulled securely over his limbs. He had a clean pair of black trousers and some hard soled, brown, leather boots that came up to his knees. A thick, dark blue cloak fell from his shoulders and he wore his weapons openly at his side. As always, he displayed the Lithuik pin proudly on his chest.

Nalia on the other hand, now wore simple brown trousers and a thick, light green tunic that split at her waist and fell to her knees. Around her hips she wore a dark belt that held her father's sword and her longbow and quiver were strapped tightly to her back. She wore her two vambraces and had found a pair of layered, leather shoulder guards also. She too wore thicker boots and had chosen a long, thick, green cloak with a lining of grey fur around the hood.

Nalia pulled her new cloak tightly around her, glad of the warmth that it provided. "They never stood a chance," she whispered. They were the first words that either of them had spoken since arriving.

"No," Brenik said distractedly. He had noticed that, even though there were many bodies lying on the frozen floor, there were not enough to account for the entire garrison. A shadow danced in his peripheral vision and he glanced nervously in its direction. "We cannot do anything for them now. We should leave this place."

"Can we not bury them?"

Brenik shook his head sadly. "No. Although I would like nothing better, we do not have time." He looked at his friend and went to place a hand on her shoulder before stopping himself, instead pulling a pair of black gloves over his cold hands. "They were true warriors, Nalia," he said simply. "They can find their way to the next life without our help."

Nalia saw Brenik retract his hands and sighed sadly as she watched him walk away. It was clear that the previous night had formed a barrier between them. She could see it in the way that Brenik recoiled from her touch and kept their conversations brief. She felt awful for driving her friend away and dared not think of what he now thought of her.

She knew Brenik hated himself for what he had done. She could see in his eyes just how uncomfortable Brenik was around her now and she hated herself for it. She hated herself for destroying the only thing that the two of them had left.

She wiped her tears away before Brenik could notice and turned to follow him back to the horse. She stopped, however, as she looked at him. She could not help but notice that he was standing taller than before and that he seemed to have regained some of the confidence that he had lost following the invasion of Cathwood. He turned to her and smiled with eyes that told her that, no matter what had happened, he would always be there for her.

She smiled softly in return and sighed to herself, not knowing what to do. It was only when Brenik called her that she hurried over to him and gingerly took his gloved hand as he helped her back onto the saddle.

The tall peaks of the Greyhelm Mountains loomed above them, casting a shadow over the already gloomy atmosphere.

"Do you really think we will find help there?" Nalia asked in a quiet voice.

Brenik was about to reply when suddenly the sound of clattering wood cut across the courtyard. He spun about and drew his sword, staring in the direction of the ruined blacksmith.

"Bren?" Nalia whispered urgently from atop Ishalla.

Brenik looked back at her and pressed his finger to his lips as he slowly advanced on the blacksmith's building. He could hear movement clearly now, a scratching sound coming from behind the remnants of the wood and stone walls. The shadow glided past in the corner of his vision again and Brenik tensed nervously, his leather gloves creaking as he tightened his grip on his sword. Gingerly he moved along the wall and stepped swiftly around the corner.

The body of an elderly border collie lay up against the stone wall, a thin line of blood trickling down her white side from where she had been fatally wounded. Standing over the body was another collie, pawing desperately at her mother. The dog was big for a collie and Brenik would have assumed her to be an elder if it were not for the obvious traces of wolf within her. Her back and head were black as were all of her legs save the front left which was white like her paws and muzzle. Her eyes glistened an icy blue and were surrounded by two circles of white that ran into her muzzle.

Brenik smiled at the collie and lowered his weapon. "Well, hello there," he said kindly.

The dog turned to face him and growled defensively.

Brenik sheathed his sword and held up his hands. "It's all right, I'm not going to hurt you," he said gently, removing his right glove and reaching out his hand to the dog who cautiously allowed the elf to stroke her head.

"What is it, Bren?" Nalia called. She gasped as she came around the corner and saw the dog.

"She must have belonged to the blacksmith. Looks like this was her mother," Brenik said as he stroked the dog affectionately.

As if to prove his point the collie nuzzled the prone dog and whimpered sadly.

Brenik carefully looked at the collar around the dog's neck. "Her name is Zephira."

"She's all alone," whispered Nalia.

A smile touched Brenik's face as Zephira lifted her white leg and placed her paw in his open palm. "Not anymore she isn't," he whispered.

Chapter 13

Yukov licked his fangs nervously as he looked around the dark clearing. Forty men and women, a far greater turnout than he had ever expected, stood before him. They were a mixture of predominantly vampires and werewolves, although a few dryads could be seen swaying amongst the crowd. They filed into their separate groups, muttering in muted tones to each other as they waited for the purpose of the gathering to be revealed.

Yukov glanced down at his neat black overcoat and flicked a speck of dust away before positioning himself in the centre of the circle. He cleared his throat loudly, causing a silence to fall over the gathered creatures.

"My friends," he began confidently. "Thank you all for coming, I know many of you have travelled far to be here and . . ."

"Skip the pleasantries, vampire!" hissed one of the dryads. "Some of us don't have time for your pointless small talk."

The dryads were a strange folk. They had neither trust nor patience with members of other races, which was why Yukov had been so surprised to see five of them turn up to the meeting. That one of them was a male surprised him even further due to the fact that dryads had a very low male birthrate. Each one of them had olive brown skin that was rippled and jagged like bark. Small branches bearing green leaves sprouted randomly from their bodies and their thick arms ended in long spindly fingers whilst their feet were wide and knobbly like the roots of a tree. Their heads sat on non-existent necks and their hair, if they had any, was often the same colour as their flaky skin and consisted of patches of moist, green moss and thin, vine-like tendrils that snaked their way around the dryads' bodies. They were naked save for the creeping vines or thin, grassy skirts that hung around their waists and breasts. Standing well over two meters tall and with large, florescent green eyes that appeared almost hypnotic, the dryads were an imposing sight to behold.

Yukov bowed politely at the dryad who had scolded him. "Of course, Tashakra," he said. "Well, in short, I called you here because I, we that is, need your help. A few days ago, I came across two elves from Cathwood City. The city has been attacked and destroyed by the Necromancers."

There was a hiss of disgust at the mention of the death wielding magi. No one in the gathered circle had any love or respect for the Necromancers.

"Heretics!" spat the nearest vampire.

"Untamed scum!" roared a broad werewolf.

Yukov held his hands up to silence the enraged crowd. "Yes, yes. The Necromancers have returned as we know. And now they have begun their assault on Justava. These two elves plan to recruit an army to oppose them. I have agreed to fight with them against this darkness, but we need your help if a stand is to be made."

A stony silence fell across the dark clearing, broken only by the creaking of the trees and the whistle of the wind as it blew through the forest.

"Why should we help?" growled a small werewolf at last.

Yukov looked into the woman's pale blue eyes. She had a soft face, but he knew that underneath was the body of a savage killer.

"Because," the vampire said at last, "many of us owe the continued existence of our race to the elves."

It was a true enough fact. Many years ago, werewolves, like vampires, had been hunted to near extinction. A common misconception about their race was that the wolves had no control over when they changed, and that once they changed they became overcome by a blood frenzy. This was true for young werewolves who had very little control over when they changed and how they acted. However, as a werewolf grew he or she slowly gained control over both these things, the only thing that they were unable to control being their change during a full moon.

It was the paladins from the Kingdoms of Men who had spread the horror stories of entire towns being ripped to shreds by rabid wolves who could not control themselves. With the paladins' stories urging them on, entire villages had begun hunting down any werewolves in their area until the elves had learnt of the truth behind the wolves' changing.

Over the next few years the elves had begun to seek out the surviving wolves and had sped them away from the pitchforks of the villagers to the safety of the Great Forest. The wolves' numbers had suffered great losses at the hands of men, but thanks to the elves, they had been able to continue a life away from the whips of the fanatical paladins.

The werewolves nodded slowly as Yukov recounted the story of their plight and the vampires also muttered their agreement, remembering how the elves had saved their kind too. Yukov smiled as voices began to rise higher and higher and cries of approval broke out from the two factions.

"We don't," hissed Tashakra, her voice cutting through the excited crowd and silencing the spreading cries of loyalty to the new cause.

Yukov fixed Tashakra's glowing eyes with his own dark pupils. "Was it not the magic of the elves that brought your people to life in the first place?"

The dryad licked her flaky lips but Yukov smiled when she did not respond to his question.

Yukov turned back to the crowd. "We sit here and talk about how powerful we once were. We sit here and curse the Necromancers for their heresy. But what good is talking when we do not act?" He looked around slowly and deliberately, picking out individuals and holding their gaze. "If you will join our cause then please, go to your parts of the forest and spread the word! We may only be a small force, but together we are unstoppable!"

A silence fell over the creatures before the vampires stood up as one. The entire pack looked Yukov directly in the eye before placing a closed fist over their hearts and bowing low, almost to the ground. Yukov returned the gesture with a smile and watched as his fellow vampires dispersed into the forest, heading back to their dark domains to recruit more of their kind to the cause.

As the vampires left Yukov noticed a few werewolves sneak out along with his kin, the task before them too much to bear. However, the majority who had remained let out loud howls to signal their allegiance.

Yukov bowed the wolves out before turning to the dryads. "And what of you and your folk?" he asked curiously.

Tashakra took a step forwards and ran her bright green eyes over the tall vampire. She shook her head defiantly, sending several dying leaves fluttering to the floor from her tangle of hair.

"You are crazy, vampire!" she hissed finally. "You give your life for people who will not care for you when the deed is done."

"Perhaps you are right," Yukov admitted. "But better we risk our lives with them, than with the cowards who would rather burn this forest down than fight us fairly."

The dryad hissed again and left silently, taking two of the other females with her. As they left, the male and remaining female swayed towards Yukov and the former extended a spindly fingered hand to the vampire.

"The trees fight with you, vampire. We have not all forgotten the ancient magic which awoke us," he whispered.

The female nodded eagerly. "More will come, we will see to that."

Yukov bowed once more. "Thank you," he said as he watched as the dryads blended expertly into the tree line and disappeared. He turned around and headed for home, a feeling of triumph building in his heart.

"And so the war begins," he whispered to himself.

*   *   *

Tashakra and her two fellow dryads ran through the forest, their powerful feet crunching against the blanket of brittle leaves bellow them. The three finally came to a second clearing, one much smaller than the one where the meeting had been held an hour ago.

Three mounted figures were waiting patiently for them. Two were identical, tall and broad shouldered with purple cloaks, silver armour and tall conical helmets. The third rider was stood several paces before her dark bodyguards. She was small and slender, sitting delicately atop her powerful grey stallion. A long cloak of black lined with rich, purple velvet was wrapped around her slim body and the hood had been pulled delicately over her long blonde hair to shadow her radiant face.

"My Lady!" Tashakra cried out as she ran to the woman.

The woman scowled as Tashakra bowed awkwardly before her. "Up!" she snapped. "Do you have what you promised me?"

Tashakra nodded excitedly. "Yes, yes! The vampire was trying to recruit the other creatures! There are elves off elsewhere who are attempting to recruit more to their cause!" Tashakra paused. "I trust this pleases you?"

"Where are the elves?"

Tashakra's face fell and she turned away from the woman's gaze. "He didn't say," she whispered.

The woman sighed, turning her hazel eyes on the creature before her. "You promised me the best, Tashakra."

"My Lady, I am sorry! I did what I could!"

The woman urged her horse forwards a few paces to draw level with the dryad. A soothing smile touched the woman's red lips as she placed a hand on Tashakra's wooden head. "Of course you did," she whispered. "But we had a deal, Tashakra. Your people would be spared if you brought me what the Master wanted." The woman sighed and glanced up at the dark trees. "I'm afraid you have failed to do that."

Tashakra's glowing eyes paled as she looked into the cold hazel eyes of the Necromancer. "Please, I beg of you! I will do anything you ask!"

The woman withdrew her hand and shook her head sadly. "It is too late for that, Tashakra." The woman flicked her wrist and turned her horse around, revealing a grey, wooden staff with a silver diamond gripped in the gnarled branches. "The Master does not tolerate failures."

Seeing the staff glowing in the Necromancer's hand, Tashakra turned and fled, barging past her two companions who screeched in agony as a plume of green fire engulfed each of them. She ran blindly through the trees, leaping from one branch to the other until she felt something snare her leg. Tashakra screamed in terror as strong vines wrapped around her legs and began to drag her back to the clearing where they pinned her to the floor.

The Necromancer appeared over Tashakra and knelt beside her. "Even in this forest, nature is mine to command," she whispered, stroking the side of the dryad's face with the back of her hand.

The woman's hands reached out and scooped up a handful of ash from the two burnt dryads. She looked coldly at Tashakra as she let the ashes slip through her fingers onto the dryad's body.

"Your people will burn," she whispered as an inferno of green fire began building in her palm. "And you will be the kindling that starts the fire!"

Chapter 14

Nalia shivered from the back of the saddle, not from the cold but rather from the loud, droning howl that cut through her like a knife and caused the hair on the back of her neck to bristle in fear.

Things had been going well up until now. For five days the elves had moved unhindered through the mountains, criss-crossing through the different passes in search of the Northern Clans. Up until now the only signs of life that they had seen were the occasional snow-hawks that circled high overhead or the snow-rabbits that Zephira would seek out at night. That afternoon, however, they had stumbled across a pack of goblin scouts.

There had been seven of them, each one no more than three feet high. They had three knobbly toes that matched three knobbly fingers and long, crooked noses. Their sickly turquoise skin was coated in grime and small tufts of wild hair sprouted from their knuckles, feet and elbows. Goblins wore very little armour and the ones that they had encountered had been wearing nothing but scraps of loose, brightly coloured clothing, although the colours had been somewhat dulled by the stains of mud, blood and excrement that covered them. When the goblins had seen the elves, their long faces had twisted into sneers and they had brandished their miniature weapons viciously at their sides, shouting war cries and spurring their mounts into pursuit.

Normally, a small pack of goblins would have proved very little difficulty to the two battle hardened elves. However, each of the goblins had been mounted on a savage wolf. The wolves were slightly larger than Zephira, with long pointed muzzles filled with yellow, saliva dripping fangs and covered in thick, grey fur matted with blood and grime. As they had begun to circle the elves and their animals, Brenik had dug his boots into Ishalla's side and they had fled into mountain passes.

Brenik gritted his teeth as he guided Ishalla through the jagged rocks of the mountains, Zephira leaping sure-footedly ahead in search of an escape route. Behind them came the blood-curdling howl of the wolves, reminding them that their pursuers were never far behind. Occasionally Brenik would pull sharply on the reins, attempting to direct Ishalla towards one of the smaller paths found by Zephira in the hope of losing their pursuers. But each time he did, a wolf rider would leap ahead of them and block their path, forcing them back onto the main pathway.

Nalia glanced over her shoulder to see three of the riders coming up behind them. Here in the deep snow the wolves could easily match Ishalla for speed and the three behind them were slowly gaining, their wolves skipping lightly over the snow whilst Ishalla was forced to drive a path through the thick banks.

Suddenly Ishalla stumbled, losing her footing in the deep snow. Although she kept her feet, the break in her stride was enough to allow one of the wolves to get alongside her. The goblin rider sneered up at Nalia and thrust his spear towards her. She reached out and batted the spear aside, taking hold of the shaft and pulling sharply. The goblin squealed as he was launched from his wolf into the snow. The wolf, seemingly unaware at the loss of his rider, snapped hungrily at Nalia's ankles.

Suddenly the wolf yelped in pain as it was tackled to floor by Zephira. She snarled viciously as she tore at the wolf with claws and teeth before sprinting back to Ishalla's side, snarling at the other goblins that chased them in defence of the two elves.

Seeing their companion fall to the unforgiving teeth of the elves' hound, the other two goblins dropped back, keeping a safe distance between themselves and the elves whilst the other four rode ahead, continuing to cut off their target's escape routes.

When the elves realised they were being herded, it was already too late.

Brenik gritted his teeth as he looked nervously around. The rocks on either side of the path had become solid walls, rising up to cut off any chance of escape. Brenik urged Ishalla to run faster but it was far too late. Already they could see figures rising up on the horizon, blocking the path in front of them whilst the six goblins lined up behind them.

"Orcs," Brenik spat under his breath.

Orcs were taller and broader than their goblin cousins. They wore rusted, mismatched scraps of armour with drab clothing underneath and brandished crude but deadly weapons. They spilled over the lip of the hill before them, filling the path with their sweaty, smelly bodies and shouting abuse at the trapped elves.

Ishalla slowed to a stop at Brenik's command, whinnying defiantly as the orcs and goblins jeered at them from in front and behind. Zephira paced back and forth in front of Ishalla, growling angrily at the tribe before them.

A tall orc with a long ponytail that was woven around two yellow bones muscled through the ranks of his kin. In one had he held a tall totem bearing the red boar emblem of the orc war-god Greyhelm the Boar, the legend from which the mountains took their name. The warlord snarled manically, sending flecks of yellow mucus flying out onto the snow before him whilst the rabble behind him pulled at invisible leads, desperate to reach the elves.

"Shut up!" the orc warlord snarled back at his troops. "Well, well. What do we got 'ere then? A couple of intruders, I says. What . . ."

The orc's voice was suddenly cut short by a sudden *"thud!"* The orc stumbled backwards several paces before falling onto his back, a small crossbow bolt protruding from his left eye. The air was suddenly filled with the whining sound of more crossbow bolts as they whizzed down from the top of the cliff walls to pepper the orcs and goblins below.

The goblins broke ranks first, fleeing down the mountains on their wolves with the orcs following not far behind them. Brenik watched as the green skinned monsters surged past them without even glancing up. Within a few seconds the rocky valley was empty save for the two elves and their animals.

"Hello!" Brenik called to the silence, pulling softly on the reigns to steady Ishalla.

No answer.

"We . . . We thank you for your help," Nalia said uncertainly.

"We are looking for the Northern Tribes!" Brenik called loudly. "We wish to speak with their Chieftain."

Zephira growled suddenly as a shadow fell across the elves and they turned to see a tall man standing silhouetted against the white sun on the cliff above them. Slowly more men began to appear, dressed in thick furs and holding heavy crossbows which they pointed threateningly at the two elves.

"Ye have found 'em," growled the silhouetted man in a thickly accented voice. "Bind their hands, and shut those animals up!"

Before Brenik could react he was suddenly pulled from the saddle and his mouth and nose covered by a damp rag. He tried to struggle, but his eyes quickly became heavy and he slipped into a deep sleep.

Chapter 15

General Guillard Terune stroked his long chin thoughtfully as he assessed the battlefield before him. The elven city of Rochelle, sat within a deep curve in the Olarian River which wound its way down from the Greyhelm Mountains in the north to open out into the wide expanse of the Eastern Sea. Rochelle was the capital city of the second Elven Kingdom, and hence of great importance to the Empire's cause. However, like Cathwood, Rochelle was extremely well defended. The river provided the city with protection from all sides whilst two walls angled at forty-five degrees to each other with a gatehouse flanked by heavy artillery positions in the centre protected the city from a frontal assault.

Guillard had positioned his troops parallel to the two walls, sending wave after wave of Kerberyn towards the white walls as he probed his enemies defences curiously.

"General!" Zahrg, the orc Necromancer who had accompanied the Masked Man in the battle with Rothule and Maleena Lithuik, rode up to Guillard. "What do I tell my troops?"

Guillard was momentarily silent before he turned in his saddle to face the orc. "My Lord," Guillard began respectfully. "Send in another wave of Kerberyn, the weaker ones as before. Then begin to form the rest of your men up into their positions."

Zahrg nodded curtly and hurried off to pass on the General's orders. The Masked Man watched irritably as the orc scurried off.

He was tired of waiting, the early days were critical to the Empire's success and they could not waste time on drawn-out sieges.

"We should move forward," he hissed impatiently as he rode up beside Guillard. "We cannot waste time starving our enemies into submission."

The General smiled from under his silver helm. "Not yet, My Lord. But I promise, this is no siege."

"So when do we attack?"

A cryptic smile crossed the General's face. "We will know to move when the time comes."

*   *   *

Arthran Reelm, Captain of the Port of Rochelle, stood nervously on the wooden decks of his great city's dock. From behind him he could hear the distant, monotonous pounding of the enemy drums mingled in with the thunderous roar as the invaders bombarded his city with stone.

"Why are we here, Captain?" one of his men grumbled. "We could be of more use up on the walls!"

Captain Reelm looked back at the elf, noticing how tense the soldier was. "We have to make sure they aren't trying to flank us, soldier," he said, trying to sound comforting. "Someone has to warn the city if that's the case." A small ripple of water made the captain turn nervously back to his watch. "Get back to your position!" he called to the soldier behind him.

Carefully, Arthran examined the water; it was a starless, pitch black night and he could not see the opposite bank of the wide river. The slow sound of flowing water usually helped to soothe his nerves. Tonight, however, every splash and ripple seemed irregular, setting his whole body on edge. Another loud splash drew his eyes to a small rocky outcrop that sat a metre out from the dock. He strained his eyes as he looked over to where large circles of water were rolling out from the point several feet in front of him. Frowning he leaned over the edge of the decking for a better look.

"Captain!"

The call came too late. Before the captain could look around a hand clamped around his ankle like a vice and pulled him forwards.

Losing his footing, Arthran tumbled into the icy water of the river. His screams were drowned out as a swathe of corpses with glowing yellow eyes fell upon him and dragged him down into the depths of the river.

*   *   *

Guillard smiled as the distinctive howl of the undead rose up from behind the walls of Rochelle and new warning bells began to ring urgently throughout the city.

"Make ready to charge!" Guillard yelled.

As his orders were repeated on down the line, Guillard drew his scimitar and spurred his horse towards the city walls. With this signal, the armies of the Necromancer Empire surged forwards, easily breaking through Rochelle's gate and engulfing the city and it's defenders.

Within the hour, Rochelle had fallen and her citizens were ready to join the Necromancer Empire, be it by their own will or by the magic of the Necromancers.

Chapter 16

Brenik blinked painfully against the yellow light as his eyes grudgingly came into focus. He was sat in a circular tent made of tough brown leathers bound over a wooden frame, his hands secured to a pole behind his back. The floor was covered with thick brown and black furs except for in the centre of the tent where a circle of rocks filled with earth allowed a small fire to flicker brightly, the thin trails of smoke rising up out of a flap in the top of the tent. To his right, Brenik could see Nalia sitting unconscious with her back to another post. On his left was another woman who Brenik realised to be a dwarf. She had thick, leathery skin with dark, ginger hair and, like all dwarfs, was broad and stocky.

"Finally awake, eh?" The dwarf grinned at Brenik. She had an accent similar to the tribesmen who had taken them, only not quite as thick.

"Where am I?" Brenik muttered groggily.

"Ye are in the glorious home of Chief Cirnan of the Northern Tribes," she said in mock regality.

"Cirnan?" Brenik blinked again, finding his eyes were steadily becoming more used to the flickering firelight. "I don't . . ."

"Don't worry laddie," the dwarf interrupted kindly. "Ye've been hit with their drug; it knocks ye out and makes things seem a wee bit hazy for a while when ye wake up."

"How long have we been out?"

"About a day, give or take." The dwarf shrugged. "Don't worry, they've taken mighty good care of ye. And yer horse and dog are fine as well. Though I can't say the same for the souls that tried to feed 'em!" She laughed softly before indicating Nalia. "Don't worry about yer friend. She'll be awake in a bit."

Brenik nodded slowly, trying to make sense of what had happened to them. "And who are you?" he asked eventually.

"Oh! Yes!" the dwarf said suddenly. "Spend a couple of days trapped in a tent and I forget me' manners. I am Alleyra, at yer service. I'd shake yer hand but . . ." Alleyra trailed off, indicating the ropes that bound their hands to the wooden frame of the tent.

"I'm Brenik," he replied with a slight smile. "That's Nalia." He tilted his head slightly to indicate his friend. "Why are you here?"

"Two elves up in the mountains, I could ask ye the same thing!" the dwarf laughed. "If ye must know I am a treasure hunter. I was having a look to see if I could find any of the goblin treasure troves when these hospitable folk found me. Not too fond of strangers these people. What about ye two?"

Before Brenik could reply, the tent flap was pushed back and a lone man walked in. He was of average height and had short, dark blonde hair and grey eyes. His strong jaw was covered in a thin layer of stubble and his large lips and round cheeks were a bright red from the cold mountain air. He wore a long, fur overcoat over a thick, red shirt and dark brown trousers. A wide belt was wrapped around his waist, secured with a broad golden clasp. A sharp dagger hung openly at his side with the hilt of another protruding from his right boot. He carried himself with an air of quiet confidence and commanded a sense of strong and fair leadership. Mixed in with the subtle yet distinctive flashes of shining jewellery on his clothing, Brenik knew the man to be Cirnan, Chieftain of the Northern Clans.

"I thought I heard voices," Cirnan said as he pulled off his black gloves. His voice was kinder than it had been in the mountain pass. "I trust ye both are comfortable?"

Alleyra sneered at the man. "Oh, I don't know. It's wee bit chilly."

"Quiet, dwarf!" Cirnan spat with sudden venom. He turned back and crouched down before Brenik. "Don't ever see elves in these parts. Mind telling me what yer doin' up here?"

Brenik cleared his throat, remembering his lessons in diplomacy. "We came to seek your people, Chief Cirnan of the Northern Clans. We need your help."

A frown touched the Chieftain's face as he held out a broad finger and ran it admiringly over the golden reflin tree on Brenik's pin. "I know where this symbol comes from," he whispered. "Which means that either ye're in big trouble or ye're thieves like her," he said with a nod towards Alleyra.

"We are no thieves," Brenik said calmly. "I come from the House of Lithuik, my friend from the Sommer House."

Cirnan lifted his head and looked into the elf's dark blue eyes. "Which makes me wonder, what could I possibly do for one such as ye?"

"The world has changed, Chief Cirnan. Already many of my kind lie dead in the ruins of our own cities. It will not be long before a similar fate befalls man and dwarf alike!"

A frown crossed the Chieftain's face. "And who would have the strength to take on elf, man and dwarf all at once I wonder?"

"A group of wizards and witches. They have learnt the forbidden magic of Necromancy."

Cirnan recoiled suddenly as if someone had run a jolt of electricity through his body. Although the Northern Tribes were largely cut off from society, the wrath and evil that spawned from Necromancy was still well known to all the inhabitants of Justava.

"How is that possible?" Cirnan demanded.

"I know not," Brenik admitted. "But what I do know is that the newly founded Necromancer Empire plans on destroying or enslaving all of Justava. No land will be safe from their deathly grip. Not even yours, Chief Cirnan."

Cirnan scratched his chin. "In that I believe ye, we would not be able to stand. But how do I know ye speak the truth in the first place? Ye could be spies, sent to draw my forces apart so that larger armies of men may crush us! I know that the Kingdom of Resgard still wishes to see our people scattered for the defiance our ancestors showed."

"My words are true, Chief Cirnan," Brenik said, maintaining a level tone. "My own parents were killed by their hoards, as were my friend's parents. If you wish to see proof then send your scouts swiftly to the elven outpost at the foot of the mountain. They will find it to be destroyed, and the bodies of elf and Kerberyn will litter the ground before them. We are not spies, Chief Cirnan. And soon Resgard will have more to worry about that the continued existence of your clans."

Cirnan looked into Brenik's face, pausing briefly before nodding. "I will do as ye say, as I am inclined to believe yer story. We have heard whispers amongst the orcs ourselves. If what ye say is true, then I will speak with the elder members of the tribe and they will advise us on how to act." Cirnan drew his dagger and cut away the bonds around Brenik's wrists. "Until then, ye're free to walk the camp. Ye may sleep in here and tend to yer friend when she wakes. I will see to it that food and drink are brought to ye."

Brenik bowed his head. "You are most generous, Chief Cirnan. I should like to see my horse as well, and my dog."

"Aye, they are indeed fine animals. I have seen to it that they have been well cared for, though neither seem to appreciate us. Come! I will take ye to them!"

Brenik stood, rubbing his wrists and smiling at Cirnan. He was beginning to get a better sense of the man. Although Cirnan was not young, he was clearly struggling with his role. His short hair had a wild flair to it and his shirt was only partially tucked in. The sheath of his dagger had not been cleaned recently nor had his belt buckle. Brenik also saw the light in the man's eyes and his readiness to trust Brenik also indicated that Cirnan either was not ready for his position or not fond of it. Either way, Brenik decided that he liked the man.

They were just passing through the tent flap when a small voice spoke up.

"I wish to help," Alleyra said.

The two men stopped and turned to look at the dwarf, Cirnan raising his eyebrow sceptically.

"Please," the dwarf begged. "I am a strong fighter; I can help ye! And I would not see the dwarfs destroyed by this evil."

"Aye, she speaks true, a good fighter she is." Cirnan scowled at the memory of the dwarf's capture. "But a dwarf and a thief she still is!"

"I never stole anything of yer's! That treasure was a goblin stash and ye bloody well know it!"

"A stash on our grounds belongs to us! Ye're a thief Alleyra!"

"And ye're a prejudice fool Cirnan!" She turned desperately to Brenik. "Brenik, ye have to help me! Let me fight with ye and protect my home!"

"With respect, Chief Cirnan," Brenik said slowly. "You yourself just admitted her to be a good fighter. And good fighters we will need plenty of if a stand is to be made against the Necromancers. What would would the punishment be for her crime?"

Cirnan sighed unhappily. "She'd probably be sold off to another tribe to work as a slave. That, or executed if the elders deem her crime severe enough. I must say, neither option appeals to me, but that is what the elders will decide and as Chief I am bound by our laws to obey them." His tone made it more than clear that was the only reason why he followed the elders' instructions.

"Then you must convince them otherwise!" Brenik said flatly. "And if not, then take from my supplies the cost you would get from selling her and I will take her into my service."

Cirnan glared at Alleyra. "We will see," he growled softly. "For now I will show ye to yer animals. Come."

Brenik followed Cirnan out of tent and into the cold. As he did he glanced back at Alleyra and winked. The dwarf grinned at him in response.

"We are well supplied up here, Brenik Lithuik!" Cirnan boasted as they walked through the camp. "These mountains are as bountiful as any forest, despite what ye might think!"

Brenik looked around the camp approvingly. It was set beside a deep ravine with the peaks of the mountains forming a semicircle around the camp's perimeter, the thin paths through the rock preventing any large army from assaulting the tribe in force. The camp itself consisted of rows of the circular tents with men and women hurrying about their daily chores. In the centre of the camp was a group of wooden structures and larger tents which included a trading post and blacksmith.

"The hub of the camp," Cirnan explained as they walked past. "The mountain gives us iron for weapons, rabbits for eating and fresh water for drinking!" Cirnan laughed and clapped Brenik on the back. "Now do ye see why we have stayed here for so many generations?"

"I do indeed," Brenik said, genuinely impressed by what he saw. "Your people have done exceedingly well."

"Aye, that we have, lad."

Brenik looked at Cirnan again and watched as he strode confidently through the camp. Men and women, soldiers and messengers parted before him and smiled at their Chief, offering a gracious salute or a call of respect. The elf smiled at the loyalty the tribesmen showed towards their leader and realised that Cirnan was indeed suited to his role. Nevertheless, he could still tell that Cirnan felt restrained by his position and that the man was holding much of his personality back in order to appear strong in front of Brenik.

"Yer animals are just over here," Cirnan said, breaking Brenik's thoughts.

Cirnan led Brenik past one of the larger tents to a small paddock where Ishalla stood braying noisily. Zephira sat beside her in a smaller paddock, growling at anyone brave enough to come close.

"These two have nearly had the hands of anyone who's tried to feed 'em," explained Cirnan as he opened the gate to the paddock. "I'm sure they'll be pleased to see ye."

Brenik slipped through the gate into the paddock and the two animals turned to face him. Ishalla gave a snort of delight and trotted happily over to the elf whilst Zephira leapt at the gate to her smaller paddock. Brenik laughed as he released the dog from her pen and she leapt towards him, nuzzling her head against his hands as he stroked the two animals affectionately.

"Take yer time Brenik!" Cirnan called cheerfully. "The camp is yer's. In the meantime I'll try and talk some sense into the elders!"

Chapter 17

The city of Emladis sat in the Seventh Kingdom of Justava, more or less in the very centre of the country. Built beside the Terrion River on a lone hill in the middle of the large plateau that sat in the centre of Justava, the city, like the Kingdom in which it was built, belonged to no race in particular, but rather was shared between all races. Known as the City of the Magi, it was in this Kingdom that witches and wizards from all races, creeds and factions would gather and share their wisdom and knowledge, free from the burdens of their societies. The city was a place of great power and as such, had been the first victim of the Necromancer Empire.

On the surface of things, nothing seemed to have changed. The white stone buildings remained standing undamaged, the walls of the city were unharmed and the great temple that stood at the very top of the lush, green hill in the centre of the city continued to shine in the morning sun.

It was only when one looked closer that the damage could be seen. Where the streets had once been filled with laughing children and market vendors from distant lands there was now silence. Where neat grass and bright flowers had lined the pathways there were now shrivelled remains of dead plants, overrun by tangled masses of weeds. In one fell swoop the Necromancers had revealed themselves, and with them they had snatched away all life in the once beautiful city.

Guillard had been to Emladis only once before and despite the destruction caused by the magi who had betrayed their order, the city was still capable of taking his breath away. As was the mighty temple which he now stood in.

He was waiting in a short corridor on the highest floor of the temple. White marble steps with thick red carpets led to the lower levels at both ends of the corridor and the two massive arched windows that stood above them let in long rays of bright sunlight. The corridor itself was lined with black marble pillars and the blood red carpet ran the length of the polished floor. A large door made of dark, varnished wood sat in the middle of the corridor, guarded by two cloaked statues holding stone staffs.

"General!" A dark elf stepped from the corridor behind the dark door and saluted Guillard respectfully. "They are ready to see you, Sir."

Guillard nodded and walked silently through the ornate doors into the smaller corridor beyond, the guard disappearing back into the main corridor after he passed.

It was in this temple that the Necromancers had first revealed themselves to the Council of Magi and Guillard could see the evidence of the battle that had ensued all around him. The white walls were marked with dark scorch marks and small fragments of marble had been chipped away in places. Charred pieces of cloth and splinters of wood from a broken staff marked the spot where their owner had fallen. The air was close and stuffy and Guillard was glad when corridor opened up slightly to another ornate wooden door with large, golden handles. His boots clicking loudly against the marble steps, Guillard walked quickly up to the wide door and pushed down on the handle, ignoring the small, dark red stain that was splattered across the golden design. He stepped through the door into the room beyond.

The circular room had once been home to the Council of Magi, a group of seven witches and wizards who were considered to be the best in each of their respective fields of magic. The circular room was ringed with a series of open arches that gave a panoramic view of Emladis whilst ancient enchantments served to protect the room from the effects of the weather. The outside of the chamber was ringed with tall candlesticks and busts of famous members from the Council's history. In a lower ring at the centre of the room sat seven high backed chairs, each with a different coloured cushion to represent the field of magic that their Council Member specialised in. The room, once proud and filled with the knowledge and strength of the seven most powerful beings in Justava, was now acting as the office of the Necromancer Emperor.

The Master and the Masked Man were stood in the centre of the room, talking quietly to each other. Standing apart from them, leaning against one of the wide arches, was a beautiful woman. She wore a long black dress that had a slit that ran the length of her right leg, revealing the soft, pale skin below. Her golden hair fell neatly about her round face and she chewed her rouged lips as she regarded Guillard with curious hazel eyes.

Guillard stared blankly at the woman, mesmerised by her beauty. She reminded him of Nalia, a delicate beauty capable of great strength. Guillard blushed as he found himself staring at the woman and stumbled quickly into the room as she turned her piercing eyes back to the Masked Man.

The Master and the Masked Man turned to Guillard as he stepped into the circle. They had been leaning on their black staffs for support as they discussed the recent events that had taken place within their new Empire and the coloured gems shone brightly in the light that flowed into the open room.

"General," the Master hissed, beckoning with a withered hand. "Come forward."

Guillard walked forward and dropped to one knee, ignoring the woman whose eyes returned to him as he moved. "My Lords," he said respectfully.

"Rise, General," the Master said softly, placing his hand on Guillard's cold forehead. "There is little time for formalities when it comes to the conquest of Justava. Now tell me, how goes the campaign?"

Guillard nodded as he stood swiftly. "Very well. As of today the last of the major elven cities was vanquished and its inhabitants made ours to turn to the cause. I have instructed our reserve forces to commence a sweep of all known remaining elven settlements to flush out any survivors whilst the main army regroups. In the meantime, messengers bearing both news and evidence of our growing power have been dispatched to the Lords of both the dwarfs and men and word was received not long ago that the orc and goblin warlords are ready to remove those in their tribes who will not readily march with our own forces."

A thin smile touched the Master's shadowed face. "And how do you presume the men and dwarfs will react to this news, General?"

Guillard paused, thinking carefully about his response. "It is hard to say, My Lord. The men may put up initial resistance out of some misguided sense of honour. The knights and paladins in particular will not bow down without a fight. However, men are fickle and as you have often pointed out, greed and self preservation is rife within their leaders. Once we utterly crush the first city they will soon bow down to us and the knights and paladins will find themselves very much alone."

"Good. Very good," the Master said with a nod. "What of the dwarfs?" he continued eagerly.

"Dwarfs care little for anything that does not shine. Promise them enough gold and they will be ours."

"And if I am unwilling to pay for their allegiance?"

Guillard shrugged. "Their understanding of magic is limited to the very few dwarfs who do manage to join the ranks of the magi, and even they are seen more as outcasts than warriors. They do not understand magic and in many cases are fearful of it. We will find no protest to the 'forbidden art of Necromancy' as it were, but we will find them to be fearful of magic in general. An adequate demonstration should provide us with an edge over the population."

The Master rubbed his smooth chin in appreciation and turned to the Masked Man. "Send Lord Zahrg to lead our armies against the dwarfs. If they are afraid of magic, then seeing an orc wielding it will only do to increase that fear."

The Masked Man bowed deeply. "I will see to it shortly, Master."

The Master smiled again and tapped his staff against the marbled floor, sending a warm glow rising into the red ruby that tipped the weapon. "It has taken time and careful planning, but the Seven Kingdoms are at last within our grip. Justava will be ours to rule."

"It has been a long road, My Lord," said the Masked Man in agreement. "But your leadership has finally led us to our true calling."

A slight cough interrupted the rejoicing and the two men turned coldly to the dark elf General.

"My Lords, forgive me but we will not have complete control." Guillard stood firmly as the two men stared at him through eyes that he could not see. "Many of the smaller factions will be able to evade our grip. Along with the Neutral States and proper leadership they could become a potential threat. Leadership that my two elven friends could provide."

"You give your young friends too much credit," the Masked Man scoffed.

"I would remind you, My Lord, that they are no older than myself. I give them the same credit I give to myself. Credit for the skill that I have seen them demonstrate over the many years that I have known them."

The Masked Man waved a hand dismissively. "You are a good General, Guillard, but this obsession with your friends is becoming a distraction."

Guillard bit his lip and bowed stiffly. "As you say, My Lord."

The Master turned to the Masked Man and smiled thinly at him. "My friend, I wish to speak to the General alone. If you could inform Lord Zahrg of his new task then I would be most grateful."

"My Lord? Must Zahrg be informed so soon?" the Masked Man said uncertainly.

"Go!" the Master said, his tone making it clear that he would not be argued with. "The General and I have matters to address in private."

The Masked Man bowed curtly. "Apologies, My Lord. I meant no offence. I shall see to it that Zahrg is informed immediately."

Guillard bowed to the Masked Man as he said farewell to the Master and left the room. "Is there something I can do for you, My Lord?" he said when they were alone.

The Master walked over to one of the chairs. Like the others it was made of a dark wood crafted with curved armrests and intricate designs. The cushions on the seat back and arms were red, signifying the chair to be the seat of the Arcane Council Member.

"I used to imagine myself ending up in this seat," the Master said distantly as he rested his staff against the back of the chair and settled down onto the plush red cushions. "General, I am inclined to agree with your assessment of your friends."

"My Lord?"

"I have, heard about them. Heard about the fight that they put up during the invasion of Cathwood and of their exploits in their earlier lives. I agree that they could be a great threat to our new position."

"What would you have me do, Master?"

The Master steepled his fingers thoughtfully. "If the entirety of Justava was out to get you, General, where would you go to hide?"

Guillard stood silently for a while before replying. "The Seven Islands, if I could. But given their location I would hazard a guess to the Great Forest," he said thoughtfully.

The Master nodded approvingly before beckoning to the blonde woman who drifted over to his side. "This is Lady Liethra," explained the Master. "She has recently learnt that the elves are indeed planning a rebellion."

"My spies caught a vampire recruiting warriors to their cause," Liethra explained in a voice as soft a silk. "But I was unable to learn where the elves were."

"I knew it!" Guillard said excitedly. "Master, forgive my boldness. But we should crush this army whilst it is still young!"

"No!" the Master said firmly. "We must give them time to regroup so that all the rebels are brought together, then we will strike. For now, go and summon the army, General. Have them prepare for battle. In the meantime, send a small force to the Great Forest to gather further intelligence."

Guillard bowed deeply. "Yes, Master. It will be done as you say."

"Of course," hissed the Master. "Fear not the smaller races, General Guillard," he then added. "Once man and dwarf are ours to command," the Master clenched his fist in triumph, "the rest of Justava will either bow at our feet or be crushed in our grip."

*   *   *

Down below in the city's catacombs the Masked Man pushed his way angrily through the ranks of dark elves going to collect their armour and past pens of Kerberyn to where Lord Zahrg was dictating orders to a tall captain.

"Lord Zahrg!" called the Masked Man bitterly. "Are your troops ready for war?"

"They are indeed," growled Zahrg. "As am I."

The Masked Man glanced at Zahrg's left arm which had been broken by Maleena Lithuik's dying spell. "Your wound is healed then?"

Zahrg nodded. "Fully. I am ready for whatever task you have for me."

"Good. The Master has asked for you to lead your men against the dwarfs. You are to use your magic and superior numbers to scare the dwarfs into joining us."

"Dwarfs!" Zahrg snorted. "I say we kill 'em all. No good hoarders; they will give little help to the Empire."

"They are miners and crafters," the Masked Man corrected the orc. "We need their metals and their war machines."

Zahrg grunted in agreement. "I'll leave by sunset."

The Masked Man placed a firm hand on Zahrg's shoulder and drew him in close. "Hear this, Lord Zahrg," he hissed in a hushed tone. "You will take the other Necromancers with you. You will empty the temple's halls until only a handful remain."

Zahrg eyed his fellow Necromancer with suspicion. "Are these the Master's orders, or yours?"

The Masked Man turned and looked at the dark elves, the soldiers whom he had converted, who had sworn their allegiance to an Empire. He then turned so that the slits in his helmet were fixed squarely on the orc's own dark eyes.

"They are the orders of the Necromancer Emperor, Lord Zahrg," the Masked Man said innocently. "You know your history, my friend. Newly formed governments are often so, unstable."

Chapter 18

Brenik carefully wiped a damp cloth over Nalia's head as he explained their situation to her. The drugs had had a worse effect on his friend and she had been suffering from a terrible headache since the day before when she had woken up.

"So we're their prisoners?" Nalia asked, glancing at Alleyra.

"No," Brenik said. "We're safe here. Don't worry." He pulled the cloth away and looked into her eyes with concern. "How are you feeling now?"

Nalia smiled and looked up. "Better," she said gratefully.

The tent flap opened and a short woman carrying a large sack walked into the tent. "The Chieftain wants to see you in his tent shortly," she said.

Brenik nodded and was about to reply when he saw the woman pull out a knife and advance on Alleyra. He reached instinctively for his sword but stopped when he saw the woman cut Alleyra's bonds and help the dwarf to her feet.

"Chief Cirnan has ordered your release," she said flatly. "Here are your things." The woman dropped the bundle of clothes at the dwarf's feet and walked quickly out of the tent.

Alleyra grinned as she reached into the sack and pulled out her armour and weapons. "Oh, thank the Gods," she whispered before turning meaningfully to Brenik. "And thank ye as well, Brenik."

Brenik smiled kindly. "Think nothing of it, my friend," he said. "We'll wait for you outside."

Alleyra emerged a few minutes later, wearing dark leather armour reinforced at the edges with bands of polished brass. Across her chest were strapped two bandoliers in the shape of a cross and upon each were a selection of knives and daggers of various shapes and sizes. A broad belt was wrapped around her waist and she had pulled her dark orange hair into several neat braids.

"Feel better?" Brenik asked as they walked towards Cirnan's tent.

Alleyra grinned fiercely. "Oh, much better."

*　　*　　*

"Stupid bloody fools!"

Nalia jumped in surprise as Cirnan and three of his fellow tribesmen stormed into the Chieftain's tent, grumbling profanities amongst themselves. Alleyra and the two elves had been waiting eagerly for the Chief to return from his meeting with the tribal elders for some time since the woman had come to get them. It did not appear to have gone well.

"What's wrong?" Nalia asked in concern.

Cirnan threw his hands up into the air in frustration. "Well as ye know our scouts have proven that what ye have told us about yer homes is true."

"Exactly, so the elders understand the danger we face," Brenik stated as he leant on the map table before him and regarded Cirnan with a look of severity.

"Aye, but they won't bloody do anythin'!" Cirnan slammed his dagger angrily into the map table, the metal tip pinning the crumpled map of Justava to the table.

Alleyra walked forward from where she had been leaning against one of the tent's supports. "So they're just goin' to sit by whilst the rest of us burn?" she muttered bitterly.

Cirnan picked at the hilt of his dagger. "I wish it were different," he said disappointedly. "But that is their word and whilst it stands ye will not have the full support of the Northern Clans."

Nalia knew that what Cirnan said was true. Although he was the Chieftain of all the Northern Clans he was still bound by their ancient laws to listen to the word of the elders when it came to matters of war. Without their say, no army would ever leave the mountains without facing severe consequences.

Brenik closed his eyes as Nalia slumped back against one of the tent supports. A long silence descended over the tent, broken only by the whistling of the wind as it was funnelled through the mountains.

"So we have wasted our time coming here," Nalia whispered at last.

Cirnan wrenched his dagger from the table and held it up before his eyes, turning the thin blade slowly in his fingers. "No, not quite. I said ye would not have the full support of the tribes." A light shone in Cirnan's eyes as a sly smile pulled at the corners of his mouth. "There are those of us who would support ye, despite what the elders say. Those of us who think our ways are outdated and stop us from doin' what is right, what will save our people."

Brenik glanced behind Cirnan as the three other men nodded in agreement. "What do you propose?" he asked curiously.

"Firstly, I will come with ye on yer travels," Cirnan began. "My presence may help ye recruit other factions to yer cause and I should like to know who else will be joinin' us in the fight."

"What about the elders?" Nalia asked.

Cirnan shrugged dismissively. "I will tell the elders that I am escortin' ye off the mountain. By the time they realise that I've gone with ye, it'll be too late for them to do anything."

"No offence, great Chief," Alleyra said sarcastically, "But one fighter won't make a damned bit of difference against an army."

Cirnan threw Alleyra a cold look before continuing with his plan. "Whilst I'm gone, these three will ride out to all the other clans up in the mountains and gather as many supporters as they can."

A grin broke out across Brenik's face as the three other men nodded their agreement. "That's fantastic!" he said joyfully.

Cirnan nodded, smiling with Brenik. "Once they have as many men as will join them, they'll head down to wherever it is that we're gatherin' at."

Brenik stopped, suddenly realising that they had not planned what to do once they secured the Northern Clans' allegiance. "We have not really decided on a meeting place," he admitted as he glanced at Nalia who shrugged in similar confusion.

"Well, we have other allies in the Great Forest," she said thoughtfully as she stepped over to the map. "I suppose that once you are ready, you could march down the mountain and set up camp along the forest's southern boarder."

"What of the monsters?" growled one of the tribesmen.

"They will not threaten you, that is a promise," said Nalia. "The Great Forest is probably the safest place in all of Justava at the moment."

"Aye, then if that's where we're meetin' we'll be there," grunted another of the tribesmen. "I ain't scared of no ghosts."

"Good," Brenik said. "Once we get back we'll . . ." He frowned as a loud horn sounded in the background, the sound of panicked screams following shortly afterwards.

"No. It can't be," Cirnan breathed as he glanced towards the entrance to his tent. "Go! Get your gear and go!" he yelled to the others.

As the three tribesmen scrambled out of the tent Cirnan turned towards his own weapons, a crossbow and a longsword, and hurried to fling the sword over his shoulder and load the crossbow.

"What's happening?" Brenik called urgently to Cirnan.

"Brellyg," Cirnan growled as he loaded a bolt into his crossbow and strapped the small quiver to his belt.

Before Brenik could ask his next question, Cirnan charged out of the tent. Glancing uncertainly at Nalia and Alleyra, Brenik quickly unslung his bow and followed the Chieftain out into the camp.

All about them, men and women were running about in panic, the men gathering their weapons whilst the women hurried the children away towards the mountains. A low rumbling noise suddenly rolled over the icy peaks and caused the children to scream in terror and the adults to duck instinctively to the floor.

"This way!" Brenik called over his shoulder, spying Cirnan through the mass of bodies.

With Nalia and Alleyra close on his heels, Brenik fought through the crowds and dashed across the snow to the large open area of ice that lay between the camp and the edge of the deep ravine. Here the men were gathering behind barriers made of wood and hardened by tightly packed snowdrifts, passing spears and crossbow bolts around and muttering silent prayers to the God. The wide plain of snow stretched out before them, dotted with huge shards of ice and ending with the sheer drop of the deep ravine. The mountains loomed high above them on both sides of the soldiers, their peaks hidden by the never ending fall of snow.

Another deep rumble filled the still air.

"Steady!" Cirnan yelled calmly down the line.

Brenik followed the voice, shouldering his way through the ranks of fur-clad warriors to the front of their lines where he found Cirnan crouched behind the most forward barricade.

"Get down, Brenik!" Cirnan yelled as he pulled the elf roughly to the floor.

"What's happening? Who is Brellyg?" Brenik hissed urgently at the Chieftain.

Another loud roar filled their ears and Cirnan nodded grimly at a small dot on the horizon. "Brellyg," he whispered.

As Brenik turned yet another ferocious roar blasted across the icy plain to echo loudly off the rock walls on either side of Cirnan's clan. The mountains responded with their own roar as large clumps of snow and ice were shaken loose by the deep vibrations, the unstoppable avalanches sliding down the mountainside to tumble into the ravine below.

Brenik watched the nervous men as they tightened their grips on their weapons and huddled closer to their barricades. He turned and his sharp elven eyes stared out over the ravine to see that the small dot had grown into the form of a huge winged creature. He gasped as he finally realised what Brellyg was.

Brellyg was a dragon.

"Hold the line!" Cirnan yelled, his voice appearing to bolster the courage of his soldiers. "Crossbows stay forward; spears prepare to move up and cover!"

Cirnan barely got his orders out before Brellyg let out another thunderous roar and came crashing down onto the small plain of ice, scattering the fragile shards all about him. The dragon stood on four legs as thick as tree trunks with huge, black, razor sharp talons curving out from his thick toes. His long body was made up of tough, red scales layered over a yellowish underbelly that ran down into a long, pointed tail. Along the length of the dragon's back and neck ran a string of shining, black spines of various sizes and the beast's two leathery wings were spread wide from points behind his muscular front legs. On top of the dragon's long neck sat its massive head; two large black spines curved up and out from above it's dark orange eyes and a pair of pointed ears protruded out from either side of the savage spikes. The dragon had a long snout with nostrils that billowed a small stream of smoke and when the beast opened its mouth it revealed a set of sharp, white teeth and a long, forked tongue.

"Get back beast!" Cirnan yelled viciously. "Like before you will find nothing but pain here!"

Brellyg snorted, sending two distinct puffs of black smoke billowing from his large, flared nostrils. He roared loudly in challenge to the Chieftain and took a slow, deliberate step forward.

"Take aim!" yelled Cirnan as he raised his own crossbow.

"Wait!" Brenik pushed Cirnan's crossbow down and looked around in confusion at the other men. "Did you not hear what it said?"

A sea of blank faces stared back at Brenik.

"It just spoke!" the elf cried uncertainly.

Cirnan pushed Brenik aside. "Have ye lost yer mind, Brenik?" he roared. "That beast cannot talk! It's a monster!"

Brenik looked desperately at Nalia "Tell me you heard him?" he pleaded.

The other elf nodded quickly. Whereas the others had apparently heard a threatening roar from Brellyg, Nalia had heard a calm, level voice. The dragon could indeed speak.

"What are ye bloody doing, Bren?" Cirnan yelled as Brenik stood up slowly from behind the safety of the barricade.

Determined to prove his point, Brenik slipped away from the tribesmen and began to walk carefully out towards the dragon, Nalia following closely behind him. The dragon tilted his head in interest as they got closer.

"You spoke?" Brenik said uncertainly, getting as close to the dragon as he dared.

"I did." The dragon's voice was a low rumbling sound that originated deep within his stomach. It sounded not dissimilar to the voice of an old man. "And it would seem that I have finally been understood," the beast finished in satisfaction.

"Why is it that we can understand you?" asked Brenik.

"You are an elf!" Brellyg said as if the answer were obvious. "As one of the elder races you see and hear things as they should be."

Brenik licked his cold lips. "Why are you here?" he said carefully.

The dragon chuckled to himself, sending bursts of white smoke shooting out of his nostrils and sounding very menacing to the men behind the elves. "If you are wondering whether I wish to eat you and these, barbarians, then you need not worry," the dragon said, making no effort to hide the disdain he felt towards Cirnan's people.

"So why are you here?" Nalia stepped forward cautiously.

"I have forever been trying to communicate with those beasts," the dragon snorted as he indicated the tribesmen with a clawed foot. "Unfortunately they try and shoot me whenever I get close. So far all I have been able to achieve is a few nasty splinters."

"What do you want with them?" Brenik asked, feeling more confident in his safety.

"Why, to warn them of course! I keep an eye out from the sky and try to warn them about those vile orcs who we've all come to hate so much these days! Not that I owe them anything mind you," Brellyg hastened to add. "However, more recently there has been something much more deadlier. A score of Kerberyn attacked the outpost of your people." The dragon stopped when neither elf showed any reaction. "You are unsurprised by this?" he asked curiously.

"We have seen the Kerberyn already," Brenik explained. "They attacked our home of Cathwood. They are being led by the Necromancers who intend to enslave all of Justava."

This time, Brellyg's roar was genuine and not a form of communication. It was a thunderous noise that echoed across the mountains and shook another clump of snow from its mountain perch. Nalia's hand clamped onto Brenik's arm as the two elves took several fearful steps backwards.

"Necromancers!" Brellyg bellowed at last. "Foul demons! Heretics! How have they returned?" he demanded.

The two elves tumbled to the snow as Brellyg's head dropped quickly down to their level and they suddenly found themselves staring into the great orange and red slit that was the dragon's eye.

"We do not know," Brenik said quickly as he and Nalia rose fearfully to their feet. "Several years ago a shrine was discovered along with teachings of Necromancy. The teachings should have been locked away but someone must have uncovered them."

Brellyg snorted again. "Those teachings should have been destroyed! Because of that failure, Justava is lost to darkness! With your kind dead there is not power enough to stand against them."

"Maybe," Nalia said slowly, attempting to calm the dragon. "But we are building a resistance. An army to fight the Necromancers! That is why we are to here, to ask for the Northern Clans' help!"

Brellyg eyed the elves carefully. "You have courage, that I will not deny." The dragon paused in thought. "But you will not get far with those people." He indicated Cirnan and his people who still sat fearfully behind their barricades.

"Actually, we have already secured the help of Cirnan and the clans," Brenik said triumphantly.

Brellyg raised a ridged eyebrow in thought. "Have you indeed? The barbarians have more spine than I would have thought." He paused in consideration before standing up to his full height and proudly spreading his wings apart. "Very well. By the Eternal Fire I hereby pledge myself to you. I will help you in your fight, and I know that the others of my kind will also be interested in aiding you against the Necromancers."

"Others?" Nalia said in disbelief.

Brellyg nodded. "Yes, I am not the only dragon left in the world. Come, and I will show you. It does not take long to fly back to my home."

Nalia looked at Brenik. "You should go with him, Bren. If we can get the help of the dragons then we will stand a far greater chance of defeating our enemies."

Brenik nodded in agreement. "Make your way back to the forest with the others. We'll catch up with you later."

From behind the barricades, Cirnan sprinted towards the elves with Alleyra and Zephira hot on his tail. His jaw dropped as he saw the dragon lower his neck and allow Brenik to climb onto his back. "What are ye doin'?" He bellowed as he charged across the open ground. But he was too late and before he could reach them, the great dragon flapped his wings and lifted off into the grey clouds.

"What does he think he's doin'?" Alleyra gasped as she ran up beside Nalia.

A small smile touched Nalia's lips as she looked up into the sky, Zephira howling loudly beside her. "He's bringing the dragons," she whispered.

Chapter 19

Brenik gritted his teeth and pressed his legs firmly against Brellyg's flanks as the dragon banked sharply to one side. It was a bad time to discover that he hated flying.

"How much farther?" Brenik yelled over the wind and driving snow that had been stinging his face for the past couple of hours.

Brellyg's chest rumbled as he shouted back a reply. "We're just beginning to land."

Brenik nodded gladly, he was sat between two spines just forward of Brellyg's massive wings and he quickly dug himself in more securely as the great dragon suddenly pitched to the left and began to fall in a slow, spiralling dive.

Once they drifted below the screen of dark clouds filled with white snow, Brenik gasped as the blizzard subsided slightly, allowing him to see much farther across the mountain ranges. Nothing that he had ever read about the dragons could have prepared him for what he saw.

The great beasts had made their home in the large crater of a dormant volcano, set far away to the west of the tribes of orcs and northerners. Whilst the huge walls of the crater were covered in snow, the floor was bare, red rock with only small patches of snow dotted here and there. No doubt a result of the great plumes of fire that the dragons produced Brenik thought.

Down below, Brenik counted twenty other dragons, some red like Brellyg whilst others were shades of blue, green or black. The elf grinned with genuine excitement.

"Something is wrong," Brellyg suddenly growled in concern.

Without warning the dragon stopped his slow, circling descent and dropped into a steep dive, catching Brenik off guard and nearly sending the elf tumbling off of the beast's back. As it happened, it was only when Brellyg slammed recklessly into the crater's bare floor at a run that Brenik lost his grip and slid off the side of the dragon, rolling as he hit the floor and barely avoiding being trampled by the dragon's powerful rear legs.

"I'm fine, thanks," Brenik grumbled as he scrambled to his feet, brushing his clothes off and adjusting his pin. "I . . ." The elf stopped. He was looking at a small green dragon lying still on the bare ground before him.

There were two types of dragon, the large four legged kind like Brellyg and the smaller, two legged kind like the one he was now staring at. The dragon was lying on the floor, her long neck stretched out in a pool of silvery gold liquid collecting around her head. As Brenik approached the beast, he saw the hilt of a dagger protruding from the dragon's right eye, the silver blood of the dragon still seeping slowly out of the open wound.

Brenik turned around to see Brellyg rolling over a yellow skinned dragon with his front foot. The elf hurried urgently over to him.

"Dead." Brellyg's powerful voice was reduced to a whisper. "They're all dead."

Brenik looked down at the dead dragon. There were pairs of tiny holes dotted all over it's neck but no blood was visible, the work of vampires undoubtedly.

"I . . . I am so sorry Brellyg," the elf whispered sorrowfully.

Brellyg looked down and turned away from Brenik. His eyes suddenly lit up as they set upon a pale blue dragon. "Karviss!" he whispered before hurrying over to the other dragon.

Karviss was older and larger than Brellyg. His scales were a soft blue and down his back ran a line of thick, white hair that also sprouted from around his chin, making it seem as though the dragon had some kind of oversized beard.

Karviss watched his friend approach before managing to whisper his name. "Brellyg."

Brellyg shot forward to his friend's side, the ground shaking under his heavy footsteps. "Karviss!" he cried again. He looked down at his friend and winced when he saw the many burns and gashes that covered the dragon's soft, white underbelly. "Who did this to you?" Brellyg whispered angrily.

Brenik appeared by Brellyg's side and Karviss suddenly roared with anger. "Them!" the dragon cried, his voice straining with the effort.

The dragon tried to turn his head towards Brenik but the movement proved too much for the wounded beast and he slumped weakly back against the rock. Brenik shifted uncomfortably as Karviss turned a suspicious gaze on the elf.

"Elves were leading the Kerberyn we saw the other day, vampires and orcs accompany them." Karviss fixed Brellyg with an intense stare. "And Necromancers, Brellyg! Necromancers were here!" Karviss' breathing was ragged and his eyes were becoming more and more unfocused.

"Easy, my friend," Brellyg said gently. "The elf is an ally, he means us no harm. You must be wrong about the elves. The Necromancers have attacked their cities, this elf lost his family to them."

Karviss shook his head weakly. "No," the dragon croaked. "They were twisted, pale skinned, skeleton like. But they were elves I am sure."

"How can that be?" Brenik said. "My people defended you! We would ever attack your kind!"

Brellyg looked sadly at the elf. "Orcs defended us once, yet we have been at war with them for hundreds of years now. And did you not tell me that your friend betrayed you? It could be possible that more of your kind have followed in his footsteps."

The wind whistled loudly and Karviss' eyes closed for a moment. "You have to go Brellyg," he said softly. "They will be back, they want our skins for their armour and our blood for their magic. Go whilst you still can. If the elf is what you say he is then help him. But you must leave now! The dragons must survive!"

"We can save you, Karviss," Brenik offered desperately. "Brellyg could help you out of the crater and we can find a place to rest and tend your wounds."

Karviss shook his head sadly. "No, it is too late for me. You must go!" He looked at Brenik. "Go with him Brellyg, see to it that these demons are forced back to whatever corner of hell that they crawled out of!"

Brellyg bowed his head sadly at his friend before turning to Brenik. "Come Brenik." The dragon bowed down to let the elf climb up onto his back before standing up to his full height and turning back to face Karviss. "Farewell, Karviss, Lord of the Dragons. May your fires burn forever in the light of the Eternal Flame," Brellyg said respectfully.

Karviss snorted a small jet of blue fire in response and bowed his heavy head. The Dragon Lord watched as Brellyg and the elf vanish into the clouds before his eyelids closed for the last time.

*   *   *

Brellyg flew silently away from his home, his head bent down against the driving snow as his great, leathery wings cut through the freezing air around them. They had not flown far when the dragon suddenly fell slowly from the sky and landed on a small plateau nestled amongst the grey mountains.

Brenik slid slowly off of the Dragon's back as they landed and looked sadly up at the beast. "I'm sorry," he whispered over the low whistle of the icy wind.

Brellyg looked away form the elf and trudged forward, coming to the edge of the plateau where he looked far out across the distant, snow covered mountains. Brenik held back for a moment before walking over to stand by Brellyg. Neither of the pair spoke for a long time, the only sound coming from the low whistle of the wind as it blew through the mountains and swept the snow about their bodies.

"I never thought this day would come." Brellyg's voice was so quiet that at first Brenik wasn't sure if he had mistaken the dragon's voice for the wind. "We dragons have been on the brink of extinction for such a long time." Brellyg sighed, causing a puff of dark grey smoke to waft slowly from his nostrils where it was quickly whipped away by the wind. "I just assumed that we'd always find a way of surviving."

"Dragons aren't extinct yet, Brellyg. Not whilst you live at least. There may even be other dragons living in Justava," Brenik said hopefully.

The great dragon shook his head. "No. I am the last, I am sure of it. More to the point I can feel it. There is a cold emptiness that runs through my body and saps my fire." The dragon looked up at the dark, starless sky. "A dark night for a dark time. What is the use of fighting the blackest night with naught but a match as a weapon? Fighting these Necromancers is folly! We will all die trying!"

Brenik stood silently throughout the dragon's outburst and continued to say nothing as the beast turned around and curled up against the rocky cliff, burying his head under his great wings. Brenik looked down and ran his hand over the golden symbol of the reflin tree that was pinned to his chest and a small but determined smile touched his lips.

The elf walked casually over to Brenik and settled down against the cliff. "The night may be dark Brellyg. And the flame may be small," he said softly. "But it is in the blackest of nights when even the smallest flame burns brightest."

Chapter 20

"So what exactly happened when they tried to take you?" Nalia asked as she and Alleyra rode slowly down the mountain together.

"Not much. I came out of the goblin trove with my arms full of gold to find a bloody group of tribesmen waitin' for me. One tried to grab me, so I took one of his fingers." The dwarf chuckled softly from the saddle behind the elf. "There was a bit of a scuffle. I injured almost all of 'em before Cirnan himself brought me down."

"And did you, well . . . Kill anyone?"

Alleyra laughed. "Nah. I make a point of only killin' orcs and goblins. Just gave 'em some scars to remember me by."

Zephira barked in approval and the two women laughed softly. Suddenly there came the sound of a horse galloping and Cirnan came flying around the corner towards them.

"They're gone!" he yelled in a panic. "All of 'em!"

"Who are gone?" Nalia asked quickly as she drew level with Cirnan.

"The bodies!" cried the excited Chieftain. "The scouts said that they had piled the bodies of the dead elves and were goin' to come back to burn 'em later on. I can see the tracks but there's not a body in sight!"

Nalia chewed her bottom lip, remembering the depleted number of dead bodies that she and Brenik had seen when they had discovered the deserted outpost. "Let's take a look," she said grimly.

They rode quickly down to the ruined outpost and looked around. The snow had eased over the past few days and they could still make out the tracks from where the scouts had dragged the bodies into the centre of the outpost. Other than the dip in the snow, however, there was no evidence that the bodies had ever been there.

Alleyra jumped down from the saddle behind Nalia, sinking up to her waist in snow, and inspected the area where the elves had been piled. "There are footprints here," she said.

"The scouts, obviously," Cirnan said dismissively.

"I don't think so," Alleyra said thoughtfully. "Not unless your scouts have started to wear . . ." The dwarf's sentence was suddenly cut off as a blue tinted hand shot out from under the snow and grabbed her by the throat.

"Alleyra!" Cirnan yelled. He swiftly drew his longsword and charged towards the dwarf, swinging the weapon down and severing the hand from the icy wrist. Alleyra fell back, gasping for breath.

Silence fell over the courtyard before a strangled scream rose up out of the snowy ground and more hands pierced the white blanket. Slowly, one by one, the corpses of the elves who had defended the outpost dragged themselves from below the snowy ground and began to limp hungrily towards the three companions.

"Get back!" Cirnan yelled as he swiftly dismounted and helped Alleyra to scramble away from the handless captain that was now rising from the ground before them.

An arrow suddenly flew between their heads and embedded itself in the captain's left eye, knocking him flat on his back. Alleyra and Cirnan turned to see Nalia sliding a second arrow from her quiver.

Nalia let the second arrow fly from her bow before turning to the others. "Go for the heads," she ordered cooly as her second arrow dropped another of the undead warriors.

Alleyra sprang to her feet and drew two of her long daggers before tackling one of the dead elves to the floor and stabbing at its grey face. Beside her, Zephira sprang at one of the Kerberyn, knocking the lumbering beast into the snow and ripping its throat out with one swift swing of her paw.

The Kerberyn were few and not as skilled as those that Nalia had faced in Cathwood. The fight did not last long.

"Bloody walking dead!" muttered Cirnan as he wiped his bloodied sword clean. "What the hell was that?"

"We aren't done yet, Cirnan," Nalia cautioned. "Someone must be in charge of this lot."

They began to move silently through the camp, keeping their weapons close as they inspected the ruined buildings. Nalia scanned the barracks, an arrow knocked against her bowstring as she glided between the empty bunks. Outside the others kicked their way through the charred remains of the outpost, ignoring the smell of rotting flesh that was creeping up their nostrils.

"Did ye see that?" Alleyra hissed suddenly as Nalia emerged from the barracks. "In the stables?"

Nalia slid an arrow from her quiver and rested it against her bowstring as she moved cautiously towards the stables. A flash of movement caught her eye as someone dove behind a haystack. "Come out! We know you're in there," she yelled through the creaking doors.

A vague silhouette appeared in the darkness and a small man shuffled his way cautiously forwards. He had wispy grey hair and a crazed look on his face. His eyes were misty and he had a tattered bandage wrapped over a wound on his head. A large scar ran across his left cheek from his lips to the bottom of his ear and his nose had been badly broken. He was wrapped in torn black robes that had been repaired many times, often with pieces of different coloured cloth. An empty satchel hung from his shoulder and in his hands he held a thin, grey staff topped with a small, green gem.

"Stay back Ugra says!" the man squealed. "Ugra powerful! Ugra raise dead men to fight!"

Cirnan glanced back at the piles of dismembered corpses. "Aye, and we killed 'em all over again," he muttered.

"Who are you?" Nalia demanded.

"Ugra!" the little man said proudly. "Ugra said stay back!" he screamed as Nalia edged closer.

"You are a Necromancer, aren't you?" Nalia asked slowly.

"Yes, yes! Other wizards laugh at Ugra! Say Ugra stupid! But Necromancers show Ugra power! Ugra show other wizards! Ugra kill them!" The Necromancer cackled triumphantly and a dark shadow fell over his face. "Ugra kill you now, yes?"

Alleyra leapt forwards, swinging her legs out and knocking the old man to the floor. She kicked his staff away and placed a foot on the man's chest. "How about Alleyra kills ye instead?" she growled as she raised one of the sharp daggers.

"Alleyra, wait!" Nalia yelled as she grabbed the dwarf's arm and pulled her away from Ugra who backed fearfully up against the stable wall as Zephira advanced threateningly towards him. "We may need him," she whispered in Alleyra's ear before turning back to the cowering Necromancer. "Ugra?" she said gently. "I am Nalia."

"Nalia? Will Nalia hurt Ugra?" he asked fearfully, looking at her through his milky-white eyes.

"If you promise to answer some questions, Ugra, then I give you my word that no harm will come to you." Nalia smiled as the Necromancer nodded quickly. "Why are you here?" she began.

"Other Necromancers go to mountains! Go speak to green-skins and to fight dragons! Ugra stopped to sleep. When Ugra woke up, everyone was gone!"

"Dragons?" Nalia said, oblivious to the Necromancer's other ramblings.

"Ugra thinks other Necromancers are missing him! They always laugh at Ugra's jokes!" Ugra beamed with pride.

"Ugra!" Nalia pressed the Necromancer. "What do you mean about the dragons?"

"Ugra says they go fight dragons! Master wants dragons to ride and dragons for armour! Necromancers have gone to kill dragons!"

Nalia looked back at the mountain in despair. "Brenik," she whispered. "We have to go back!"

"Go back?" Cirnan snorted. "Did ye not hear him? The mountains are crawlin' with Necromancers! It's a wonder we got through unseen!"

"What about Brenik?" Nalia protested angrily.

"He's got a dragon, I think he can handle himself," Alleyra said with a smile. "Besides, what if we go back and he's sat at the feet of the mountains waitin' for us?"

Nalia looked down at her feet and nodded, knowing that the other two were right. "Yes. I'm sorry," she mumbled. But what if he's not? she thought fearfully.

"Don't be daft!" Cirnan said, slapping her on her shoulder. "Now, what do we do with this lad? Tie him up and leave him?"

"Ugra would not like that," the little Necromancer protested.

"Well to be honest, Cirnan doesn't bloody care whether Ugra likes it or not!"

"Cirnan certainly didn't bloody care about what Alleyra thought," muttered the dwarf.

Nalia turned and slapped the dwarf on the arm. "Really? You choose now to start another argument? What is it with you two?" she cried in exasperation.

"Hey! I'm not the one that tried to steal from someone," Cirnan said, holding his hands up defensively.

"They didn't belong to ye!" the dwarf retorted angrily.

"Enough!" Nalia yelled. "Cirnan, find some rope and tie his hands together. Alleyra, come and help me burn these bodies." As the two trudged off to follow their orders Nalia looked down at Zephira and sighed. "This is what our great resistance is made out of," she muttered. Zephira merely barked cheerfully in response.

Chapter 21

The Masked Man ran a hand over the thick, leather bound book that rested on the table before him. A simple rune was depicted on the front, three straight lines passing through a circle. He opened the book, taking care not to damage the ancient pages as he flipped to the back of the book. The pages here were newer and the seam fresher. It was in these pages that the Masked Man had recorded his own histories alongside those of his many ancestors. More recently the entries had been getting longer.

"Are you still up?"

The Masked Man flinched at the soft voice and almost knocked his inkwell over as he turned to the speaker. "Liethra," he said softly.

Liethra stood in the doorway to her lover's chambers. Her blonde hair fell loosely about her body and the low cut dress that she wore left little to the imagination. She looked at the Masked Man and bit her lip seductively. "It's my last night," she purred. "I'm leaving for Malin tomorrow."

The Masked Man gently closed the crumbling book and turned to her, the eyes behind the mask moving slowly over the curves of her body. "I know," he said, holding back his lust.

Liethra walked slowly into the room, kicking off her heeled shoes and curling a lock of her hair around her index finger. "You will miss me," she said knowingly.

The Masked Man paused before striding across the room and pulling Liethra towards him so that their bodies were pressed closely together. "You don't give me orders," he hissed as she let out a gasp of air.

Liethra lifted her head up and placed the tips of her fingers on the cheek of her lover's mask. "Don't I, Jarus?"

Jarus snarled at the use of his first name and pushed Liethra against the cold, stone wall. "Do not think that you can control me," he growled threateningly.

Liethra lifted her legs and wrapped them around Jarus' waist. She smiled innocently as she took his mask in her hand and lifted it off of his scarred face. "And you can't control me," she whispered before she pressed her lips against his.

*   *   *

Nalia sighed as Alleyra and Cirnan began to bicker once more. Ever since the earlier battle at the outpost where Cirnan had saved the dwarf they had been at each others throats constantly, refusing to allow the age old prejudices that existed between their two factions to die with this simple act of kindness.

She rolled her eyes as she slipped tiredly down from Ishalla's back and looked around. They were just over a days ride from the outpost but the ground was already far flatter here and what little snow there was had become thin and patchy. Several hardy reflin trees sat across from them and the rocky ground was dotted with patches of dry gorse bushes and green grass.

Nalia nodded approvingly at the cover that the trees could provide them. "We'll make camp and wait for Brenik here," she said. However, her voice fell upon deaf ears as her two companions began to bicker even more fiercely.

"Ye never stop to think that outsiders might be lookin' to help ye!" Alleyra bellowed from the saddle behind Cirnan.

"Oh aye, because clearly anyone stupid enough to wander the mountains out of choice is only out to help everyone else! We have survived so long because we're careful about who we trust!" Cirnan roared.

Alleyra spat a curse at the Chieftain who tried unsuccessfully to elbow her in the ribs. Earlier, Nalia had lost her patience with the two and had refused to share her saddle with Alleyra. Swapping the dwarf for the babbling Ugra who had been trudging glumly along by the horses with Zephira snapping warningly at his heels every so often. She now regretted this decision as their close proximity had only served to increase the severity of their arguments.

"Fine," Nalia muttered. "I'll do it myself. Ugra, give me a hand."

"Ugra help! Ugra help! Just keep dog away!" he whimpered.

Nalia grinned as Zephira herded Ugra towards the horse and sat with her eyes fixed on the tiny man as he unpacked Ishalla's saddle. As the two worked, Cirnan and Alleyra continued their heated argument, it was only when the tent had collapsed on Nalia for the third time that they stopped fighting long enough to realise they had come to a stop.

"Do ye want a hand with that?" asked Cirnan innocently.

Nalia pushed the fabric off of her head and brushed the hair out of her face. "Oh, you're helping now?" she snapped sarcastically.

Rather embarrassed, Cirnan and Alleyra slid quickly off of their shared horse and helped the other two to set up their small camp. As Cirnan made sure Ugra would not run off, Nalia sat down with her back to a stone and closed her eyes. She missed Brenik. Throughout her life her friend had never been far from her side, now he was off hunting dragons with an army of Necromancers on his tail whilst she was babysitting two bickering children and a crazed Necromancer.

"Bren'll be back soon." Alleyra's voice was gentle and when Nalia opened her eyes she saw that Cirnan had left Ugra under Zephira's watchful gaze and had now gone to gather kindling from a nearby thicket of gorse.

"Yes. He'd better be," she smiled.

Alleyra smiled knowingly. "Ye like him, don't ye?"

Nalia could feel her cheeks colour slightly and she looked down into her lap. "I . . . I don't know. But even if I did then nothing would happen."

"Why?"

"Because," Nalia laughed softly. "He's my friend. That's it. Anything else would just be ridiculous."

"But something has happened hasn't it?" Alleyra said after a careful pause.

Now Nalia's cheeks really were beginning to burn. "There was one night, on the way up to the mountain. But the next morning was just awful, it was like we'd built this barrier between us. I've wanted to speak to him, but he always deflects the conversation away. I think he wishes that it hadn't happened."

Alleyra was about to reply when Cirnan returned, his arms empty of any wood.

"Ye do understand that the point of goin' to get firewood is to bring it back when ye cut it down?" the dwarf taunted.

Cirnan ignored her and looked urgently at Nalia. "There's someone comin' up the road," he said.

Chapter 22

The three companions grabbed their weapons and hurried to hide behind the gorse bushes that lined the roadside. Looking down the beaten track they could see a figure mounted on a white horse riding swiftly in their direction.

"Doesn't look like a Necromancer," Alleyra said slowly.

Nalia stroked the feathers of the arrow that she held against her bowstring. "Looks can be deceiving," she said quietly.

"Aye," Cirnan muttered. "Even so, we have him outnumbered. I say we find out what he's up to."

Before either of the two women could stop him, Cirnan stood up and marched out of the bushes onto the road, raising his crossbow and aiming it at the rider. At the sight of the massive man and the two women that followed him onto the road, the rider's horse whinnied loudly and reared up onto its strong back legs. There was a flash of light as the rider drew his sword and turned to face the three figures standing aggressively before him.

"Stand down!" the rider ordered. "I am a Knight of Resgard and I command you to lower your weapons!" His deep voice echoed loudly in his shining, silver helmet.

Nalia saw Cirnan tense as the knight declared his title.

"Oh! A big, brave knight!" Cirnan taunted sarcastically. "Let's see where that title gets ye when ye have a crossbow bolt in yer heart!"

The knight angled his blade towards Cirnan's heart. "Who are you who dares speak to me so boldly?" he demanded.

"Travellers," Cirnan replied gruffly, tightening his grip on his crossbow, his fingers hovering over the hair trigger.

Recognising how close Cirnan was to shooting the knight on sheer principal, Nalia lowered her bow and placed herself between the two men. "We mean you no harm if you do not mean to harm us," she said calmly to the knight.

The rider paused for a moment before turning his horse and spurring it into a brisk trot. As he came closer Nalia was able to get a better look at the man. He was tall and broad shouldered and wore thick, silver plate armour that gleamed in the moonlight. A round helmet with a white plume sat upon the man's head, hiding his face behind its metal visor. Across his back was tied a light blue cloak and a white kite shield with a blue cross the same colour as the cloak hung across his shoulders. The man's horse was white, although its flanks and socks were splattered with mud and grime from their long and hard ride. Like its rider, the horse wore shining armour on its head and neck and its reins and saddle were trimmed in the same light blue and white as the rider's cape and shield.

"I mean you no harm," the knight said truthfully. At this distance they could hear the man's voice echo more clearly in his helmet. "Please, tell me your names."

Nalia nodded at Alleyra. "This is Alleyra of Orinar City and this is Cirnan, Chieftain of the Northern Clans. I am Nalia Sommer of Cathwood City."

As he listened to the travellers' introductions, the man suddenly became very interested in Nalia. "You are from Cathwood?" he asked excitedly. "Thank the Almighty!" At the elf's confused look he quickly continued. "My name is Sir Ornith Denware. I am a knight of King William Resgard the Sixth, Lord of the Kingdom of Resgard."

"King Resgard?" Nalia frowned. Resgard the Sixth was King of the largest and most dominant of the Kingdoms of Men, a land that lay far to the west of Cathwood. "What is King Resgard doing sending one of his knights all the way out here?" she asked.

"My King was betrayed by members of his own court," Ornith explained. "Several of his aides were able to sneak assassins into the castle. Fortunately we saved our King and were able to capture one of the assassins. From him we learned of a group of evil magi known as the Necromancers and of their plans to attack the elves. I was sent to Cathwood to warn your people, but when I got there I found that your fair city was in ruins. I now ride to the outpost to warn them of what has happened."

Nalia looked down sadly. "Whilst your warning is appreciated, Sir Ornith, you have already seen that it comes too late. The Elven Kingdoms have already fallen. Many elves, including our rulers, are already dead."

Sir Ornith reached up and removed his helmet, revealing a youthful face with thick, blonde hair swept casually to one side. His eyes shone green and his strong jaw was smoothly shaven. The knight swung easily from his horse and walked towards Nalia where he knelt before her, took her hand in his and kissed it delicately. He looked up at her with genuine sorrow in his eyes.

"I am sorry, milady," Ornith whispered. "I was not quick enough. I have failed your people."

Nalia, who was now blushing slightly, shook her head dismissively. "No, no! Not at all, Sir Ornith! There was nothing that you could have done to save us."

"Maybe not," the knight admitted. "But I was sent to help your people by my King, and I intend to do just that! I will take you safely from this place, back to my King who will provide you with shelter and will treat you with great care."

Cirnan rolled his eyes angrily and turned to Alleyra. "I might have found someone to hate more than ye," he whispered.

Alleyra winked at Cirnan. "I'm surprised he didn't turn his sword on ye when she said yer name."

"I think he's a little distracted," Cirnan muttered, listening as Ornith dove into a long-winded speech about how much safer Nalia would be in Resgard.

"We have indefinite supplies of food and water," the knight boasted. "The walls are high and well manned, the Necromancers will not . . ."

"Sir Ornith!" Nalia gently cut the man off. "Thank you for your kind offer, but we are on our own mission. My two friends here are the start of an army of resistance fighters. Chief Cirnan here has called for his tribesmen to take up arms and another friend of mine is still in the mountains recruiting other warriors to our cause."

"A resistance?" The knight glanced towards Cirnan and sneered. "You will not get far without the support of the Seven Kingdoms."

"I'm afraid we will have to," Nalia said. "The Necromancers plan to destroy the Kingdoms, Emladis and the Elven Kingdoms have fallen already. I fear that your own Kingdom does not have long to stand."

"All the more reason for us to return now!" Ornith urged the others. "Resgard is prepared to fight, as are Malin and Angelis! You will find more skilled warriors there than you will in the mountains," he said with a bitter glance at Cirnan.

"I'd take a hundred of my men over a thousand of yours," Cirnan spat angrily. "As ye pointed out, your Kingdoms are filled with traitors! And I would not seek the aid of captains who butcher their own people!" Cirnan glared at Ornith as he thought back to the violence that had erupted during the time of his ancestors' long protests. "So thank ye for yer offer, but we're doin' just fine on our own," he growled.

The knight looked at the Chieftain with contempt before turning back to Nalia. "I was sent here to help in anyway possible. Whilst I do not agree with your view that our armies are corrupt, nor do I agree with your choice of friends," he muttered as he glanced again at Cirnan, "I do see what you are attempting to do. I have much experience in war and I hope that I can be of service to you and your people." The knight bowed low again, resulting in a snort from Cirnan.

Nalia couldn't help but smile at the knight's excessive chivalry and threw Cirnan a warning glare as he laughed. "Any help we can get is greatly appreciated," she said as she pulled the knight to his feet. "We thank you, Sir Ornith, for your kind offer and gladly accept your experience and knowledge."

"The honour is mine, milady," the knight said proudly.

"We do not have much as you can imagine," Nalia said as she led the way back to the camp.

"I am sure that whatever you . . ." The knight trailed off as his eyes fell upon Ugra who was cowering in the corner of the camp under Zephira's watchful gaze. "What is that?" he said in a low voice.

"His name is Ugra," explained Alleyra. "He's some crazy Necromancer that we captured up at the outpost."

"Is there a reason as to why he is still alive?" Ornith said bitterly.

"I gave him my word that no harm would come to him if he revealed why the Necromancers were in the mountains," explained Nalia.

Ornith snorted. "Word or not, his kind deserves death for what they are doing."

"I am a lady of my word, Sir Ornith," Nalia said. "I will not have him harmed." The tone of her voice did not leave the matter open to discussion.

Ornith chewed his tongue as he looked disapprovingly at the Necromancer. "As you wish," he finally muttered. "But if he puts one toe out of line, then I shall deal with him swiftly."

"Somethin' we can actually agree on," Cirnan murmured under his breath.

Ornith quickly settled down into the camp, laying out his own things and preparing his own meal in a small, black pot. As he cooked he watched curiously as Nalia wandered off to the edge of the camp and folded her arms as she looked up into the distant, star filled sky.

"She seems sad," Ornith commented thoughtfully.

Cirnan sighed. "Look," he growled angrily, "let's get this straight. I don't like ye and ye don't like me. The girl is fine, she doesn't need yer help. None of us do!"

"Then why am I still here?" the knight shot back.

"Nalia's too nice to say anythin' bad!" Cirnan muttered. "And she doesn't know what ye people are like!"

"What's that supposed to mean?"

"Ye knights pretend to care! Ye act like gentlemen but underneath ye're all cowards! When ye really see people suffer, ye just turn yer backs and look the other way!" Cirnan shouted.

"How dare you insult my order!" Ornith hissed in a threatening tone. "The Knights of Resgard are the most honourable warriors in Justava!"

Cirnan snorted and rolled his eyes. "Aye! Tell that to the women and children who ye cut down in the cathedral grounds! Or the families who you drove out of their homes to starve in the wilds!"

"You . . ." Ornith began before biting his lip. "This is our ancestors' fight, not ours," he reasoned. "I have said nothing to offend you!"

"Ye didn't have to!" Cirnan growled. "I saw the look ye gave me earlier."

"You know, at least I am trying to put our differences aside," Ornith said after a long period of silence.

"Oh, aye! So ye're the great peacekeeper now?" Cirnan mocked. "When ye want somethin', we can talk. But if we want somethin', ye turn yer swords on us!"

Ornith scowled at Cirnan's mocking tone. "You defied an order from the King! Your ancestors deserved . . ." The knight stopped himself again and took a deep breath to calm his temper. "Look. Taxes and politics are of no concern out here. This is a pointless argument. I am just trying to get to know you all a little better. Is that really so bad?"

"Fine!" Cirnan snorted.

"So?" Ornith said after Cirnan gave no other response. "What's wrong with her?"

Cirnan shrugged. "If ye must know, she misses her friend, Brenik."

Ornith dipped his spoon into his pot and dished himself out a generous serving of stew. "Brenik? Are they together?" he asked thoughtfully.

"Who?" Cirnan asked, clearly he had not been listening.

"The two elves?"

"I thought Knights of Resgard were sworn off desires of the flesh," Cirnan chortled as he adopted the accent of the upper class of Resgard. "They're just friends. Don't you go gettin' any ideas lad. She's got standards that you could never meet!"

Ornith ignored the insult and watched Cirnan frown as he picked a leaf from his bowl, not noticing the knight slip off towards where Nalia was standing.

As Cirnan threw the leaf dismissively into the fire and sat back he jumped when he found Alleyra glaring at him from the seat beside him.

"Where's he off to?" she asked suspiciously.

Cirnan shrugged as he spooned an oversized helping of stew into his mouth. "Dunno. Gone to speak to Nalia I think. Wanted to know if she and Brenik were together or somethin'," he said, spraying food into the fire.

Alleyra glared at Cirnan before knocking his bowl out of his hands. "Ye got no bloody sense man!" she growled.

"Oi!" Cirnan yelled, looking down at the spilled remnants of his stew. "What was that for?"

"Nalia does like Bren!" Alleyra exclaimed. "And I'm damned sure that he likes her as well!"

"So what?" Cirnan said, spooning out another helping of stew. "If that's the case then they'll end up together anyway."

Alleyra glared angrily at Cirnan before knocking his bowl out of his hands once more.

*   *   *

Nalia rolled her eyes as she heard Alleyra and Cirnan start another row. In the distance a wolf howled and she shivered at the long and eerie noise.

"You look cold," said a gentle voice.

Nalia turned to see Ornith stood behind her. He had removed his armour and now wore dark brown trousers and a pale blue, padded shirt. In his hands he held his cloak which he was now offering to Nalia.

She smiled as he placed it across her shoulders. "Thank you," she whispered softly, pulling the cloak tightly around her body.

"I hope you aren't too worried about your friend," Ornith said softly.

Nalia chuckled dryly. "He's been through so much worse than this. He'll be alright, I'm sure."

"Worse? What could be worse than being stuck in the mountains with those demons?" Ornith jabbed a finger in Ugra's direction as he spoke. The little man was scurrying about the camp as Cirnan shouted at him to clear up the mess he had made.

Nalia's eyes dropped to the floor, she was unsure whether she should reveal Brenik's troubled past to the stranger, it was a story that very few people knew. "It's a long story," she said reluctantly.

Ornith smiled. "I think we have the time."

Nalia looked at Ornith, she could not explain why, but something about the man made her trust him. She sighed as she began to speak. "Brenik is the son of Rothule Lithuik, one of the Lords of Cathwood.

He is a highly skilled physician and on top of that he is an expert warrior and has often led parts of Cathwood's army in battle."

Ornith nodded slowly. "Yes, I know of the Lithuik family. I thought I recognised the name."

Nalia continued. "Several years ago, Brenik was travelling back to Cathwood with his fiancé and a group of soldiers after visiting the Kingdom of Rochelle. On their way home they were ambushed by a group of bandits who captured Brenik and the others. When they were taken back to the bandit's camp, they made Brenik choose between the life of his fiancé or the lives of his men."

Ornith tilted his head to one side as a small tear began to slide down Nalia's face. "Which did he choose?" he asked, already knowing the answer.

"He chose to save his men. I think . . . I think he knew that if he had tried to save his fiancé then she would have been made a slave instead, and his men killed in horrible ways. They killed her in front of him and then threw him in with the rest of his men."

"How did they escape?"

"Overnight they managed to break free and steal some horses, but the bandits soon caught up with them and began to pick them off." Nalia sighed. "Of the thirty men that Brenik gave the life of his fiancé to save, only two made it back to the outpost with him. One died from his wounds later that day. The other, Guillard Terune, became a good friend of Brenik's but ended up betraying the entire elven race to the Necromancers that we are now fighting. So Brenik sacrificed his future wife for nothing, and in doing so he saved the man who turned our people over to the enemy. That, Sir Ornith, is what is worse than what he faces now."

Ornith nodded slowly at the tragic tale. "His fiancé, she was close to you?" he guessed.

"Her name was Gwyyn and she was one of my closest friends. She and Brenik were perfect for each other; it just seems so wrong that they were torn apart." Nalia turned to look at Sir Ornith. "Several days after he returned, a parcel arrived for Brenik. Inside was Gwyyn's severed head. A 'gift' from the bandit leader. Brenik gathered an army and led them in the destruction of the bandit camp. They captured the leader, the man who killed Gwyyn. When they brought the man before him, Brenik could have executed the leader right there, but instead he showed him mercy." Tears now rolled freely down Nalia's soft cheeks. "He was so strong, so brave even though this man had torn his world apart."

Ornith nodded thoughtfully. Often it took more courage to spare a life than to take one.

Nalia sniffed and wiped her tears away before handing Ornith back his cloak. "Thank you for the use of your cloak, Sir Ornith, but I think I shall turn in for the night."

Before Ornith could reply, Nalia bundled the cloak into his arms and hurried off into her tent, holding back the fresh tears that threatened her eyes. She threw herself onto her sleeping mat and wrapped herself in her own arms.

Brenik's story always made here feel this way. It had been when he had first shown an interest in his future fiancé that Nalia had first come to realise her own feelings for him. Of course she had been happy for them both, but she had always known that a small part of her had secretly wanted them to break apart. She knew that what had happened was not her fault at all, but nevertheless, a small part of her always felt very guilty whenever she thought of the sad tale.

For a long time, Nalia lay silently in her tent, unable to sleep. She was confused about so many things, chief amongst which were her feelings for Brenik. She cared deeply for him but she was confident that nothing would ever come from it, especially given the awkwardness that now seemed to fill the silences that they frequently shared. On the other hand there was Sir Ornith, the dashing knight who had swept into her life and had shown her nothing but kindness since first meeting with her. She could tell he had taken an interest in her and she could not deny that she found him to be attractive. But she still had feelings for Brenik.

Nalia sighed as she closed her eyes and tried to sleep once more, her mind reeling with images of Brenik and their time together.

Outside, Sir Ornith scratched his chin thoughtfully. He liked the girl, she seemed kind and she was indeed very beautiful. But he was fairly confident that she had feelings for the other elf. Whether he shared those feelings for her, however, Ornith would have to wait until they met to find out.

Chapter 23

It was early morning when Nalia was awoken by a far off roar that echoed within the mountains and rolled down into the road where they camped. Zephira growled uncertainly in response to the foreign noise as the young elf grabbed her green cloak and dashed excitedly out of her tent, grinning when she caught sight of the small, distant dot that was speeding towards their campsite. She quickly roused the others and they watched in awe as the giant dragon and his rider circled the camp once before dropping smoothly to the floor. The dragon growled softly and bowed his head, allowing Brenik to slide nimbly off of Brellyg's scaled back.

As soon as the elf hit the floor he was swept up in a hug from Nalia. "I missed you," she whispered in his ear, glad to see that Brenik no longer recoiled from her embrace.

Brenik held the hug for a long while and then smiled as they released each other. "I missed you as well," he said kindly. "Did you run into any trouble?"

Nalia shook her head. "Nothing we couldn't handle. We met some Kerberyn at the outpost," she said, nodding in Ugra's direction. "Cirnan kept us safe though and we captured their leader."

"Good," Brenik said in relief before turning curiously to Ugra. "I'll have to have a word with our new friend later on."

"Good luck," Nalia muttered. "He's crazy."

Brenik chuckled softly before looking up as the others walked quickly over to the pair of elves. Zephira bounded happily between them and jumped up at Brenik, panting happily as Brenik wrestled playfully with her.

"Did ye find anythin'?" Alleyra asked excitedly when Brenik had calmed the dog down.

Behind the elves, Brellyg looked away sadly. Over their long flight he had gradually begun to come to terms with the loss of his kin with the help of Brenik's comforting words. Nevertheless, the pain was still very near and the dragon still felt a surge of emotions whenever someone mentioned his lost brethren.

Brenik placed a comforting hand on the great beast's leg. "The dragons are gone," the elf said sadly. "When we reached their home we found them butchered by the Necromancers. We saw them on the way back, that's why we're late. They're all over the mountains. It looks as though they are calling the orcs to war."

Nalia sighed and placed a hand on Brenik's strong arm. "Ugra told us that that was their plan. I had hoped you would reach the dragons before the Necromancers arrived."

"I'm sorry," said a confused voice. "But is the destruction of the dragons not a good thing?"

Brellyg snorted angrily and Brenik frowned as he suddenly noticed the newcomer in their midst. The man was tall and handsome and carried an air of arrogance with him as he stepped forwards.

"It is in no way a good thing," the elf said curtly as he fixed the man with suspicious eyes. "An entire species has been pushed to the brink of extinction! There is nothing good about that."

Ornith shouldered his way past Cirnan and regarded Brenik with a calculating stare. "Dragons once roamed my Kingdom, killing innocents on a whim without any sign of remorse. You can understand why I am inclined to disagree with you, can you not?"

The dragon growled threateningly from behind Brenik but once more the elf quickly placed a restraining hand on the beast's thigh. "Who are you?" he questioned.

The knight bowed extravagantly. "Sir Ornith Denware. Knight of King William Resgard the Sixth, Lord of the Kingdom of Resgard. I am here to join your fight against the Necromancer Empire."

From behind the elves Brellyg muttered something inaudible at the young knight, sounding to everyone but the elves like a short, angry snort.

"Well, Sir Ornith," Brenik said with a hint of sarcasm. "I recall a time when humans drove the dragons away, driving them to the brink of extinction until we put an end to your madness. If I recall correctly, the dragons were hunted and culled without a shred of remorse."

Ornith bit back his anger. "I know my history. And I also know that the dragons needed to be driven off."

Brellyg continued to glare threateningly at the knight as Brenik fixed Ornith with a cold stare. "Well, regardless of your views, Sir Ornith, we need all the help we can get," Brenik said curtly. "Brellyg here has offered to aid us in our fight and I am more than happy to have the aid of a dragon when we go to fight giants and other foul beasts! I am sure a fire-breathing dragon will be a lot more useful to us than one of Resgard's knights!"

Cirnan grinned at Alleyra as Ornith's eyes grew cold. "Not so big now," he muttered, enjoying seeing the knight battle with Brenik.

Ornith glared angrily at the elf. "He has offered to help? How can you possibly know that?" he scoffed.

Nalia stepped quickly between the two men, breaking the tension between them with her presence. "Elves are able to speak with the dragons, we understand each other," she explained as she reached out a hand to stroke Brellyg's long snout. "How are you?" she whispered kindly.

"Tired," Brellyg said with a gentle snort. "My heart is heavy with anger and sorrow."

"I am sorry, Brellyg," Nalia said sadly.

The dragon shook his great head. "You have enough burdens, Nalia. Do not trouble yourself with the weight of the dead as well."

Ornith's expression softened as he watched Nalia smile affectionately up at the dragon. "I see," he said slowly. "Well as you said, we need all the help we can get." Ornith suddenly stuck out his hand towards Brenik. "Forgive me, Brenik. It seems that we have got off to a bad start. I meant no offence to you, or to the dragon."

Brenik shook Ornith's hand carefully. "None taken, Sir Ornith. Your reaction was, as you said, understandable." Although Brenik's voice was calm there was an unmistakable edge to his words.

Cirnan clapped his hands together eagerly and grinned. "Good, we're all friends again! Now can we please get some breakfast going? I'm starvin'!"

Brenik threw Cirnan a wide grin and the five companions settled down to a breakfast of cold stew and slightly stale bread. Brellyg in the meantime, disappeared off into the wilderness in search of a more adequate meal to suit his appetite, his loud roars echoing off the mountains to the east as he hunted his prey.

Cirnan nodded at Ornith. "Charmin' fellow isn't he?" he said to Brenik as they began to clear away.

"Oh yes, just lovely," Brenik said sarcastically. "Has he been like this all the time?"

Cirnan snorted. "Aye, of course! He's a knight, what do ye expect? I'm surprised they found a helmet big enough to fit his ego."

Brenik laughed. "Well you never know, a few days with you might bring him down to your level!"

"Aye, I'm countin' on it," Cirnan grinned.

Having eaten and cleared up all evidence of their campsite, the group set out on the long ride back to the Great Forest. When they had left the mountains, Cirnan had brought a spare horse along with them in preparation for Brenik's return, allowing the four larger companions to ride their own horse whilst Alleyra and Ugra were shared between them.

They rode in single file to hide their numbers and ran the horses at a brisk but measured pace, not wishing to tire their mounts out. As they rode, Brellyg flew high up in the skies above them, keeping up easily with the horses as if they were barely moving. During the first day he would occasionally turn back and swoop high over the mountains, bringing news that the tribesmen were indeed defying the elders and were preparing to follow their small company down towards the Great Forest.

With the forest getting ever closer, the group eventually broke their single file rule and began to ride in groups. Brenik took his opportunity to hold back and speak with Ugra, who he had just acquired from Nalia's saddle. He glanced over his shoulder at the Necromancer who was shifting uncomfortably behind him. The Necromancer had said virtually nothing of use since his capture, spending most nights babbling nonsense to himself. But there was something about Brenik that seemed to calm the little man and he was now sat silently behind the elf, staring into the sky through his cloudy eyes.

"So, what's your story?" Brenik asked casually. "I hear you were left behind?"

"Yes, Ugra was forgotten," the mad mage sighed sadly. "Ugra is used to it though. Ugra was always forgotten when Ugra was young."

"Why?" Brenik asked curiously.

"Ugra was sent to learn magic; Ugra used to be very, very, very clever! A witch, Ugra forgets her name, wanted to teach Ugra chaos magic! Ugra felt very, very special!"

Brenik could not help but nod in agreement. Chaos was one of the seven branches of magic and the closest legal form of magic to the forbidden powers. Only the very best witches and wizards were trained in its use due to the dangers of the corrupting spells.

"So what happened?" Brenik pressed the little man.

"Ugra got spell wrong. Tried to make special rune, but spell bounced back and hit Ugra! Since then, Ugra is not so clever. Council wanted to banish Ugra from the order! Said Ugra was mad!" he sighed sadly before breaking into a grin. "But the Necromancers changed that!" he finished happily.

"How?"

"How what? Ugra said distantly.

"How did they make you strong again?" Brenik said patiently.

"Oh! They gave Ugra much power! Made Ugra feel strong again! All Ugra had to do was distract the Council. Ugra did it very well!"

"You distracted the Council of Magi?" Brenik said, clearly impressed. "That was no small task. How did you do it?"

"Simple! Ugra killed one of them!" Ugra beamed proudly.

Brenik raised an eyebrow. "You killed one of the Council Members?"

"Yes! Ugra shown special chaos spell! Ugra used it to kill Light Mage!"

Brenik looked back at the small, crazed man behind him. "There's a lot more to you than meets the eye isn't there?"

Ugra simply beamed happily again. "Ugra is special!" he declared proudly.

Chapter 24

Night fell on the third day of their journey and the companions settled down for the night, pitching their tents before sitting around their modest fire with their increasingly bland meals.

"If there's one thing I hate about travellin'," Cirnan grumbled as he turned the cold, stodgy stew over with his spoon, "it's the food."

"Don't ye ever think of anythin' besides food?" Alleyra asked tiredly, although she herself had to admit that the stew was beginning to wear very thin.

"I do!" Cirnan said defensively. "The drink isn't strong enough either," he muttered as he swirled his half empty mug of cold, weak tea.

"Aye," Alleyra agreed as she thought longingly of the sweet dwarf ales, "I'm with ye on that one."

Nalia smiled at her two friends, glad to see that they were finally beginning to calm down and treat each other with respect and even kindness. She then glanced over at Brenik and Ornith who were hunched over a crumpled map, talking tactics. Brenik and Ornith were both strong characters and it was clear Ornith was not enjoying having to defer to Brenik's decisions. Despite their trying to get along, a tense atmosphere had formed between the two warriors and the resentment that they felt towards each other was obvious in the way they spoke to each other.

"When we get back to the forest we should hopefully have a small army awaiting us," Brenik was saying to Ornith.

"We aren't actually going into the forest are we?" Ornith inquired as if the mere thought were enough to put him off his food.

"Well of course we are," Brenik said as he picked at his dinner. "That is where we shall meet Yukov."

Ornith crinkled his nose as he set his bowl down. "Yukov?" he asked.

"Yukov is the vampire that Nalia and I met after we escaped Cathwood. He took us in and provided us with shelter before agreeing to help our cause. Whilst we have been in the mountains, he has been recruiting the people of the forest to fight for us."

"People?" Ornith raised an eyebrow. "Brenik, you know as well as I that there are no people in that forest. The only things that live there are monsters!" Silence fell over the other three as Ornith's voice rose and adopted a harsh edge.

Brenik glanced at Nalia before turning back to Ornith. "We thought the same as you, Ornith. But Yukov proved us wrong. He took us in, gave us food and shelter and helped us organise ourselves. All this was Yukov's idea," he said calmly.

"No doubt he was playing some kind of trick on you," Ornith muttered dismissively. "He probably wants you to gather an army so that he and the other savages will have something decent to feast upon!"

"Ornith, you don't know that," Brenik said flatly. "You have not met Yukov. I doubt you have ever met a vampire."

"I've read the stories, Brenik!" Ornith growled. "I know all about the vampires and the werewolves!"

"You know the paladins twist those stories, Ornith."

"The paladins protect us from the unjust and unholy. I will not become a snack for those beasts!"

"Perhaps if you give them a chance you will realise you don't have to!" Brenik replied, standing up suddenly. "We are going to the forest!"

Ornith jumped to his feet, pressing his index finger into Brenik's chest. "Who put you in charge anyway? Why should we be listening to you?"

"No one asked for your help, Ornith!" Brenik snarled. "Since you joined us all you have been doing is sticking your nose into our business! You think you know what is best for everybody but you don't!"

"Well at least I am trying to help! I don't sit back and let things just happen like you!" the knight snapped.

"When have I ever done that?" Brenik cried in frustration.

Ornith sneered at Brenik. "Well, lets just say I wouldn't have just sat there whilst someone beheaded the woman who I loved!"

Nalia gasped as a cold silence descended over the pair. She watched as Brenik glared at Ornith, his face a mixture of anger, surprise and grief, before shoving his way past the knight and storming off into the darkness.

Ornith watched him go and his face suddenly fell in horror as he realised what he had said. "Brenik!" he called out in shame. "Brenik I'm sorry! I didn't mean . . ."

Nalia stood up and pushed past Ornith. "Why did you say that?" she hissed.

"Nalia?" Ornith called desperately.

"Let me talk to him," she snapped back at the knight.

*   *   *

Brenik leant silently against a lone tree not far from the road's edge. Behind him he could hear Nalia's soft footsteps. "How did he know?" Brenik asked when his friend was in earshot.

Nalia walked up beside him and looked sadly up at the full moon above them. "I told him, Bren," she admitted. "I'm so sorry, but he wanted to know about you. I never thought . . ." She trailed off as her friend looked sadly at the ground.

"It's fine," Brenik whispered. "I know he's right."

Nalia reached out and slipped her arms around Brenik, resting her head on his broad chest. "No, he's not," she said strongly. "You did everything you could. No one could have saved her."

"I could have," Brenik whispered. He hugged her weakly, his arms drained of strength. "Or I should have tried harder."

"Bren, no one could have tried harder," Nalia said as Brenik turned away. "Ornith has no idea what he's talking about," she insisted.

Brenik nodded and stared silently at the floor. Nalia stood closely beside him, watching him carefully as the silence dragged on.

"You like him don't you?" Brenik said suddenly.

"What?" Nalia said, slightly taken aback by the abruptness of her friend's question.

"Ornith," Brenik said gently. "I've seen you talking, seen the way you look at him. I know you have feelings for him. I know you," he added and smiled down at his friend as she laughed softly.

"Sometimes I think you know me better than I do," she admitted. "I don't know how I feel about Ornith. I mean, he is a good man at heart. But, there's something that is stopping me. I can't explain it."

Brenik resisted the urge to laugh. "I understand," he whispered. "What will you do?"

Nalia shrugged. "I don't know. What do you think?"

Brenik looked down at his friend and squeezed her tightly in his arms. "I think you should do whatever your heart tells you to do."

Nalia looked up into Brenik's deep blue eyes and opened her mouth to speak. She was about to tell him how she felt but something stopped her. She still loved Brenik deeply but the time had come for her to try to move on. Brenik was her friend and that was all he would ever be. So instead of speaking she simply smiled and hugged him a little tighter.

Brenik sighed as his friend pulled him closer. As she did so he could smell the sweet scent of her golden hair and feel the soft touch of her skin against his. He was still very much in love with her. For a moment he considered telling Nalia how he felt but he stopped himself before any words could begin to form. If she was happy with Ornith then Brenik would not interfere. As always he would continue as her friend and would be there for her whenever she needed him. It was time for him to try to move on.

Chapter 25

On the fourth day of their journey, when the tall trees of the Great Forest were just beginning to pierce the horizon, Brenik found himself riding alongside Ornith. Since the night of their argument, Brenik had been doing his best to avoid talking to the knight, but it seemed that the inevitable conversation had finally caught up with him.

"We're finally here," Ornith said in relief.

"Yes, finally," Brenik replied plainly.

A silence passed between them before Ornith spoke up again. "I am sorry about the other night, Brenik. You must understand that I did not mean what I said."

Brenik sighed and looked down at Ishalla's reigns. "I understand, Ornith. In the heat of the moment I think we both got a bit carried away." In truth Brenik hated the knight for what he had said. He hated him because deep down, Brenik knew that Ornith had been right, knew that he had failed Gwyyn.

Ornith nodded solemnly before changing the topic of their conversation. "So, will this vampire be waiting for us when we arrive?"

"I hope so," Brenik said. "Have you come to terms with the situation now?" He glanced sideways at Ornith as he spoke, curious to see how the knight would react.

"I have," Ornith admitted. "I realise that in times of great need one must put aside personal feelings and prejudices for the greater good. However, I hope you don't expect me to trust this vampire of yours."

Brenik shrugged indifferently. "Whether you trust him or not does not matter to me. So long as you can fight beside him without turning on him then we won't have a problem."

Ornith chuckled. "I will do my best," he joked, although Brenik did not smile.

An awkward silence descended over the pair and Brenik hoped that that was the end of their conversation. After a while though, Ornith spoke up once more.

"You and Nalia are close aren't you?" the knight asked curiously.

Brenik eyed Ornith suspiciously. "She is my oldest and closest friend."

"Yes, but is that it?" Ornith pressed him. "Are you just friends, or is there something else going on?"

Brenik felt his chest tighten. "Why do you want to know?"

Ornith smiled innocently and ran a hand through his long, golden hair and down onto his smooth chin. "Well, she is a beautiful woman. I wanted to make sure I wouldn't be stepping on anyone's toes as it were."

Brenik looked at Ornith in stunned silence, a wave of nausea running over him. Even Ishalla seemed to slow down and she dropped several paces behind Ornith's white stallion before Brenik was able to compose himself and urge her back up to speed. "I don't think that would be a good idea," he said as he caught up with the knight. "Not until things are more settled at least."

Ornith frowned. "Why not?"

"I . . . I just don't think that either of you would have the time for a relationship, what with the resistance and everything else that is going on," Brenik said, stumbling over his words. "Things might be a bit difficult for the both of you and I would hate to see her get hurt."

Ornith nodded slowly at the elf's response. Brenik clearly had feelings for Nalia, that much was obvious to Ornith even if no one else seemed to have noticed it. If Ornith wanted a chance to be with Nalia he realised he'd have to act fast to prevent anything happening between her and Brenik.

"I'll bear that in mind, Brenik. Thank you for your advice," the knight said. Pulling back on his reigns Ornith carefully slowed the pace of his horse and dropped conveniently back to ride beside Nalia, a place where he stayed for the rest of the journey.

*   *   *

The midday sun hung high above the company as they galloped across the wide plain before the Great Forest, relieved to be at their journey's end. Brellyg swooped low over their heads as he flew on and circled twice over the green hills that were nestled against the Boar's Tusk before turning back and diving down to meet the group.

Realising that something was wrong, Brenik urged Ishalla forwards to meet the dragon as he landed heavily on the grassy plains. "Is everything alright?" he yelled up at the mighty beast.

"There are a group of people on the hill. It appears as though they are trying to signal you," the dragon rumbled, nodding up towards the rolling hills.

"What's goin' on?" Cirnan growled curiously as he and the others rode up beside Brenik.

"Looks like a welcoming party up in the hills," Brenik said suspiciously. He turned back to Brellyg. "Keep an eye out from the skies. We'll go and take a look."

They turned their horses and galloped over to the small depression in the side of the mountains where Brenik and Nalia had arrived at after escaping Cathwood City. A group of mismatched figures stood awaiting their arrival. There were two vampires hidden from the sun under the shade of the reflin trees, a pair of werewolves and a tall, male dryad.

The dryad quickly approached the riders as they climbed up the hill. "You are the friends of Yukov?" he hissed as he pointed at Brenik with a long, twig-like finger.

"I am," Brenik replied cautiously as he dismounted. "Where is he?"

The dryad looked sadly towards the forest. "Gone," he whispered.

"Gone?" Brenik asked in confusion. "Gone where?"

The dryad turned his luminous green eyes back to Brenik. "The Necromancers. They have taken him!"

Chapter 26

Yukov gasped as a bucket of ice cold water was thrown across his bruised face, causing him to cough violently as he was awoken from his state of semi-consciousness. He was still in the dungeon, strapped to a table at a forty-five degree angle to the floor. The small room was lit by two murky torches which, combined with the drugs that he had been steadily fed over the past hours, made it difficult for even the vampire's sharp eyes to focus on details. A shadow moved in the corner of his eye, the dim light making it impossible to see who it had been. But Yukov already knew who his tormentor was.

"Where are the elves?" Guillard Terune's cold voice cut through the still air of the stuffy room.

This was Guillard's third interrogation and Yukov had steadily grown used to the elf's increasingly direct questioning. So far, Yukov had withstood each of Guillard's previous attempts and the elf had grown more and more frustrated each time. Yukov had sat silently as Guillard questioned him, enduring the pain that came with each question as he waited patiently to be drugged again and then awakened a few hours later by the impolite, icy splash of the water.

"My answer has not changed, traitor," Yukov said bitterly.

Guillard now appeared as a blurry haze in the corner of Yukov's vision. "I am running out of patience," he hissed, bringing his face closer to the vampire's.

Yukov suddenly lunged forwards, baring his fangs as he pulled against the iron restraints that held him to the table. Guillard flinched and pulled back, but not before the sweet taste of blood filled Yukov's mouth as one of his fangs drew a long scratch down the elf's shallow cheek.

"Funny," Yukov joked as he licked the sweet blood from his lips. "I could do this all night."

Guillard clutched the cut on his cheek, wiping the blackened blood away in anger. "That was a very costly mistake!" he said in a threatening hiss. "I am tired of waiting! You will suffer, you will break, and then you will die!"

"I have lived through far more than you can imagine, traitor!" Yukov spat venomously. "You have nothing that you can use against me."

A thin smile touched Guillard's lips. "That remains to be seen," he whispered into Yukov's ear.

Yukov watched as Guillard pulled a thin knife from his belt and walked over to the corner of the room where a large sand bag hung suspended from the ceiling. With a quick flick of his wrist Guillard's blade poked a tiny hole in the bottom of the bag, sending a steady trickle of sand spilling out onto the stone floor below. Above Yukov there came the sound of stone grating against stone and a section of the roof began to slide slowly backwards. There was a flash of blue sky and a thin ray of sunlight penetrated the still air of stone prison, casting a bright line a meter across on the slab floor in front of the vampire.

Guillard smiled victoriously. "As more sand leaves the bag the roof will slide farther and farther back. Eventually, the light of the sun will be on you." Guillard regard Yukov's state, unclothed save for a small pair of tattered shorts. "You know what that will do to you, vampire. The pain will be unbearable, even for you. Tell me what I want to know and you won't have to suffer needlessly."

Yukov stared at the line of sunlight. He knew what contact meant for him. It was the fate that he feared most of all; the sun would sear his flesh and turn it to ash if not treated properly. As Guillard had pointed out, the pain would be excruciating.

Yukov slowly raised his dark eyes and stared calmly at the elven General. "I will tell you nothing!" he said boldly.

Guillard chuckled harshly as he turned towards the door. "Courage and defiance will only get you so far, vampire."

"And how far will betrayal get you until the knife is pointed at your own back?" Yukov called after the elf.

Guillard turned in the doorway and glared at Yukov. "You think you know me. But you cannot begin to comprehend what I am planning. You shall soon tell me what I want to know, not even you can endure what is to come." Sliding the door shut, General Guillard turned and marched down the corridor towards the Master's chambers, leaving the vampire to his fate.

*   *   *

Brenik rubbed his temples as he looked down from the hill at the army below. The sky above was grey, matching the elf's mood. "This is all that would come?" he asked the dryad behind him.

Behind him, Hisseda, the male dryad who had informed him of Yukov's capture, nodded grimly. Despite all that had been done by the creatures that Yukov had gathered, only a fraction of the Great Forest's inhabitants had offered their aid to the resistance. One hundred and fifty vampires, two hundred werewolves and thirty dryads.

"It simply isn't enough," Brenik sighed.

"How can four hundred stand against the Empire?" Alleyra said despairingly.

Cirnan placed a broad hand on Brenik's shoulder and looked confidently at his two friends. "Don't forget, my men are marchin' down to help us as well. Soon these fields will be filled with armed men rearin' for a good fight!"

"If they get here in time," Alleyra pointed out.

The others nodded grimly. They had to assume that their position had been compromised and that the Necromancer army was on its way to crush them as they spoke. It would be a simple matter for their small force to break up and disappear into the forest. But with Brellyg off scouting the roads to Justava's central regions, there was no way to get word to the Northern Clans on the march to the forest. Even if they could run, the Necromancers would most likely burn the Great Forest to the ground when they arrived at the empty fields.

Brenik turned his back on the small army and looked grimly at his fellow commanders. "Alleyra is right. We must assume the worst. Cirnan's men will not arrive on time and we will be severely outnumbered."

"How do we even know that they are coming?" Cirnan asked suddenly.

Ornith snorted. "He's a vampire, he's not going to protect our location if they torture him."

Brenik ignored the comment. "They captured him in the forest. Even if he doesn't give up our location they will assume we are here. We cannot leave the forest unprotected, it is our only safe haven."

Cirnan nodded in understanding. "So what's our plan then?" he asked. "Fight until we can fight no more?"

Brenik shook his head and pointed towards the forest. "We cannot fight them on open ground. But we can use it as a ploy." He now indicated the table before him upon which sat a crudely drawn map of the Great Forest's southern boarder. "We'll position ourselves and the wolves on the plains before the forest. When the Necromancers arrive we will feign a charge to draw their attention before beginning a fighting retreat until we are in the trees. I am hoping that our enemy will follow us once they think we're on the run. Once inside the forest, the Necromancer's numbers will count for very little. We can let the vampires lose upon their ranks whilst the dryads keep herding them in the right direction. They will lose all form of order in the forest, all we have to do is close the door on them."

"A valiant strategy," Ornith remarked. "What makes you think the Necromancers will take the bait though?"

Brenik looked back up at the group, his face was drained and dark circles had formed under his tired eyes. Nevertheless, his blue eyes still shone and the other commanders could not help but feel a surge of inspiration run through their bodies as he fixed them with his piercing gaze.

"Guillard will undoubtedly be leading the attack," Brenik said confidently. "If he knows Nalia and I are here then at least there will be some honour to the fight. He is not as far gone to deny us that. Plus I am counting largely on the lack of skill of the Kerberyn. Once they have a taste of flesh they are less easily controlled and I am hoping we can goad them into a frenzy."

There was a nod of agreement. No one was for a moment saying they would be victorious in their fight. But they all knew that this was not one that they could simply run away from. They would stand together in their final hour, or they would not stand at all. All they could do was hope that Yukov did not reveal too much about their plans in the mountains.

*   *   *

The Masked Man turned on his feet as the door to the Chambers of the Council of Magi creaked open. The Master and his most trusted advisor had been discussing the possibility of constructing a series of concentration camps in order to hold the human and dwarf prisoners that had been captured during the initial invasion of the Western Kingdoms but now they found themselves interrupted by the unannounced arrival of General Guillard.

"General!" The Masked Man hissed deeply. "You were not summoned. What is the meaning of this intrusion?"

Guillard strode swiftly across the marble floor to stand amongst the ring of chairs. He looked confidently into the black sockets of the Masked Man's iron mask. "You told me I need not worry about my two elven friends and that I was wrong to be 'obsessed' with them. Well I have just learnt that my fears were justified."

The Masked Man tilted his head, regarding Guillard through the hollow eye sockets of his spiked mask. "What do you mean?" he asked curiously.

"The elves are forming a resistance movement," Guillard declared triumphantly.

The Master stood up, his long, black robe hanging down around his thin frame as he pointed a withered finger at Guillard. "You are sure of this?" he asked slowly.

"How?" the Masked Man demanded when Guillard nodded.

Guillard turned to one side and with a clap of his hands the door to the Council Chambers opened again. The General raised a hand and pointed to a creature being dragged across the floor by two dark elves. When the guards threw the figure roughly to the floor, the Master and Masked Man saw him to be a vampire. The creature wore nothing but a pair of ragged shorts and from the knee down his pale skin was black and twisted like burnt wood.

"This vampire," Guillard said, grabbing a fistful of the vampire's hair and pulling his head back so that they could see the creature's beaten face, "was caught in the Great Forest attempting to recruit its creatures to a resistance movement formed by a pair of elves. After my interrogation he revealed to me that the elves had left for the Kingdoms of Men several days ago and will be returning very shortly to the forest to gather their army and fortify their position."

The Masked Man turned excitedly to the Master. "Liethra has just moved her army through the Kingdoms of Men, she would have known of any large forces leaving the boarders. They must have failed in their attempt to recruit their army!"

"They could have slipped across the boarder to the Dwarf Kingdom," reasoned the Master.

"But Zahrg is there as we speak," the Masked Man countered. "Almost all of the Necromancers are either in one of the Kingdoms of Men or the Dwarf Kingdom." He shook his head confidently. "No, if the elves had succeeded in rallying an army they would have been spotted. I am sure that they have failed!"

Guillard turned to the Master. "Regardless of how much support they have or have not gained we must crush this resistance whilst it is still young!"

"I agree," the Master whispered at last. He extended his hand and his black staff snapped into his withered palm from where it had been resting against the red cushioned chair of the former Arcane Council Member. "I will personally see to it that an example is made of these upstarts!" the Master declared. "General, prepare my troops. Tomorrow, we march to war!"

Guillard nodded before indicating the vampire. "What do we do with him? He is of little use to us anymore."

A cruel smile touched the Master's thin lips as he met Yukov's defeated eyes. "He must be dear to the elves and their warriors for them to have entrusted him with recruiting people to their cause. It would be, unfair on them if we did not show them what has become of their beloved monster."

Chapter 27

Brenik guided Ishalla slowly through the ranks of mismatched men and women that stood mingling on the open grassland. Here and there a few people would glance up at him and nod in respect as he rode past before returning to whatever task they had found to keep themselves busy. It had been five days since their return to the Great Forest and already the group of companions, now the leaders of the resistance, had grown to be respected by the creatures of the forest. Brenik glanced over to where Ornith was waving away a pair of werewolves as though they were his personal servants and corrected himself. Most of them had grown to be respected.

A gruff voice from behind spoke quietly to Brenik. "I think they missed a spot when they polished his armour."

Brenik smiled as he looked back to see Cirnan riding slowly up to him. Like the other companions, the creatures of the forest had provided the Chieftain with a suit of armour from their personal hoards of treasure. Cirnan had been given a suit of light scale armour that had been painted dark brown and decorated with golden trimmings in a simple pattern. The chieftain still wore his long fur coat over the top of the armour and both his crossbow and longsword were slung over his back in the shape of a cross.

"Heaven forbid he might actually get dirty!" Brenik said in an overly horrified voice.

The two friends laughed together as Ornith strode arrogantly away from the muttering werewolves. A silence passed between the pair as they looked around the field of disjointed warriors. Eventually Cirnan spoke again, although this time his voice was quieter and his words more serious.

"They are with ye to the end, Brenik," the Chieftain said respectfully. "As am I."

"I don't ask you to stay Cirnan," Brenik said as he stared out across the plains. "You could go and warn your people to turn back. You could return to the mountains and pretend that none of this ever happened."

A small smile touched Cirnan's fat lips. "I never told ye the truth behind what I did, Brenik. There's a reason why I was able to leave so easily."

Brenik frowned. "What are you talking about?"

"When the elders said we would not help ye, I told 'em that I was goin' to anyway. They told me that if I did, that I and anyone who followed me would be cast out from the tribe. I'm no longer the Chieftain, Brenik. I gave up that title when I left the mountain."

Brenik stared in stunned silence at Cirnan. "You did all of that for us?" he finally managed to say, feeling overwhelmed by the loyalty and trust that Cirnan had placed in him.

Cirnan shrugged. "At first I thought I was doing it out of logic. Either I helped ye or I stayed Chieftain 'till the Necromancers came to us. But as I got to know ye, I began to realise that I did it for more than that. Ye're a natural leader Brenik. Ye're fair, kind and one of the bravest men I've ever met. I'd follow ye to hell and back if ye asked me."

Brenik smiled at Cirnan. "One demon at a time, my friend," he laughed before becoming serious again. "Thank you, Cirnan. That truly means a lot to me."

Cirnan grinned fiercely. "Aye! So you won't be gettin' rid of me any time soon!" he joked as he waggled a fat finger at the elf.

Brenik laughed. "Fair enough. That armour does suit you I guess."

Cirnan grinned at the complement as he looked down admiringly at the smart suit. "Aye, Alleyra picked it out. She's got good taste ye know. I'm not sure about yer's though."

Brenik looked down at his own armour. Even though he had been offered suits of shining silver mail and golden plate armour he had refused all of the offers. Instead he had selected a new pair of elegant, leather vambraces decorated with the heads of golden dragons, some thick, leather boots and a light but tough shirt of chainmail to wear under his clothes. As always, the golden pin of his broken house shone brightly on the dark blue cloak that hung from his broad body.

"What's wrong with my armour?" the elf protested.

"There's nothin' of it!" Cirnan said, jabbing at the lose mail with his finger. "What's the point of it?"

Brenik reached across and slapped his northern friend on the back. "Well, I just count on the fact that I'm not stupid enough to get hit!"

The two laughed together as they rode through the ranks of wolves towards the rest of the command group. Sat on their horses, talking and laughing together, they could see Nalia and Ornith sitting slightly apart from the others.

"How are ye copin' with that?" Cirnan asked seriously as he nodded towards the unofficial couple.

Brenik shrugged. "She seems to like him. But nothing's happened yet so . . ." He trailed off and shrugged. "Well who knows, eh?"

Cirnan nodded slowly. A few days ago Brenik had explained his feelings for Nalia to him. The art of romance had never been one that Cirnan had had much understanding in. He had his share of women but he had never experienced the feelings that Brenik had described to him. Even so, Cirnan could tell that seeing Nalia and Ornith growing increasingly close to one another was making his friend uncomfortable and he was not enjoying watching Nalia fall for the knight.

Cirnan smiled reassuringly at Brenik. "Ye're right lad," he said kindly. "She's a clever girl, she wouldn't make a stupid decision. Unless she picks ye that is!" he added with a broad smile.

The two were chuckling with laughter when Alleyra approached them. "Hope I'm not interrupting?" she said over the deep chuckles.

Brenik turned and looked down at the dwarf. "What's up?" he asked casually.

"Well, down in this case," Cirnan said, snorting with laughter at his own joke.

Alleyra rolled her eyes and ignored the chortling man, turning instead to Brenik. "Ugra wants a word," she said uncertainly.

* * *

They found Ugra sat at the rear of the resistance's lines, bound tightly to one of the smaller trees on the edge of the forest. Zephira lay watchfully at his feet but when the three companions approached she jumped up excitedly and charged at Brenik.

Brenik laughed and stroked the dog affectionately before turning to Ugra. "You wished to speak to me?" he said rather more coldly than he had intended.

"Yes, yes!" Ugra babbled. "Ugra wants to say sorry! Ugra on wrong side, he sees this now! Ugra wants to make things right!"

"He says he wants to join us," Alleyra said, not bothering to hide her skepticism.

Brenik stared at the deranged Necromancer for a long time. "Why?" he asked finally.

"Because you are strong! Ugra wants to help! You can beat Necromancers!" Ugra looked down sadly. "They will probably kill Ugra if you send him back to them."

"How do we know we can trust you?" Brenik asked hesitantly.

"Ugra will swear! Ugra does swear! On . . . On anything you want!"

Brenik thought for a moment before nodding. "Cut him loose," he said.

"Bren!" Alleyra protested. "You can't seriously be . . ."

"I said cut him loose!" Brenik interrupted gently. He watched as Alleyra reluctantly sliced through the ropes that secured Ugra to the tree.

"Oh, thank you! Thank you, thank you!" Ugra whimpered, stroking Brenik's feet.

Brenik moved in a flash, driving his arm under Ugra's chin and pinning him to the trunk of the tree. "You listen to me," Brenik hissed threateningly, bringing his face close to Ugra's and ignoring the rancid breath of the Necromancer. "I don't trust you. If I get even the slightest hint that you are going to betray us, then I swear, I will hunt you down and kill you myself. Do I make myself clear?"

Ugra managed to swallow and nodded fearfully. "Ugra understands," he whimpered. "Ugra will be good."

Brenik glanced down at Zephira. "Keep an eye on him, will you?" He asked and laughed when the dog barked happily in response.

A loud roar suddenly sounded from high up above them. Brenik turned around slowly, his eyes narrowing and his lips coming tightly together. In the distance, rising out of the horizon he could just begin to make out the tips of a sea of spears.

Cirnan's face became grim. "So it begins," he growled. "Good luck lad, we're all goin' to need it."

Brenik gritted his teeth and gingerly mounted Ishalla, drawing his sword as he did. "They're here!" he bellowed as he rode towards the front line. "Get to your positions!"

Chapter 28

Rank upon rank of Imperial forces began to form into their predetermined positions on the wide, open plain before the forest and the ragged ranks of the resistance. Looking out amongst the ordered lines, Brenik could see the hoards of Kerberyn snarling and gnashing their yellow teeth in anticipation of the taste of flesh. The dark elves stood behind them, holding their wicked halberds tightly at their sides whilst square banners bearing silver skulls on purple and black fields flew proudly over their heads.

At the centre of the rows of dark elves was a group of men mounted on horses. One of the men raised his sword and led several of the horses in a brisk gallop away from the army and out into the centre of the field. Looking back, Brenik nodded and spurred Ishalla forward, riding at the head of his own command group to meet the leaders of their enemy.

When they arrived before the Necromancers, Brenik quickly scanned the enemy ranks and his eyes narrowed as he picked out the leaders. The Master sat in the centre of the group, looking small but imposing on a huge, heavily armoured, black horse. The man himself was cloaked in nothing more than a shadowy black robe with a rich, red lining. The hood of his cloak was pulled up high to hide his olive skinned face and in his hand he gripped his long, black staff tipped with the red ruby. Underneath him, the black horse snorted angrily and rose up proudly, kicking up a spray of mud into the faces of the resistance leaders.

To the Master's left was the Masked Man and on his right was General Guillard Terune. Also with them were two other Necromancers, one human, the other goblin. The bald human was short but broad shouldered. His chest was bare save for two fat bandoliers that formed a cross over his bulging muscles. In one hand he gripped the reins of his horse whilst in the other he held a twisted, grey staff. In contrast, the little goblin that sat beside him was skinny and hunched over in his saddle. He was dressed in stained, yellow rags and held a spiked staff with a red gem embedded into the tip. He muttered a string of curses as he struggled to maintain control of the wolf that he was mounted on.

"This is who would oppose me?" The Master chuckled as he looked upon the group, analysing the opposing leaders as Brenik had just done. "I must admit, I had expected more."

"That's funny," Brenik said, unfazed by the cold words, "I was expecting the great Master of the Necromancer Empire to look a little grander than an old man in an oversized cloak."

The Master cackled. "My dear boy, surely you of all people have learnt by now to not judge by what is on the outside."

Brenik glanced at Guillard who stared at him through empty eyes. "I have indeed," he conceded. "Fortunately, however, I know that you are just as black on the inside as you are on the outside."

A knowing smile touched the Master's lips. "Indeed? Perhaps you should consider looking inside yourself, boy. To know one's heart is to know one's actions. And to know one's actions is to know one's beliefs. Look at your own actions, have you always done what is right? Can you say that you have never considered what I have achieved?"

"Enough!" Brenik snapped before the Master could twist his words any further. "We did not come here to listen to your riddles!"

"Then why are you here I wonder?"

Brenik glared into the black confines of the Master's hood, searching the deep shadows for the man's hidden eyes. "You and your army are to disband and leave Justava and never return. You will undo the wrong that has been done to the elves and you will return the lands that you have taken and the people who you have forced into slavery."

"Strong demands," the Master said thoughtfully. He nodded to the army behind Brenik. "Do you think you have the strength here to make us do that though? You are nothing. Your power is wasted here, your people outnumbered and outmatched. You are all going to die."

Brenik shrugged indifferently. "If we must die then we will die. But we will have made a stand worthy of recognition."

The Master chuckled once more. "Courage. You and your people are so pathetically fond of it. Let me show you the price of your courage."

The Master turned and nodded at the goblin who quickly produced a small horn and blew a short, sharp note from the instrument. Behind the Master the ranks of the Necromancer army parted and a lone dark elf rode out, his horse pulling a small wooden cart that bore a tall, crudely fashioned cross. Brenik gasped in horror as he saw that Yukov was tied to the wooden poles by his wrists and ankles.

"Cut him down," Brenik hissed as the dark elf drew up beside the Master. The sun was currently obscured behind a dark bank of grey clouds but Brenik could see the spotted blisters that covered the vampire's skin from times when he had been exposed to the harsh rays of light.

The Master smiled, ignoring Brenik's demand. "The last remaining elves, a fat dwarf, a lost knight and a scruffy northerner?" The Master regarded Ugra who sat uneasily behind Brenik. "And a coward and traitor to round it off. This is, without doubt, the worst army I have ever seen."

"I'm not scruffy," Cirnan muttered indignantly.

"At least he didn't call ye fat," Alleyra said from the saddle behind him, rubbing her stomach self-consciously.

Brenik ignored his friends and glared at the Master "I said cut him down!" The force behind his shout made several of the Necromancers and his friends jump.

The Master chuckled again, a horrid ragged sound that caught in his throat, before turning to the dark elf. "Do as he says," he ordered before turning back to regard Brenik. "Pathetic. This is nothing more than one rabble leading another!"

Brenik watched with concern as Cirnan and Ornith whisked the injured vampire from the dark elf and helped him up onto Nalia's horse. With a shout, the young elf turned her horse about and galloped back towards the camp.

Brenik watched her go before turning back to face the Master. "Perhaps we are not the greatest army to have graced the lands," he admitted, struggling to control his anger. "But no matter what happens today, we will have shown Justava that there is still hope left! And that people are always willing to fight and die for their freedom!"

The Master chuckled. "You are brave and idealistic, boy. But what happens when the story surfaces that your forces were decimated? That an army of thousands attempted to battle the Empire only to be crushed and wiped from existence?" From under the shadow of his cowl the Master smiled wickedly. "No. Your defeat will be so final, so crushing that no one will dare to follow your example. Whatever happens today, the resistance will die, along with you and all of your friends."

Brenik watched as the Master whipped his horse about and began to ride back to his army. "What happens when you are not there though?" the elf suddenly called out. "What happens when you are dead? When your masked advisor lies lifeless on the ground? When your treacherous General is no longer able to lead your forces?"

Guillard glanced nervously at the Masked Man as the Master's victory was taken away from him. The Masked Man said nothing, however, merely watching their leader closely as his horse slowed and stopped.

Brenik shook his head defiantly as the Necromancers turned back to face him. "We don't have to destroy your army to win this battle. No, we only have to destroy you and your henchmen." Brenik turned Ishalla around and glanced back over his shoulder. "Look for me on the battlefield," he warned. "I may be the last thing you see." With a loud shout, Brenik set Ishalla to a gallop and returned to his own army.

From behind Cirnan, Alleyra let out a low whistle. "Imagine what he would have said if he'd called him fat!" she muttered.

*   *   *

Brenik jumped off of Ishalla's saddle when he reached his own lines and sprinted over to where several werewolves were gathered around Nalia's horse, easing Yukov down from the saddle. The vampire lay in a state of semi-consciousness as they lowered him onto the grass and held a dark cloak above him to shade him from the sun that was beginning to slide out from the cover of the clouds. Nalia held his head in her lap whilst one of the wolves gently fed him sips of water from his canteen.

"How is he?" Brenik asked as he dropped to the floor beside his friend.

"He'll live," the werewolf said gruffly. "But we need to move him back into the forest as soon as we can."

"Brenik." The weak voice cut Brenik's response short and he looked down as Yukov raised a sun blistered hand to the elf. "Brenik I am so sorry. I have failed you," he whispered.

Brenik gently lowered Yukov's hand back to his side. "Lay still, my friend. We will save you, do not worry. And this is not your fault, I swear to you."

A pair of werewolves appeared holding a wooden stretcher between them. Carefully they eased the vampire onto the sheet suspended between the two bars and lifted him up.

Brenik squeezed Yukov's hand reassuringly. "Get him as far away from here as possible," he instructed the werewolves. "Seek out the other vampires and see if they can help him."

The two werewolves nodded grimly at Brenik and hurried off, keeping the cloak draped over the vampire to protect him from the harsh sun.

Brenik watched them go before turning to Nalia, wanting to tell her that Yukov would be alright and that they would see their friend soon to calm his own nerves as much as hers. But when he turned he found Ornith already telling her the exact same thing, holding her tightly against his armour and stroking her golden hair. Gritting his teeth in frustration, Brenik turned angrily away and climbed up onto Ishalla's back. He busied himself by drawing his bow and selecting an arrow from his quiver.

"Bren?" Alleyra whispered in concern.

In no mood to talk, Brenik ignored the dwarf and dug his boots into Ishalla's sides. "Make ready!" he yelled as he rode back towards the front lines.

Ishalla rose up onto her back legs and pivoted so that Brenik could look back across his forces. His eyes scanned the faces around him, men and women looking up at him expectantly, searching for any trace of emotion in their leader's face. Brenik set his features, trying his best to look strong and confident.

He then began to speak. "Today is a day of blood, and of sacrifice! A day when we turn as one in defiance to those who have wronged us!" He paused and looked across his army, picking out faces and holding gazes. "Justava once cast you from her societies to live your lives in the shadows of those that would oppress you! But today it is you, not them who will stand against this threat! Today we show Justava that she belongs to all of us! And that no matter what race we are, what beliefs we hold, we will stand united in her defence!" Brenik stood in his stirrups and raised his bow high into the air. "For Justava!" he bellowed.

Behind him the wolves repeated Brenik's cry. "For Justava!" they echoed.

Brenik settled back into his saddle and watched in awe as the wolves began to change. Some dropped to their knees whilst others clutched at their heads as their bodies began to contort and spasm. Then they stood up straight and began to grow in height, their skin disappearing under a sea of thick fur whilst their faces developed long snouts and their eyes shrunk to beady, black orbs. As one the werewolves howled in response to Brenik's speech and they began to charge towards the Necromancers.

The Battle of the Great Forest had begun.

Chapter 29

Brenik loosed the black-shafted arrow and watched it fly gracefully through the air before it pierced the forehead of a charging Kerberyn, dropping the broken beast instantly. Beside him a grey furred werewolf howled in approval of the shot and Brenik grinned in response.

The elf glanced around as he slipped another arrow from his back. He was mounted high on Ishalla, surrounded by a sea of the huge werewolves that were easily able to match the great horse for speed. The wolves stood as tall as horses and Brenik could just pick out the shapes of his companions, surfing the wave of dark fur as they charged bravely into battle.

Not too far behind Brenik, Cirnan fired off a crossbow bolt that felled another of the Kerberyn. With a shout of approval, he tossed the useless weapon aside and pulled his longsword from his back before turning and grinning at Alleyra.

"Never thought I'd say this," Cirnan yelled over the roar of the charging armies. "But look after yerself!"

"Aye," Alleyra yelled back as she spun a pair of long knives in her padded hands. "Ye too, Cirnan."

Vicious, unforgiving cries came from the Kerberyn as they swarmed forwards, urged on by the mental will of the Necromancers that controlled them. The werewolves howled once more, their own snarling roars drowning out the deathly shrieks of the enemy, and the two armies met.

The first clash was a bloody one. The werewolves tore into the Kerberyn as though the walking corpses were made of nothing but rags. Dead limbs were ripped out of sockets, heads were swiped off of the necks which they sat upon and sharp claws easily splintered the rusted weapons that the Kerberyn wielded.

In the centre of the resistance's line, the commanders attacked with just as much ferocity. Swords split skulls open whilst expertly placed arrows zipped through the air to drive deeply into their targets' rotting flesh.

Alleyra cackled in approval as she pounced off the saddle and landed on top of a Kerberyn, gouging its yellow eyes from their sunken sockets with a quick stab of her blades. The dwarf moved back to stand beside Cirnan and his horse, jumping and cutting the throats of two more Kerberyn as she charged past.

"This is more like it!" she yelled as she sent a throwing knife spinning into the the collapsed remnants of another corpse's spine.

Cirnan pulled sharply on his horse's reins as he dodged a clumsy spear thrust. He spun around to face his attacker but found himself watching as the owner was ripped in two by a massive werewolf.

"Aye! But the wolves keep stealin' ma' kills!" he complained as the wolf tore apart another body.

Alleyra grunted as she rolled out of the way of a Kerberyn's sword and jumped up to stab it in the back of the skull. "Don't be such a baby!" she teased as she wiped her pus covered hands on her bloodied armour.

At the tip of the resistance's lines Brenik's sword rained blows down onto the Kerberyn from the back of Ishalla, hacking a swathe of destruction on either side of him. Ishalla herself lashed out with her feet, her powerful hind legs driving into the Kerberyn behind her and splintering their rigid bones. Brenik looked around confidently as the Kerberyn began to slowly fall back, overwhelmed by the superior skill of the resistance fighters.

"Rip them apart!" Brenik yelled above the cries of battle. He turned and saw Ugra cowering behind a werewolf as the beast ripped through a group of Kerberyn. "Ugra! You'd better start doing something useful or I'll set Zephira on you!"

Ugra glanced nervously over to where Zephira had a Kerberyn pinned to the floor. His eyes widened as she tore the beast's throat out with one swipe of her paw and looked fearfully up at Brenik and nodded quickly. "Alright! Ugra help! Ugra help!" he blabbered hysterically.

Brenik nodded in satisfaction as Ugra began to fire off weak bolts of crackling, black energy, one of the simplest chaos spells. As they hit the Kerberyn the beasts became overcome by a series of sudden muscle spasms, leaving them defenceless to the rampaging werewolves. It wasn't much of an attack, the werewolves needed no assistance against the Kerberyn, but Brenik was glad to see that the former Necromancer was doing something useful.

Brenik turned his attention back to the battlefield. More of the Kerberyn were turning in retreat and the werewolves were howling in triumph as they drove easily through the small number of beasts that remained to fight. "Keep pushing forwards!" the elf yelled in encouragement. "We have them on the run!"

*   *   *

The Masked Man allowed a thin smile to spread under his mask as he silently called the Kerberyn back to the Imperial lines.

"I thought you said that the Kerberyn had no fear," Guillard said angrily as he rode over to the Masked Man.

"I am not the one controlling them, Guillard," the Masked Man lied. "It is the Master's will that they respond to." Another smile touched his lips as he saw the flash of doubt cross Guillard's face.

"The Master's will is absolute," Guillard said rigidly.

"Is it, General?" the Masked Man asked softly. "Was it not I who created his army? Was it not I who sought you and his other leaders out?"

Guillard looked at the Master, suddenly noticing how frail the man looked. "He needed you to do that," Guillard protested. "His power is too great to trouble with such matters!"

The Masked Man turned his horse and began to trot towards the Master. As he passed he looked at Guillard. "Then why are we losing?" he asked.

The Master scowled as the resistance pulled back and the extent of the damage that they had done was revealed. Only a handful of Kerberyn had managed to stumble back to the Imperial lines.

The soft sound of a horse's hooves snapped the Master back to attention. "They retreated," he hissed in disgust as the Masked Man drew level with him.

"I can't explain it." the Masked Man said uncertainly. "It's like something is blocking my connection to them."

"Or someone," the Master whispered thoughtfully as he turned back to the commanders who sat behind him. "General, send in the next wave. Tyranar, I want you to lead them. Bring me the head of one of their leaders and you will have your choice of any of the Seven Kingdoms."

The bare chested man urged his horse forwards and ran a hand over his bald head. "And if I bring you them all?" he growled softly.

The Master glanced at the Masked Man as he rode off and lowed his voice so that only Tyranar could hear him. "Then my right hand will find that the left has become more capable," he said curtly.

Chapter 30

Despite the success, the Kerberyn had only been the beginning of the Necromancer's attack and the resistance remained uneasy as they reformed their lines.

From the rear of the Imperial ranks there came a loud roar as five huge giants lumbered forwards, paying no attention to the fleeing Kerberyn that they crushed underfoot. The beasts bellowed loud war cries as they crashed into the werewolves, tossing the wolves aside or crushing them with their huge fists and feet. The werewolves could not hold against both the giants and the renewed spirit of the Kerberyn and soon began to fall into a fighting retreat.

Concern etched Brenik's blood-splattered face, the retreat had come much sooner than he had expected, as had the great giants. Swiftly he selected an arrow for his bow and spun Ishalla back to face the forest. "Fall back!" he yelled to the nearby wolves. "Get back to the forest!"

Brenik pushed his boots against Ishalla's side and guided her towards Ugra where he leant down and plucked the Necromancer from the ground and hauled him up into the saddle behind him. With a sharp whistle to Zephira, Brenik turned Ishalla and began to ride swiftly down the resistance lines, passing on the order to retreat.

"Look out!"

Brenik pulled sharply on Ishalla's reins as Ornith's warning filled his ears. The ground before his horse suddenly erupted in a shower of golden shards as three shimmering crystals rose out of the damp ground. He glanced to his right to see the bald Necromancer glaring at him with hate burning in his eyes.

"Get the order out!" Ornith called as he rode past the elf. "I'll hold this one off!" The knight did not wait for Brenik to reply. Instead he spurred his horse onwards to meet the charging Necromancer.

The Necromancer glared at Ornith as he chanted and large fragments of fine, crystal shards appeared above his head as he summoned another spell.

Ornith shrugged his shield off of his shoulder just in time to block two of the shards which shattered harmlessly against his white shield. However, his horse suddenly lurched underneath him, broke step and stumbled to the floor. Ornith grunted as he threw himself clear from the stallion, just catching the glint of the last crystal shard as it faded from his horse's still body.

The Necromancer sneered down at Ornith as he rode slowly past. "Take away a knight's horse and what do you have? A pathetic boy playing at being a soldier!"

Ornith dove aside as several crystals erupted from the ground below him. "Visionary magic," he whispered to himself.

"Saying goodbye to your horse?" the bald man goaded. "Not to worry, you'll be with the beast soon." The man kicked his legs into his horse's side and charged towards Ornith, hurling groups of the golden blades at the knight.

Ornith crouched defensively behind his tall shield as the rider drew ever closer, the crystal weapons smashing against his shield and littering the floor with their broken shards. As the rider drew level with Ornith, the knight scooped up a handful of crystals in his right hand and threw them in the Necromancer's direction. The man let out a howl of pain before falling from his dark horse.

Ornith stepped over the Necromancer who was clawing helplessly at the bloodstained shards that had peppered his face. "Take away my horse and I'm still a knight. Take away a visionary's eyes," Ornith muttered as he drove his blade into the man's bare chest, "and you are nothing," he spat angrily.

As Ornith looked up he saw Brenik riding back down the frontline. "Need a lift?" the elf called when he saw Ornith's fallen steed.

"No, I'm good," Ornith said as he attempted to wipe the blood from his armour. "Go, get the order out! I'll carry on on foot."

"Suit yourself," Brenik said with a nod of respect as he rode off down the line, continuing to order the retreat.

*   *   *

In the centre of the fight, Nalia heard Brenik's voice carry across the field as she fired off a pair of arrows, impaling two of the monstrous Kerberyn with her shots. A roar from her left drew her attention and she turned to see one of the giants charging towards her. She scrambled out of the way but her foot caught on the limb of one of the dead creatures and she tumbled to the floor.

The giant bellowed in triumph and was about to crush her with a massive fist when it was suddenly tackled by Brellyg. The dragon crashed into the giant, knocking it to the floor where he pinned the beast's arms to the blood sodden turf with his powerful front legs. Brellyg arced his long neck down and blew a blast of searing hot fire into the giant's face before relinquishing his grip on the beast's arms and slashing at its face with his vicious claws. The giant howled in pain as the hair on his head burst into flame and began to burn his open wounds. The beast writhed and twitched for a moment but soon became still. With a snort, Brellyg spread his wings and took to the sky once more, barely catching the thanks that Nalia called out to him.

"Nalia!" someone shouted.

Nalia turned to see Ornith hurrying towards her, his silver armour smeared with blood and his blonde hair matted with mud. Like her, she gathered that Ornith had lost his horse during the battle.

"Ornith!" Nalia cried in relief as she saw her friend stumble towards her. "Come on, we have to get out of here!"

Ornith nodded and gripped her soft hand as she pulled him away from a lumbering Kerberyn. He swiftly slung his shield onto his back and drew his sword in his right hand, the weight of the weapon a comforting presence in his hand.

"Let's go!" He called to Nalia, spying a second giant drawing ever closer to the pair.

* * *

Farther down the line, Cirnan and Alleyra were facing another of the giants. At the sound of retreat, Alleyra had leapt back onto their shared horse and they had attempted to fall back when one of the giants had suddenly marched into their path. Now their horse swerved desperately around the beast's massive limbs as he attempted to crush both the horse and it's riders.

"Go left!" Alleyra yelled urgently.

Cirnan gritted his teeth and tugged on the reins, pulling their grey horse out of the way of the giant's heavy right fist. As they rode past he swung his sword, cutting a deep gash along the giant's thumb. The beast roared and stamped his feet in anger, flattening several unfortunate Kerberyn.

"Get behind it!" Alleyra called again.

The dwarf pulled a pair of long knives from her back, spinning them expertly in her small hands. As they came around behind the giant's legs she slashed her blades across the backs of the beast's knees, severing its tendons in one fluid slash. The giant roared in pain and fell flailing to the floor where he was soon swarmed by the werewolves and the two riders.

"Ye're an ugly fellow!" Cirnan yelled as he jumped from the horse and drove his sword into the giant's head. The beast twitched violently before lying still.

"Well, don't just stand there!" Alleyra yelled as Cirnan slid his sword from the giant's head. "We're goin' to get left behind!"

Cirnan nodded and climbed back onto their horse. Looking around he saw that three of the giants were still standing along with the seemingly never ending army of Kerberyn. However, even as Cirnan was about to comment on their situation, two of the giants went down. One was felled by a torrent of flame from Brellyg whilst the second was claimed by one of Brenik's arrows which pierced the giant's one good eye. It did not take long for the final giant to eventually go down and for the Kerberyn to begin to return sheepishly to their masters for a second time.

* * *

Following the fall of the giants, the field became quiet as the broken Kerberyn fell back to their masters. Brenik looked around his weary lines, watching his warriors drop to the floor to cradle dead friends and hurry the wounded to safety. It was a grim scene, but although the resistance had been forced to fall back much earlier than he had anticipated they had held off the first waves of the Empire and their casualties were not as high as expected. Despite everything, morale was high.

"You are doing well," Brellyg commented as he touched down beside the elf. "It seems that I mistook the flame for match after all."

Brenik smiled as he remembered their conversation on the lonely plateau and looked down at the small wound he had sustained on his left arm. "You just watch. This flame will grow into an inferno," he said as he wiped the blood away.

"I have no doubt," the dragon chuckled.

"Pity the vampires are stuck in the forest," Brenik muttered as he glanced up at the high, midday sun.

"We may not be able to use the vampires," Brellyg rumbled, "but what of the dryads?"

"I've already sent word to the forest." Brenik indicated the tree line with his chin. "Look, they're coming now," he said.

Brellyg turned and nodded in approval as the silent group of tree-like figures glided slowly from the forest to join the resistance lines. He turned back to face the Necromancer lines which were now shrouded in a veil of green fog, making it impossible to see what their enemy was preparing.

"I was going to save them for when we pulled back to the forest," Brenik explained.

Brellyg shook his head. "No plan, no matter how flawless, survives contact with the enemy." The dragon nodded approvingly at the dryads. "It's a good job they're here. I think we are going to need them now more than ever," he rumbled grimly.

Brenik's eyes darted nervously to the fog before falling back to Cirnan and the other resistance leaders. He beckoned them over.

"Well done, all of you," Brenik said proudly as they approached. "We have held back the first waves and the death toll is low. We've even managed to take out one of their wizards thanks to Ornith." Brenik waited patiently as the others congratulated the knight. "As you can see, the dryads have joined us out here now so we should be able to make an even stronger stand than before," he finished when they had quietened down.

"Aye, but that was only the beginnin'," Alleyra muttered.

As if on cue, the green fog suddenly began to descend over the companions, drowning everything in a haze of eerie, green mist.

"This fog is not natural," Ornith whispered as green wisps of smoke clawed at his armour.

"It's the Necromancers," Brellyg whispered. "They are coming."

From the depths of the mist came the solid sound of drums, each beat signalling the single noted advance of the Necromancer leaders.

Chapter 31

Even as the dragon spoke they could see the dark figures beginning to emerge from the ghostly fog. Brenik recognised the dark elves instantly. Clad in their silver armour and rich purple clothing, each of them held their halberds tightly across their chests and wore cold expressions on their thin faces. In the centre of their ranks strode Guillard and the magi of Necromancer army.

"Fight well, all of you," Brenik said softly to his friends as he strode forward and slowly drew his sword. He then raised his voice so that every member of his army might hear his words. "We make our stand now!" he cried. "Fight for your homes! Fight for your families! Fight, and know that if you find yourselves in fields of green, with the sun warming your backs, that you have brought freedom and peace upon yourself, and that you are home at last!"

The wolves howled once more as the dryads slipped into their ranks. They waited patiently as Brenik wound his way through their lines and stepped out onto the empty plain between the two armies. A long silence filled the still air before Brenik raised his sword and gave the simple order. As one, the mismatched army surged forwards to meet their new enemy.

Brenik charged forwards, his sword held high above his head as he met the enemy forces. A dark elf lunged at his heart with his halberd but Brenik rolled nimbly out of the way, springing quickly to his feet and cutting the man down. A second elf lunged at Brenik but he swiftly batted the halberd aside a drove his sword through the gap in the dark elf's armour.

Brenik turned and found himself facing an elf with the insignia of a captain etched onto his armour. The elf charged at Brenik with a snarl, aiming his halberd at Brenik's heart. Brenik stepped back and swung his sword, splintering the shaft of the captain's weapon. The elf threw his useless halberd aside and drew his short sword which he began to swing before his body in a deadly arc. Brenik hesitated before crossing blades with the captain. They traded a few swift strikes before their swords locked and they began to push against each other. The captain grinned triumphantly and then spat in Brenik's face before swinging his left leg out and knocking Brenik to the floor.

Brenik grunted as he hit the sodden turf, losing his grip on his blade. He fumbled in the mud as he reached for his fallen sword, the dark elf looming above him, ready to drive his weapon into Brenik's chest, when suddenly he was tackled by a tall dryad. Brenik looked up in surprise to see Hisseda lashing out at his attacker with his powerful limbs and sharpened vines. When the dryad left the dark elf captain, Brenik saw that the man was covered in hundreds of viscous slashes and lacerations which covered his exposed skin.

"Good timing!" Brenik breathed in relief as Hisseda pulled him to his feet.

"Don't mention it," the dryad hissed. "I . . ." Hisseda suddenly let out a shriek of pain as a bolt of ghostly green energy struck him between his gnarled shoulders.

Brenik watched helplessly as the dryad was lifted into the air by the glowing beams of energy. His bark slowly began to flake away, the moss and leaves that sprouted from his body shrivelled and died and eventually Hisseda withered and was no more.

As the twisted remains of the dryad clattered to the floor Brenik spun around in an attempt to find the one responsible for the Hisseda's death. His eyes narrowed as he saw the gap in the battle and the dark figure that stood alone amongst the carnage.

Standing in the centre of a ring of his dark elves, the Master was revelling in the death that was occurring all about him. He cackled joyfully as he sent a bolt of green energy shooting forth from his withered hand, sapping the life of a young werewolf. Brenik again watched as the wolf was lifted into air and engulfed by the eerie green energy, unable to do anything to save the creature. Slowly, the wolf's black fur began to turn grey, the strong muscles in his arms shrank away and his sharp eyes became clouded. Within a few seconds the bones of the wolf clattered to the floor, his life completely drained from his cracked skeleton.

Gritting his teeth and holding back his fear, Brenik spun his sword nervously in his hand and ran through the crowd towards the Master. A dark elf suddenly lunged at Brenik with his halberd, the wicked blade slamming into the grassy turf a few inches before the elf. Without breaking his stride Brenik slashed at the man's chest, killing him in one fluid movement. A second elf charged towards Brenik but he quickly met the same fate as his companion. Brenik pulled his sword out of the elf's body and turned to face the Master.

A bolt of green energy lanced towards Brenik and stuck him squarely in the chest. Brenik grunted as his sword was thrown from his hand and he was lifted off of the ground. A strange sensation came over him and he suddenly found himself feeling drained of all energy. When he looked down at his body he saw his skin beginning to wrinkle and pale and his brown hair turning a shimmering grey.

From his circle below the Master smiled wickedly up at the elf. "I gave you every chance to join me! You could have been my greatest ally! But now, you will die. Your life will become my life. Everything you know . . ."

In the distance a horn blasted across the skies. The Master, taken by surprise, instinctively turned towards the noise, causing his spell to falter as his concentration was broken. Brenik gasped as he dropped to the floor, feeling life suddenly flowing back into his young bones. His hair returned to its usual dark colour and his skin once more became youthful and tanned. By the time the Master turned back to face the elf, Brenik had vanished into the battle.

*   *   *

The deep blast of the horn echoed loudly across the battlefield and Cirnan watched with pride as scores of tribesmen appeared on the hill above them, weapons brandished and instruments bellowing out above the roar of their battle cries. The tribesmen had arrived just in time, the creatures of the Great Forest had been pushed right back to the very border of the forest and many of them had fallen in the fight.

But now, as often happens in war, the balance of luck had turned to favour the resistance. As the tribesmen moved forwards a wall of black clouds pursued their advance, blotting out the harsh sunlight and replacing it with a light sprinkling of rain. With the sun hidden, the vampires could at last venture out of the shadows of the forest and join the fray. Cirnan could already hear them racing through the trees, uttering their death cries as the smell of fresh blood pulled invitingly at their sharpened senses.

From above, the tribesmen let out a united roar. "Death! Death! Death!" they chanted over and over, beating their fists against their exposed chests.

A sharp blast of a war horn blew out across the plains and with one final roar the northerners charged down the hill and crashed into the side of the Necromancer forces. The Necromancer reserves buckled under the sudden attack, devoid of leaders they struggled to organise and protect their flank. The tribesmen howled in joy as they hacked their way through the Kerberyn and burst through the frontline of the enemy's rearguard, the warriors continuing on their charge to attack the dark elves. Cirnan watched proudly as huge tribesmen, some sporting nothing more than a plain pair of shorts and a wide array of graphic tattoos, crashed into the rear of the Necromancer ranks, supported by the arrival of the fearsome vampires at the enemy's front.

With the enemy closing on both flanks, the Necromancers faltered under the new attacks and the resistance surged forwards, reclaiming much of the ground that they had lost. The fighting was brutal and even the magically enhanced dark elves could not ignore the very real sense of fear that ran through their bodies as they saw vampires tearing into and drinking the blood of their allies whilst the dryads and wolves lashed out at others in a wild frenzy of vines and claws. It was not in a dark elf to run in fear, but even if it had been they would have done no better, for behind their ranks the war clubs and axes of the northerners sung their deadly death songs as they crashed through the skulls of the Empire's rear lines.

The Masked Man scowled as a broad shouldered tribesman charged towards him, swirling a pair of axes around his body and shouting abuse at the Necromancer. When the warrior drew closer, the Masked Man uttered a short spell and his body began to divide into a series of mirages. The tribesman's face fell as he found himself surrounded by four exact copies of his opponent. With a roar, he lashed out at one of the apparitions, but his axes met nothing but thin air as they passed through the mirror image of the Necromancer.

"Ye coward!" the tribesman bellowed. "Fight me!"

Suddenly, the tribesman let out a gasp of surprise as the Masked Man materialised before him. With a quick jerk of his arms, the Masked Man's staff came crashing down onto the tribesman's skull, ending his life.

The Masked Man looked around the battlefield at the empowered resistance, the scowl on his hidden face growing steadily wider. He could feel the fear of his warriors, the threat of panic descending over his men. They were facing barbarians and losing! The Master had promised him the best, but the Masked Man was yet to see any evidence of his Emperor's promise. He had been right to proceed with his plan then.

A small man suddenly stumbled into his view. "Ugra!" the Masked Man hissed. He strode forwards, snatching up the little man and uttering a spell under his breath. The Masked Man closed his eyes as he felt his whole body lurch forwards. When he opened his eyes he and Ugra were stood upon one of the small hills above the battlefield.

Ugra bowed low as the Masked Man released him from his iron grip. "Master," he squeaked in his high pitched voice. "Ugra is at your command!"

The Masked Man glanced down to where the Master stood amongst death, uncaring about what was occurring around him. "The resistance is growing stronger. They are regaining ground," the Masked Man said distantly. "The Master cannot see our peril." A thin smile touched the cracked lips hidden under the mask. "All is going to plan, my little friend."

"Ugra do good?" the Necromancer asked quickly.

"For now," the Masked Man hissed impatiently.

Ugra beamed with pride. "Elves are nice!" he declared happily. "Ugra happy to be with them!"

The Masked Man turned to face Ugra, looming over the little mage and grabbing him roughly by the collar. "Do not forget that you still serve me!" he hissed. "Remember, I was the one who gave you your power back. I can just as easily take it away! Do you understand?"

Ugra nodded fearfully. "Yes! Ugra knows! Ugra is loyal!" he stammered.

The Masked Man released Ugra and glanced around the hill, his eyes settling on the entrance to a partially obscured tunnel behind them. "Maintain your cover, keep me informed about the elves and their allies. When the time comes, I will send word for you to strike."

"What about Master?" Ugra whispered.

The Masked Man touched the purple amethyst that tipped his staff as he prepared to teleport himself and Ugra back to the battle. "His time is at hand," he whispered sinisterly as the pair of Necromancers vanished from the hill.

Chapter 32

Brenik, who had fully recovered from the effects of the draining spell, was back in the fight and making his way back towards the Master's new location, determined to face the leader of the enemy. Dark elves charged towards him on both sides but Brenik's skill proved too much for them and he swiftly cut them down. He did not feel right killing his own brethren, but there was nothing that he could do about it right now.

The crowd parted slightly and Brenik caught a glimpse of the Master's swirling black cloak and he began to run towards the leader when suddenly someone stepped out in front of him. Brenik threw himself to the floor just in time to avoid the razor sharp blade of the scimitar as it passed inches over his head. Scrambling to his feet, Brenik turned to face Guillard.

"Finally we meet, Brenik," Guillard sneered.

"Give it up, Guillard!" Brenik pleaded. "You've lost! Can't you see that?"

"Does it really matter?" Guillard scoffed. "We will simply return with a bigger, more powerful army to crush you! And if you aren't here then we'll simply burn down your precious forest!"

Brenik shook his head sadly. "You are lost to us, Guillard. You are not the friend I once knew. Please, I don't want to have to kill you."

A dark shadow crossed Guillard's face as he lifted his scimitar above his head. "You won't have to."

Guillard swung his scimitar with a hiss of anger, the blade clashing against Brenik's own sword. The two elves pushed against each other's blades, glaring into the other's eyes, Guillard's full of burning hatred, Brenik's of quiet calmness.

"I have taken all of this for myself!" Guillard boasted. "I have more than you could ever dream of, Brenik!"

"Your new clothes are nice, Guillard," Brenik said sarcastically. He nodded at the helmet hanging from Guillard's belt. "But you know, you should really consider wearing that," he growled.

Before Guillard could reply, Brenik swung his head forwards, slamming his forehead down onto Guillard's hooked nose. The General grunted in pain as he stumbled backwards, clutching his bloodied nose with his free hand. When he looked up his eyes widened in surprise as he watched Brenik swing his fist towards his jaw. Brenik's punch knocked Guillard off of his feet, sending him sprawling to the floor where he lay unconscious amongst the other bodies.

Brenik winced as he shook his fist. He glanced down to see Zephira looking inquisitively up at him. "He has a hard head," Brenik muttered before reaching out and grabbing the nearest tribesman. "Make sure he doesn't get away," Brenik yelled out to the warrior.

The warrior looked down at the unconscious General and nodded his understanding.

Brenik clapped the man on the shoulder and disappeared into the battle, Zephira hot on his tail.

*　　*　　*

The Master stood in the centre of the battle, a fierce grin spread across his unshadowed chin as he drained the life of a vampire with one hand and kept the other warriors at bay with blasts of green lightning and red fire from his other.

"This is no place for you," Brenik said to Zephira as they approached the deadly circle. "Go find Ugra, keep an eye on him."

The dog barked and cocked her head before running off into the fight. Brenik watched her go before he turned determinedly and charged into the circle of bones that surrounded the Master. At the last moment, Brenik saw the Master's head snap towards him and the glimmer of light sparkle in his hidden eyes as he raised his crackling hands.

The lightning bolt struck Brenik's sword, throwing the weapon from his hand and knocking the elf flat on his back once more. The goblin Necromancer appeared in Brenik's vision, the wizard's spiked staff poised for the killing blow, when suddenly a mass of grey fur leapt over Brenik and tackled the Necromancer. The goblin howled in pain as Zephira pinned him to the floor and buried her teeth into his neck. She snarled defensively as she tore through the goblin's sickly skin before looking up and trotting happily over to Brenik, her tongue hanging lazily out from her blood-covered muzzle.

Brenik sat up quickly, wincing at the pain in his side. He gingerly touched his cracked ribs before pressing his hands to his temples and shaking his head. Reaching out a shaky hand he stroked Zephira's bloodied snout and grinned fiercely at her as she licked his face. She barked quizzically, almost as if she was asking for Brenik's approval.

"Well, as you're here," the elf chuckled, causing a stabbing pain to run down his right hand side.

Zephira suddenly barked in warning and Brenik turned to see a streak of blonde hair running through the battle. To his right he watched as Nalia ran up a jagged rock and launched herself into the circle of bones, an arrow drawn back on her bowstring and aimed at the Master's heart. But with one swift movement the Master turned around and fired off a magical blast of his life draining energy attack.

"No!" Brenik yelled, raising his hand in despair.

The deadly green bolt of energy snaked towards Nalia, burning the air which it passed through. The bolt was about to engulf the elf when suddenly it exploded in a shower of sparks as it struck an invisible barrier. The Master turned his head in surprise as did Nalia. Both were looking at Brenik whose raised hand was glowing with a bright, white light.

The Master tilted his head and smiled. "So, at last the magic within you surfaces," he whispered. "This will be interesting."

Nalia watched as Brenik limped into the circle. "Bren," she whispered worriedly.

Brenik placed a comforting hand on her shoulder as he walked uneasily past her. "Stay back," he said. His voice was kind but not open to argument so Nalia nodded and reluctantly drew back out of the circle to stand with Zephira.

The Master began to pace the ground before Brenik, staring at the elf from the shadows of his black hood. "So, it turns out that you are not the failure that I have always thought of you as," the Master chuckled to himself. He raised his hand and Brenik watched as green energy crackled between his fingers. "But do you really think that just because you have suddenly discovered your talents that you are capable of defeating me?" he hissed.

Brenik looked down at his bloody hands, a pale glow still shining through the smears of blood and dirt. "There's only one way to find out," he muttered as he thrust his hands forwards.

* * *

Acting on pure instinct, Brenik raised his hands. A red glow burned across his palm as a shower of small, red hot fireballs shot from his fingertips. The Master quickly threw up an energy barrier which easily deflected the weak magical attack, the fireballs disintegrating as they passed through the invisible barrier. Raising his own hands, the Master once more summoned his life draining spell. The beam of green energy shot from the tip of his staff towards Brenik's chest but, acting again on instinct, the elf raised his hands and fired off a bolt of bright blue lightning. The two spells collided in mid air, showering sparks all around them as they fought against each other for dominance. Eventually, however, the Master's spell proved stronger and Brenik was forced to dive painfully out of the way as the combined energy bolts struck the grass where he had only just been standing, sending a shower of mud and grass raining down around the battered elf.

The Master cackled loudly. "Your magic is strong, Brenik Lithuik, much like your father before you." The Master's cackle rung in Brenik's ears as he stood up, his back to the Master. "But even so, how could you possibly hope to defeat me. What do you have in your arsenal that I could not counter?"

Brenik turned around, a huge flaming ball of fire building in his cupped hands. He smiled dryly at the Master. "Surprise!" he whispered.

The Master hastily threw up an energy barrier but even that was not enough to stop the fireball's unchecked power. Brenik's spell slammed into the magical barricade and the ground shook as the unstoppable force collided with the barrier. The air began to crackle with energy and the magical barrier suddenly buckled as the fireball exploded, sending the Master flying into the air where he disappeared in a veil of black smoke.

Silence descended over the field as curious eyes turned to take in the scene unfolding in the muddy crater that the explosion had created. The thick smoke slowly began to dissipate, revealing the crooked form of the Master lying on the scorched earth. His black robes were singed, his smoking staff had been split in half and the shadowy hood had fallen from the man's tired head.

Brenik stepped forwards slowly, his hands spread wide in preparation to block any counterattack from the Master. "Now. Let's find out who you really are," he said as he drew closer to the figure.

The Master rose slowly to his feet, pushing the strands of his long, wild, silver-grey hair back over his shoulder and brushing the flecks of mud from his shining, olive skin.

When the Master turned slowly around, Brenik gasped as he found himself staring into a familiar pair of dark, midnight-blue eyes. "It can't be," he whispered, staggering backwards several paces in shock.

Rothule Lithuik, Master of the Necromancer Empire, smiled dryly. "Hello, son," he muttered.

Chapter 33

Brenik stared in disbelief at his father. "It's you! All along, it's been you! But how? We saw you die!"

Rothule slowly shook his head. He looked younger than before, although his hair was still a silvery grey, his blue eyes shone brighter than ever and his olive skin was smoother and lined with fewer wrinkles than Brenik remembered. However, his hands were withered and blackened like charred wood, twisted and disfigured by the massive amount of dark power that had been channelled through them over the past weeks.

"You saw what I wanted you to see. You saw me vanish, Brenik," Rothule corrected his son. "The Masked Man is well trained in the arts of illusion, more specifically in the magic of teleportation. When his spell hit me, I shattered my old staff before I was teleported outside of the city walls. You only assumed that I had died. You did exactly what I wanted you to do."

Brenik was shaking his head in confusion, trying to make sense of what he was being told. "Why? Why have you done all of this?"

"Because, Brenik, we deserve better! We are elves, the greatest civilisation in Justava! But more increasingly we are expected to bow down to the lesser Kingdoms. To men and women not fit for the power that they wield. I ask you why men deserve the power that they have amassed? Why do the dwarfs deserve the riches that they mine for? Why we elves, the very people that made Justava what it is, are slowly losing our hold on the land whilst the influence of men spreads like poison?"

Brenik glared coldly at his father. "So by killing and deforming your own people you think that we will regain our strength? You would destroy the very world you claim we created?" Brenik shook his head angrily. "You killed my mother, your own wife, for what? Power? Revenge?"

Rothule sighed, looking genuinely sad for a brief moment. "Your mother's death was, regrettable. But she would never have joined us and she was too powerful to be left alive! I wish she could have understood. I did truly love her."

"Don't you dare say that!" Brenik yelled angrily, ignoring the throbbing pain in his ribs. "If you loved her then none of this would have ever happened and she would still be alive! You cannot claim to have loved her after what you have done!"

Rothule snarled, baring a row of sharp teeth. "We may not see eye to eye now, my son, but do not presume that you know my feelings!" he spat. "I did what I had to do! For us! For the elves! For Justava!" Rothule fixed his son with a cold look. "No matter what you think, I am still your father, and you will respect my legacy."

Brenik shook his head. "No," he said flatly. "No, I have no father. My father, my real father that is, died at Cathwood when the Necromancers invaded. It is that man's legacy which I give my respect to."

Rothule sighed and a shadow fell across his face as he looked down in regret. "Then in that case, I have no son. You are nothing but my enemy, which makes you a threat to all that I have worked for. Goodbye, Brenik. You have always been my greatest disappointment."

Before Brenik could reply, Rothule fired off a blast of crackling, green lightning. Brenik quickly formed a barrier to block the spell before returning fire, struggling to match his father's skill and speed.

Nalia watched nervously as lights flashed between the two wizards as they fired spell after spell at each other. Rothule's spells were by far the most impressive. Whilst Brenik's knowledge was limited to simple spells like the fireball and lightning strikes, Rothule's knowledge was far broader, allowing him to summon tornadoes of ghostly green fire or to bring the bones that surrounded them to life to fight beside him.

Nalia winced as Brenik took a bolt to his shin, the magical energy ripping his armour from his leg and searing the flesh below. A sinking feeling settled in her stomach as she realised that Brenik could not win this battle.

Brenik grunted as he was knocked onto his back by another lightning strike sent from his father. He had been hit several times now and his skin was bruised and burnt, his clothes seared onto his flesh in places. The pressure on his lungs from his broken ribs was almost too much to bear and Brenik's breaths were short and ragged. He swayed slightly as he rose to his feet, feeling his bruised and broken bones burning with every step that he took. A haze of fatigue passed across his vision and he was vaguely aware of his father summoning another life draining spell, one that was intended to finish him. Instinct alone caused Brenik's hands to shoot up and fire off a blast of lightning to counter the spell and once more, the two powers began to battle for dominance, sparks of lightning lancing through the air as the wizards pushed their powers to the limit. Sweat trickled down Brenik's brow as he fought to hold off his father's attack. In his heart he knew it was a useless attempt; his father was too strong for him. Brenik knew he could not win this fight.

"Son." Brenik jumped as his mother's soft voice suddenly filled his ears. "Do not give in, my son. My wonderful, wonderful son."

In the corner of his eye, Brenik saw Nalia watching him from the gathered crowd, her face etched with concern. He realised now that much of the fighting had stopped, and that the two opposing sides were now gathered around the lip of the crater to watch the final battle between the Master and the leader of the resistance. Brenik closed his eyes and his mind drifted to thoughts of his friends, his people and of his army. Finally an image of Gwyyn drifted across his subconscious, surrounded by a glowing light. The ghostly apparition stood calmly beside a similar, angelic image of his mother.

Brenik met their gazes before looking shamefully away. "I am sorry. I have failed you both," he said in defeat.

Gwyyn reached forwards and placed a glowing hand on Brenik's smooth face, fixing him with her loving eyes as she tenderly stroked his cheek. "No, my love. I am so very proud of you," she said soothingly.

"I can't do this though!" Brenik protested. "I am no hero! He's too strong for me!"

"Son," Maleena said calmly, "Look around you."

Brenik looked around, seeing the faces of the men and women that he commanded staring at him with hope in their eyes.

"You already are a hero, Brenik," his mother said proudly. "You are stronger than your father. You have only to look to those who follow you to find your strength."

Brenik turned to Gwyyn, his eyes meeting hers. "I wasn't strong enough to save you though," he whispered. "Can you ever forgive me?"

Brenik felt a surge of warmth run through his body and ease the pain in his side as Gwyyn brushed her lips against his. "There is nothing to forgive, Brenik," she purred. "Now go. Your time has come, my love."

The glowing images gradually faded and Brenik was back on the gloomy battlefield facing his father. He watched Gwyyn's face as it disappeared and suddenly found himself staring at Nalia. She looked at him, her beautiful face strained with worry.

Gwyyn's voice returned to Brenik's ears. "Remember, Brenik," she began.

"There is always hope," Brenik finished in unison with his mother as Nalia nodded bravely at him and Brenik turned to face his father.

Rothule grinned fiercely as his own spell pushed ever closer to Brenik. The boy had put up a surprisingly strong fight but Rothule was by far the stronger wizard. Gradually the blue streaks of lightning began to shrink and Brenik was pushed ever closer to the lip of the crater as Rothule's power steadily overwhelmed his son.

Then suddenly the two spells exploded in a shower of white sparks as some sort of inexplicable barrier stopped Rothule's spell in its tracks. Rothule looked around for the new wizard when he suddenly felt his son's spell forcing his own beam of magic back. Rothule's eyes widened in surprise. There had never been any doubt in his mind about the outcome of the battle.

Until now.

With new found strength, Brenik fought with his father for dominance. The blue lightning bolts began to extend as the green beam of energy was compressed, the crackling centre of the two spells edging closer and closer to Rothule. Rothule's eyes widened in fear as his son slowly began to overpower him, his own magic crumbling before the strength of Brenik's spell.

With one final roar, Brenik's spell suddenly lurched forwards, the blue beams snaking around Rothule's spell before rearing up and slamming into the Necromancer's chest. The Emperor gasped as he was lifted off of his feet by the combination of the lightning and his own draining spell. Rothule slowly began to feel his own spell take effect; the lives that he had claimed began to leave his body; wrinkles returned to his skin and his eyes lost their magical shine. For a long while he hung limply in the air, watching as the spirits of the dead that he had claimed left his body in the forms of pale green wisps of smoke and his life faded away before his tired eyes.

Rothule looked around hopelessly until his eyes settled upon the Masked Man. He was stood behind the gathered crowd, staring into Rothule's clouded eyes, fully capable of rushing to his Emperor's defence. But instead the Masked Man merely reached up and removed his spiked mask, revealing a crooked smile set upon his scarred face. In that moment, Rothule Lithuik at last understood that no matter the outcome of the battle, he would never have remained Emperor. This had been Jarus' plan all along.

In his final moments, once every life that the Master had taken had slipped away from his body, there was a brilliant flash of green light and Rothule Lithuik withered and finally fell silent.

Stunned silence descended over the battlefield as all eyes turned to take in the crumpled body of the dead Necromancer Emperor. No one spoke for a long time until at last, a cheer of triumph rose up from the resistance and its soldiers surged forwards.

The Battle of the Great Forest was over, and, against all the odds, the resistance had won.

Chapter 34

The death of the Master was like the falling of small stones that bring a mighty avalanche in their wake. As the resistance surged forwards in triumph the remaining forces of the Necromancer army quickly fell into chaos and began a barely ordered retreat. The Kerberyn clattered to the ground where they stood, the magic bond that the Master had held over them shattering, causing their brittle bones to collapse as what little life was contained within them left the animated corpses. Without leadership and with a large amount of their army now reduced to dust, the rest of the Necromancers faltered and the horns of retreat sounded across the wide plains.

Brenik stood weakly in the crater as he was swamped with werewolves, tribesmen and the other creatures of the resistance, all of whom were eager to congratulate their leader on his great victory. The elf moved slowly through the jostling crowd, politely pushing people aside as he scanned the triumphant faces for Nalia. He was desperate to see her. He realised only now how foolish he had been to keep his feelings hidden, especially after the night they had shared in the cave. It had been Nalia that had given Brenik the strength to defeat his father and now that he had found her, he was not about to give her up again.

His father. Brenik was still having difficulty coming to terms with that part of the tale and he felt a wave of dizziness pass over him as he recalled the first moments of their fight. His heart was heavy with the loss of the man he had once respected, and Rothule's cold words still filled Brenik's ears. But for now he would push them aside and enjoy his victory.

A loud roar, this time not from the cheering victors, broke Brenik's train of thought as it echoed across the field and the elf turned to see Brellyg landing gracefully at the edge of the resistance fighters. The great dragon met Brenik's eyes with his own and bowed his head low in respect. Brenik smiled warmly and returned the gesture with his own grateful nod.

"Oi! Let him through!" a familiar voice suddenly shouted over the cheering crowd.

The crowd parted before him as Brenik turned in the direction of the voice, allowing him to step into a small circle where he found Cirnan and Alleyra waiting for him. Cirnan lay on his back, a large bandage wrapped around his thigh.

"What happened to you?" Brenik yelled over the roar of the crowd as he knelt down beside his two friends.

Cirnan shrugged. "This big dark elf," he said, spreading his arms wide to emphasise the size of his attacker. "Huge he was. Came along and caught me with his halberd. But, ye know, I fought him off," he finished proudly.

Beside him, Alleyra looked up at Brenik with raised eyebrows. "It was a Kerberyn. Tiny little thing." She put her fingers close together to emphasise the lack of size of the beast that had wounded her friend.

Despite his injured ribs Brenik couldn't help but laugh at Cirnan's scowl and he patted his two friends warmly on the shoulder. "Well I'm just glad you're both safe," he said tiredly.

Cirnan smiled and looked quickly at Alleyra. "Aye. Me too."

A group of men moved into the circle and Brenik looked up to see two vampires standing with their arms around Yukov for support. Yukov still looked incredibly weak but some of the colour had returned to his face and his blisters had been treated with thick layers of cream. A third vampire approached him and gingerly draped Yukov's smart overcoat over his shoulders.

"That's better," Yukov said as he pulled the warm coat snugly around his body.

Brenik stood uneasily and began to limp slowly over to Yukov. The crowd suddenly broke and a frail figure burst into the circle. At first Brenik thought it was his father and he reached for the sword he had lost in the battle, but then he noticed the man's wild stance and relaxed as Ugra beamed at him.

"We win! We win!" Ugra yelled, dancing manically on the spot.

Brenik laughed despite himself. "You did well Ugra," he admitted. "I guess we had nothing to fear from you after all."

As Brenik patted Ugra on the shoulder and walked painfully past him, no one noticed the cruel smile that touched the little man's dry lips. "For now," he whispered.

Yukov looked up as Brenik made his way over. The two vampires had set him down on the floor and were applying fresh cream to the blisters on his left leg.

"What are you doing out here?" Brenik asked when the vampire was in earshot.

Yukov smiled, showing his still deadly fangs. "Well I couldn't let you have all the glory now could I?" he joked.

Brenik smiled warmly at the wounded vampire. "We could have used you in that fight."

Yukov returned the smile. "It looks like you did pretty well without me." He frowned as Brenik clutched painfully at his ribs. "Well, mostly."

"Here," one of the vampires said distractedly as he waved a small, dried leaf in Brenik's direction. "It'll help with the pain."

Yukov watched Brenik chew the leaf slowly. "Looks like I made the right decision when I chose not to eat you," he chuckled.

"I probably don't taste very good anyway," Brenik reasoned.

Yukov smiled but his eyes suddenly darted to something behind Brenik and the elf turned around to see Nalia standing on the edge of the circle.

A smile broke out across Brenik's face. "Excuse me," he whispered as he began to walk towards Nalia, wanting nothing more than to sweep her up in his arms and never let her go again.

Suddenly, Ornith stepped out of the circle a few paces from Nalia. His armour was even more heavily smeared with blood but it still shone brightly nonetheless. He looked at Brenik and winked once before crossing the short distance to Nalia where he placed a broad hand on her cheek and kissed her firmly on the lips.

Brenik watched as Nalia returned the kiss, feeling as though someone had just wrenched his heart out. As they pulled apart Nalia looked lovingly up into Ornith's soft eyes and smiled happily before leaning her head on his broad shoulder, not caring about the blood stains that were splattered across it. The two turned around and Nalia smiled widely at Brenik, her cheeks colouring slightly as she looked giddily at her old friend.

Brenik swallowed hard as he forced himself to smile in return. Beside him he felt the comforting press of Zephira's body. He ran his hand slowly through her fur and sighed. He had fought an army of undead that day and had duelled his own father to the death. But nothing quite compared to the pain that he was now feeling in his chest.

Epilogue

A week passed and the Great Forest became silent once more. The tall trees receded to the shadows where they were once more shrouded in mysteries that few dared to investigate and the mists rolled back into the woods. Despite everything though, something had changed. The forest was no longer as threatening, the trees no longer so dark. It was as if a new life had taken hold of the forest.

On a lonely tree-covered hill not far from the stretching coastline, Brenik Lithuik smiled as he looked calmly out across the sea of green that was laid out before him. It was the perfect place to conceal the Justavan Resistance. The Resistance was still young and did not have the power to begin a full scale attack on the Empire, so they had retreated into the depths of the Great Forest, here to this hill where they would wait and grow strong until such a time when they could strike out at the tyrants beyond their boarders.

A strong gust of wind blew from behind Brenik and he smiled as he watched the trees ripple across the forest. "Hope is spreading," he whispered as he turned on his heels and walked swiftly down the steps of the watchtower, Zephira plodding along faithfully at his side.

At the bottom of the tower, the watchman nodded respectfully at him. "General!" the watchman said as he passed.

The elf smiled and nodded in response. *"General."* He was still getting used to his new title: Brenik Lithuik, General of the Justavan Resistance. *The Justavan Resistance.* Brenik laughed, it was certainly a mouthful. They needed a better name than that, but the name of his army was the last thing on Brenik's mind as he thought of all the work that would need to be done over the next few weeks.

As he walked through the camp, Brenik looked around approvingly. Men and monsters were working side by side, erecting walls, blacksmiths and other buildings whilst guards patrolled the camp watchfully. The hill was slowly becoming a fortress.

Brenik's command tent rose up before him as he walked into the busy centre of the camp. He nodded at the two guards flanking the entrance and pushed the tent flap aside. Inside he found Nalia waiting for him. She smiled gracefully as Brenik walked in.

"Well, what can do for you?" Brenik asked cheerfully.

"I have something for you," she said softly.

She stepped to one side and Brenik walked towards the table behind her. A dark blue banner was laid out across the rough wooden surface.

"Every army needs a symbol to march behind," Nalia said proudly. "This will be ours."

Brenik smiled as he looked at the design on the banner, a golden bough of a reflin tree, its branches reaching out to touch the circle of gold rope that surrounded it in seven separate places.

* * *

Jarus sighed as he stared into the cold, unblinking eyes of his mask, his mind replaying the events of the battle that had taken place only a week ago. He was not displeased with the results of the battle. He had been ready to lose to the resistance, he had been ready to see Rothule die. What he had not expected was the boy. Of course there were some advantages to Brenik killing his father, chief amongst which being that Jarus was not involved so no one had dared question him when he took the throne. But nevertheless, the boy had become dangerous. Of course there was always the possibility that Jarus could turn him; Brenik's power was wild and Jarus could easily manipulate him. But there were complications there, he would have to get someone close enough to Brenik to plant the seeds of doubt and then he would need to actually convince him to join the Empire! The defiance that the boy had shown towards his father made Jarus doubt that he would achieve any of these things.

A knock on the heavy wooden doors of the Council Chambers snapped the Necromancer out of his trace and he hastily slipped the mask over his dry features before summoning his uninvited guest.

A dark elf stepped respectfully into the room. "My Lord, General Guillard has awoken. He is insisting that he must speak with you now."

"Send him in," the Masked Man said quickly.

The wooden door opened wider and Guillard hobbled urgently in. After the battle the General had managed to escape from his captors after a heated fight. During the fight, however, Guillard had taken an arrow to his chest and the wound had become badly infected during his long ride back to Emladis in pursuit of the surviving Necromancers. It had taken all the skills of several of the Empire's best healers to keep the General from succumbing to his wound.

"General. You should be resting," the Masked Man remarked distantly.

"Does it really matter now?" Guillard spat venomously. "We have failed! The Master is dead! We have nothing!"

The Masked Man cocked his head slowly. "We have an Empire, General. Do you really think that only one man can rule it?"

Guillard swayed uncertainly on his feet. "The Master was strong. He was fair. He knew what he was doing."

"The Master was a tired, old fool!" hissed the Masked Man impatiently. "He would never have led us to our true calling."

"But, he was a symbol!" Guillard protested.

The Masked Man snorted as he rose from his seat. He walked slowly behind Guillard and put his arms around him to support the General. "Few people ever saw the Master," the Masked Man whispered. "Tell me General, what is more of a symbol? A frail old man in a cloak, or this?"

Guillard looked up as the Masked Man held his mask out before him, the pale light from the morning sun shining through the eye holes and slit between the metal lips. Guillard turned around, anxious to finally see the face of the Masked Man. However, when he turned he found that the mask was already back in place on the man's face.

"Come, Guillard. I have something to show you."

Guillard allowed himself to be led slowly out of the Council Chambers onto a wide balcony that overlooked the square below

197

them. His eyes widened as he looked down to see an army standing below them. There were men in heavy armour, dwarfs stood around complicated war machines, goblins and orcs standing in strangely organised groups and the ever present dark elves whose numbers seemed even greater than before.

For a long time, there was silence. Then the army raised their fists and pressed them to their chests.

"All hail the Emperor!" they chanted in unison.

"How is this possible?" Guillard breathed.

The Masked Man squeezed the General's shoulder as he turned away. "The land has grown dark, General. Where light falls, a shadow is never far behind."

About the Author

Harry Sherwin was born in Southampton, England and raised not far away in the small village of Whiteparish. Harry has always had a keen interest in reading and writing and spent much of his childhood coming up with wild stories of dragons and knights.

The idea of the Seven Kingdoms came to Harry whilst on holiday and at last he decided to pursue his passion and write his story down. Despite working on A levels at the same time, Harry persevered with help from his friends, family and teachers and at last produced the first book in what he hopes will be a series of successful novels.